AF485751

DETECTIVE LAFLEUR MYSTERIES

BY

STEVE ABBOTT AND JOHN FOUNTAIN

*O.R.*

*Firesign*

*Hot Gold*

*Old Man in a Hurry*

*Murder in Moonlight*

# *The Curse*
## *of the*
# *Moonlight Meteorite*

## A Detective LaFleur Novel

JOHN FOUNTAIN

———

STEVE ABBOTT

*To Matthew Gloag & Son, original distillers of The Famous Grouse Scotch whisky, which made long nights of typing even longer.*

That which mathematically has an extremely low
probability also has this characteristic: that it may
nevertheless sometimes happen.
~ Stanislaw Lem

CONTENTS

# The Curse
## of the
# Moonlight Meteorite

# PART ONE: FALLING SKIES

"…diamonds are a girl's best friend."
—as sung by Marilyn Monroe

# Avalauncher

"BIG SKY, Mont. -- To the dangers of skiing, add the possibility of getting hit by shrapnel." [*Wall Street Journal, March 17, 2004*]

The avalanche-prevention blasting feud is at its peak in the spring of 2004. The Big Sky and Moonlight Basin ski resorts are at odds over Moonlight's use of their "avalauncher"—a nitrogen-powered cannon used to blast unstable masses of snow on the slopes of the mountains. Big Sky is afraid Moonlight's cannon shots may go astray and land on the Big Sky side of Lone Peak, the eleven-thousand-foot mountain that looms above both areas.

As quoted in the Journal, Lee Poole, co-owner of Moonlight, is skeptical. "Could we launch a round over the top of that?" he asks, staring up at the lofty peak. 'It's about as possible as getting hit by a meteor."

# Getting Hit by a Meteor(ite)

**AUGUST, 2019**

They call Montana Big Sky Country. There are times when it seems to be nearly all sky—on the grasslands when a storm is moving in and the hills shade to goldenrod and ocher, and the clouds become rolling heaps of blowing pink and granite red; at the top of an oxygen-starved peak, gray rock under tough-skinned boots sloping off out of sight, the fierce blue sky overarching the entire planet; and at night, the black stretching out all around, and overhead, without limit, a deeper black made visible only by swarms of stars.

Dr. Michael "Doc" Fuentes and his long-time companion Jamila Sayvetz were out on the deck of their Moonlight Basin, Montana, home, stargazing. It was the beginning of August, approaching the time of the annual Perseid meteor shower and they were hoping to see a few early arrivals. That night in August, the conversation had shifted from stars to meteors. "Both meteors and meteorites start out as what are called meteoroids," explained Jamila, in answer to a question prompted by the sighting of a falling star. "Meteoroid is just a technical name for a small chunk of rock floating around in space," she continued, "sometimes very small, like a grain of sand. Sometimes larger."

"That's what we see as a falling star?" asked Fuentes. "A

meteoroid?"

"Right. A meteoroid hits the Earth's atmosphere going very fast—tens of thousands of miles per hour—and when it hits the atmosphere, it burns up. That's what leaves the luminous trail. Then it becomes a meteor."

Fuentes leaned over towards the deck railing to get a better look at the sky. "This meteor shower coming up, why are there so many all at once?"

"Because we're going through the tail of a comet."

"You're kidding!"

"No, really. Comet Swift/Tuttle; it was last visible from Earth in 1993. Won't be back until 2120-something, but it leaves a trail of dust behind; we pass through it every year."

"Comet dust? That's all it is?"

"This time, yes."

Fuentes considered the meaning of "this time" for a moment, then asked, "But those other bigger chunks, not comet dust, they do hit the atmosphere sometimes?"

"Oh, yes, all the time. Millions every day. Occasionally something big enough hits that doesn't burn up completely and it makes it all the way to the ground. Then it's called a meteorite."

"I think I'll just call everything a meteor and be done with it. Who's going to know the difference? Besides you."

Jamila laughed. "Meteoroid, meteor, meteorite. You're right, it doesn't matter all that much in casual conversation."

Fuentes counted this as a victory against overcomplication, of which he sometimes, playfully, accused her. But he was still curious about the bigger chunks, the not-comet-dust chunks. "So, how big can a meteorite be?" he asked. "Really big?"

"Oh, yeah. Like the Tunguska Event, in Siberia, in 1908; that one flattened all the trees for eighty square miles. It apparently exploded in the atmosphere without hitting the ground and making a crater, but it was like detonating an atomic bomb. Maybe megatons in size. Then there's Chelyabinsk, again in Russia—"

"They have all the luck," said Fuentes.

"—in 2013. It was probably several meters in size, several tons, much smaller than what they estimate Tunguska to have been.

But it made a big bang."

"But we're safe now, because these are just dust and nothing big is going to hit us, right?" he asked, only half facetiously.

"Right."

Fuentes stood and stretched. Tall and broad-shouldered—a swimmer's physique, he liked to say, though now admitting laps were more likely to be swum in the hot tub rather than Ulery's Lake. With short, dark, curly hair, and a perpetual tan, he made a good match for Jamila, who, though smaller, was also athletically built, and very fit. Fuentes sometimes had a hard time keeping up with her on the local trails, summer or winter. Jamila's hair was long and straight, a dark shining black, which accentuated her olive complexion. She and Fuentes had become acquainted back in Oswego, New York, where Fuentes had lived before retiring to Montana. They'd met while assisting a friend with an investigation into a decades-old murder—the kind of thing Fuentes got himself involved in all too often, in her opinion.

After Fuentes had moved to Montana, she'd come to visit him while on sabbatical from SUNY Oswego—this was after a long spell as a professor of electromechanical engineering at Rochester Institute of Technology—and had fallen under the spell of Montana, and Moonlight, within hours of her first visit. She'd returned to New York periodically to work since then, but her trips back had become shorter and less frequent as time went by. There had been much talk of making her relocation to Moonlight permanent, but even though she was becoming more and more attuned to her life in Moonlight, and to her attachment to Fuentes, nothing had been decided.

Fuentes settled back into his chair and they fell into a companionable silence, staring out at the dark sky looming above Spanish Peaks, the mountain range to the north, barely visible across the valley. A few minutes later, a couple of meteors flared high in the sky, leaving thin, luminous trails which faded quickly.

"Think you're getting some good pictures?" Fuentes asked.

"Oh, I'm sure I'm getting something, but it's hard to say how good they'll be. It's pretty much a matter of luck, even though I've oriented the camera in such a way that it should maximize my chances. I've aimed it at a dark portion of the sky away from the radiant point—the apparent source of the meteors, in the constellation Perseus—and it's taking long-exposure frames almost continuously, so I should get some nice trails. It's all streamed wirelessly to my computer and I've got terabytes of disk space allocated. I'll have a *lot* of imaging to sift through, but I wrote an AI program to do the processing."

"Can I help with it at all? I'd love to know more about what you're doing. Meteors are a lot more interesting than I imagined."

"Sure. I run the image processing in batches, and sometimes I'm busy or down in Ennis shopping when a job completes. You could restart the process on the next batch of data. I'll show you what to do. Basically, it's just the click of a button. I can set up some automatic notifications for you, too; like, if the next dataset in the queue isn't processed after a certain amount of time passes, the system will ping you to log in and start it."

"Won't I need your passwords to get into the computer?"

"Oh, I set that encryption up when I was still at RIT, working on some sensitive projects. Out here, I don't worry about it. Everything is local to the disk array—nothing in the cloud, and I've got a good firewall, so no hacking worries—so I leave the computer unlocked, but with the protocols saved. I was afraid I'd forget the encryption codes and get locked out myself. But the imaging data is secure—every access to the database is captured in a log file, in case I need to reconstruct a particular run for any reason. I'm also deleting any raw data that is of no use as I go, and automatically caching any significant results onto a special compressed disk sector. I'll show you how to access that as well. And if you really want to get into it—"

"I do."

"I can even show you how the AI analysis programs work."

"It sounds fascinating, but complicated. Are you sure?"

"Yes! I'm happy you're showing such an interest! It will be great fun working on it together. Don't worry about running programs if I'm not here. You can't screw anything up, and it could be a big help."

"Okay, show me tomorrow," he said. "I'll bet your pictures will be great!"

***

About an hour later, Fuentes was semi-dozing and Jamila was stretching languidly after getting up from her chair, preparing to go to bed, when the sky lit up.

Jamila let out a small shriek. Fuentes started forward with a loud, "Oh, my God," punctuating Jamila's cry of surprise.

This was no ordinary meteor.

"Oh, my God," Jamila automatically echoed Fuentes. "Oh, my."

A huge fireball seared its way across the sky, west to east, with a bright tail streaming out behind it. The trees cast dark shadows on the wide ski trail below the house. The violence in the sky was marked by an eerie silence.

They'd barely had time to register what they were seeing when a fierce flash of incredibly bright light temporarily blinded them. With a nearly simultaneous, deafening sonic boom, the shock wave hit. Jamila was thrown across the deck, hitting the back railing before falling to the floor. Fuentes was knocked back in his chair. The sound of the explosion rolled over the mountains, clear sky thunder heard as far away as Ennis, West Yellowstone, and Bozeman.

Seconds later, there was an explosive crash as something slammed through the ceiling and the deck floor, sending debris flying in all directions. Jamila managed to scream, full-throated this time.

Stunned, they could only stand and stare at the hole in the deck floor. After some minutes, looking at one another in disbelief, they slowly made their way into the house and walked to the living room. The floor was an inch deep in broken glass. They stood staring out, awestruck and silent, through the empty space where floor-to-ceiling windows used to be.

For the next few minutes, accompanied by the sound of car alarms echoing across the valley, stardust and diamonds rained down all over Moonlight Basin.

# The Arm Bone's Connected...

**EARLY FEBRUARY, 2020**

From the top of Lone Peak on a really clear day, Fuentes swore he could see more than any other human at that moment (excepting possibly the space station astronauts). The tourist brochures for the Lone Peak Tram claimed only three states (Idaho, Montana, and Wyoming), two National Parks (Yellowstone and Grand Teton), and a raft of mountain ranges (Absaroka, Beartooth, Bridger, Gallatin, Madison, Tobacco Root) were visible.

Fuentes somewhat reluctantly turned his attention away from the view and to the task at hand. He was attempting the North Summit Snowfield for the first time in more than two years. He didn't want any mistakes today. Since a partner is required in order to ski the North Summit, he had asked his friends Ashley "Bomber" Quande and Bridget "Race Chick" French to ski him down safely. Guys might be tempted to ski for themselves if conditions were great and leave a slower skier behind.

He checked his skis and adjusted his goggles, got a thumbs up from his ski buddies, and then followed them to the backcountry access gate. A minute later he was racing down the side of Lone Peak. It was only a couple of minutes down to the first decision point, the intersection of the "Rips" and "Great Falls" runs. The slightly safer route was Great Falls. Rips was the more demanding for several reasons, first of which was the necessity for very precise and deliberate navigation, and the fact that the more confined route becomes somewhat hard-packed. Then there are the lower rock cliffs. They had previously decided to take Great Falls; it offered less time in Deepwater Bowl, at the lower end of both routes, but was the more straightforward and so posed less risk.

After traversing Great Falls with no real difficulty, Fuentes hit the powder of Deepwater Bowl at high speed and then, with some relief, banked right near the bottom of the bowl on the way to Horseshoe and his easy path down. But just as he finished the turn, he was violently thrown high into the air, and one ski was ripped off.

After landing head first in the deep powder, it took some time to dislodge himself, all the while wondering what the hell had happened. It had been going so well. Shaken but unhurt, he looked downhill for the girls to wave to them that he was okay. He saw only ski tracks. He shrugged his shoulders, then turned and clawed his way thirty feet or so back up the side of the mountain.

He reached the point of his fall and found his ski, then looked around for whatever it was that had tripped him up. There appeared to be a disturbance just above him. He edged closer and looked down into a depression in the snow, a foot or so deep.

Under a light layer of powdery snow at the bottom of the pit, he saw a small object of some kind, glowing with a dim, green light. Despite the warm sun on his back, he felt a sudden chill. He knelt, trying to shake off the eerie feeling, and carefully brushed away the snow. The dim glow suddenly became a bright flare in the sunlight, and he found himself looking down at a silver ring set with a brilliant, chartreuse-green gem.

Looking closer, he saw gray shadows of something much larger lying just underneath the ring. He hesitantly began to clear the snow away from the ring, and soon uncovered the skeletal hand it adorned.

He swept the snow around the hand in a large arc and hit something about a foot to one side. Carefully extracting what he now saw to be the remains of an unattached arm, he subconsciously, yet deliberately, began to examine it as if he were back in anatomy lab in med school. The arm was intact from shoulder to hand; somewhat surprisingly, he thought, given that it had probably been dragged here from some other location, presumably by wolves—bears did not leave small bones behind, or move their prey long distances.

Based on its size and weight, the arm was from an adult male, he was sure. There was no flesh at all remaining, just some thin scraps of tendon, and one oddly colored patch on the protrusions on the upper part of the humerus, the tubercles, which he surmised might be remnants of cloth. There were obvious bite and gnaw marks all along both the upper and lower bones; the ulna, the narrower of the two lower bones, was splintered just above the wrist. The wrist and hand, again somewhat surprisingly, were nearly complete, missing only some small carpal bones and the ends of two fingers. The finger bones were tightly curled, accounting for the fact the ring had stayed on regardless of the ravaging the arm had undergone. The ring finger itself showed clear indications of a spiral fracture.

He uncurled the ring finger, taut with desiccated tendon, and slipped the heavy, masculine-style ring off and held it up to examine it more closely. There were no inscriptions other than a minute jeweler's mark on the inside of the band. The gem was set very simply. It was heavily faceted, scintillating in the bright white light reflecting off the snow. When he'd first uncovered it, he'd thought "emerald," but now as he held it in his hand, he saw it was much lighter in hue than a typical emerald—a yellow-green, a spring green, not the darker blue-green of emerald. He'd never seen anything like it. Obviously not costume jewelry—the gem had such depth, such a deep reflective glow, he suspected it must be something special.

He made a quick search around the general area but found no sign of anything else buried there; no other body parts, and no body, confirming his initial impression the arm had been carried here. For a moment he considered taking the arm down the hill with him to turn over to the authorities, but then thought better of it— the exact spot where it was found may be important in a later search for additional remains. Besides, he might drop it. Better to leave it here.

He had a sudden thought and looked around almost furtively. *What to do with the ring? Can't take the chance it will get lost somehow when the ski patrol carries it down*. It could be crucial in identifying the victim. These could be the only remains ever found, depending on precisely where the presumed backcountry accident had occurred. It occasionally happened that a climber or hiker was reported missing and never seen or heard from again. More often than most people knew.

He didn't think for a moment the ring would be "intentionally" lost—the ski patrollers up here were among the best he'd known over his long skiing career, all over the world. No, there was no chance one of them would lift it. But what if in the meantime, before they could get back up here, some other skier noticed the disturbance in the snow and stopped to take a look? Though normally a trusting sort, Fuentes was also a realist. It was a small chance, he knew; but still, better to be sure.

He put the ring into an inside pocket of his parka and zipped it shut. After gingerly placing the bones back into the small cavity in the powder, he stabbed a ski pole into the snow beside it as a marker. The ski patrol should have no trouble finding it.

*Wonder if they'll ever find the rest of him? Certainly not until summer.*

***

It had been over three weeks, and still no word.

The ski patrol had found the pole marking the location of the arm easily. The bones, wrapped in a plastic bag, had been turned over to the Madison County sheriff's department within the hour. What had happened to them after that point was still something of a mystery.

Jamila glanced up from her laptop as Fuentes waited on hold for the third time in the same call. "What now?"

"I've just been transferred back to the person I talked with ten minutes ago. No one seems to know—hold on." He bent his head down, holding the phone tightly to his ear. "I'm sorry? I can barely hear you. Yes, Dr. Michael Fuentes. I just talked to you—yes, the remains found on the side of Lone Peak. Alright, thank you."

He gave Jamila a sardonic look. "I've been referred to the

14

Gallatin County sheriff's department. It's like the opposite of turf wars is going on, no one wants to take responsibility." After another long pause and a quick "Thanks," he hung up. "Asked if I knew how many missing persons reports are active this month."

"How many?"

"A hundred-and-eighty. They said they'll have someone call me back."

It was another three weeks before someone from the Gallatin County Medical Examiner's office called. The remains had been transferred to the Montana State Forensic Science morgue in Billings. A hopeful sign, but a call there was as fruitless as his previous attempts with the local county offices. He tried to convince the examiner of the significance of the spiral fracture of the ring finger but was unsuccessful. By this time, COVID had really started picking up speed, and investigations were being backburnered whenever possible. Since this case was not urgent, he was told, it would be shelved indefinitely unless someone came forward with new, credible, information. He did not appreciate the emphasis the examiner had put on "credible."

In the meantime, given the uncertainty surrounding the disposition of the remains, he'd decided to hold on to the ring a while longer. He checked the community bulletin boards in the grocery store and deli periodically, but there were no posts regarding a lost ring of matching description. After a while, he gave up looking.

The ring, wrapped in a soft cloth, sat in the corner of a little-used dresser drawer, out of sight but not forgotten.

# What are the Odds?

**JUNE, 2020**

The trip to Moonlight Basin from the small Bozeman Yellowstone International Airport typically takes slightly over an hour, barring wildfires, which were, this early in the year, unlikely. Fuentes had just picked up his good friends A.C. LaFleur and his wife Maggie Malone, who had come in from Oswego, New York, where they owned a restaurant called the 1850 House. Fuentes had introduced A.C. to Maggie many years before, when he worked at Oswego Hospital and where she had been head nurse. It had been right after A.C. had retired from the detective division of the Oswego police force. Maggie had asked for help in solving a mystery at the hospital, and Fuentes had known A.C. would be perfect for the job.

As they made their way south down through the Gallatin Canyon towards Big Sky, Fuentes explained the current situation in Moonlight, post-meteorite. An early winter had set in not long after the strike the previous year, putting a temporary halt to what had been a rather frenzied search for large fragments, or even the main body, which was thought to have hit somewhere in the general area. In the spring, as soon as the snows had melted sufficiently, a treasure-hunting mania had descended on Moonlight like a plague. Plague was not an inappropriate metaphor, he suddenly realized, given the recent COVID situation—in fact, that was why A.C. and Maggie were here, to get out of New York to shelter in the downstairs apartment of Doc's house. Together they'd create their own "safe pod." If they needed to go out, they could use one of Doc's cars. With visitors like A.C. and Maggie, and the influx of second- and third-home owners—who normally spent just a few weeks per year in Moonlight, but who were now also sheltering long-term—Moonlight was busier and more populous than ever. The treasure hunters were an added complication.

"You won't believe it," said Fuentes. "People have gone nuts." He looked over at A.C. with a wry look. "Even Big Frank."

Frank Ivanovich, a long-time friend and sometime co-conspirator of both Fuentes and A.C., had arrived in Moonlight several weeks earlier from the Washington, D.C. area. He was also fleeing the densely populated East Coast in search of isolation and had rented a four-bedroom house near Fuentes, something called the Silvertip model. He'd quickly become interested in meteorite hunting, serious enough about his new prospecting venture to have built his own sluices. He'd rented a gigantic Dodge 4X4 crew cab pickup to haul what he called the "meteorite ore" he collected back to the house. At over six-feet tall and weighing around two-hundred-thirty pounds (thus "Big" Frank), he made an excellent prospector—he could load more dirt into those sluices in an hour than Fuentes could in three.

A.C. grinned. "Sounds like Frank," he said. "What's he up to?"

"He just finished building sluices in both of the little creeks flanking the house," Fuentes explained. "Works them constantly. He nearly went apoplectic the other day when he panned some big flakes of gold and what appear to be small diamonds from his concentrates."

"Diamonds?" asked Maggie, with both interest and incredulity. "Real diamonds?"

"Yeah, they're real. The gold might be local, but the diamonds are from the meteorite. As for the treasure hunting—you can't help getting a bit caught up in it. Especially since there really are things to be found, as Frank has already proved."

"How close did it hit?" asked Maggie. "I mean, do you think someone will find it?"

"You mean the mother lode?" asked Fuentes, with a quick smile.

"Well, yes," she answered. "Aren't you looking for it too?"

"I already have a pretty big piece of it," said Fuentes." It went through the roof—and the floor—of our deck."

"Oh, my God. You could have been killed!"

"Well, as far as I know, that's very rare. The chance of an individual being hit or killed by a meteorite is much lower than being killed by lightning."

"That's reassuring," said Maggie dubiously.

"As soon as we're settled in at the house, I'll show you our personal meteorite."

"The one that went through the deck? It's still intact?" A.C. asked.

"A fairly big piece of it, yeah. It went through the roof and the deck floor and embedded itself in the concrete patio below. We're going to turn it into a decorative feature—build a little stone border around it, shine an art spot on it—it's really quite attractive."

"Doesn't it just look like a chunk of rock?" asked A.C., again, rather skeptically.

"Just wait until you see it, A.C.," Fuentes said enthusiastically. "It's really something—when the sun hits it just right, the diamonds in it flash right up into the sky."

"So, what's it worth?"

"Oh, hard to tell; we'd have to pull it out of the concrete and break it up for a complete analysis. I think it has more intrinsic value the way it sits. Especially with the commercial diamond market the way it is now. Anyway, it already has some local notoriety. Around here they're calling it 'Doc's Rock.' Not everyone has their own house meteorite, after all."

The conversation the rest of the way turned to queries about common friends and acquaintances back in Oswego, A.C.'s plans for finally divesting himself of the restaurant, and Maggie's volunteer nursing work.

Jamila was waiting out front with a big smile of greeting—

she hadn't seen A.C. and Maggie for over two years now, since the last time they'd been in Moonlight. A.C. was a little slow getting out of the car, helped along by Maggie, but other than that she saw that he hadn't changed much—his hair was longer than usual, swept back in what Jamila guessed was a homemade COVID cut, and he wore the same heavy, black-framed glasses, but still looked great. She was glad to see he'd retired the ragged old Detroit Tigers ball cap he used to wear constantly and replaced it with the MSU Wildcats cap Fuentes had sent him.

Maggie had changed not at all, Jamila decided. Only a couple of inches shorter than A.C.'s six-feet even, her long auburn hair still showed very little silver, and Jamila knew she didn't dye. As Fuentes got the luggage out of the back, Maggie stood off to one side and stretched, limbering herself up after the hour in the car, displaying a figure A.C. like to describe as "statuesque." Jamila could tell she had not let the pandemic interfere with her yoga or exercise routines.

The last time they were here, she couldn't help thinking, they'd almost all been killed. Not by a meteorite, of course, but by a criminal gang A.C. had been on the verge of exposing. It had been another one of Doc's escapades, one that had begun in the Pony Bar, of all places, brought about by his never-ending desire to see justice served, as always aided and abetted by A.C.

There would be a lot of reminiscing done over the next few weeks. *But please*, she silently begged, *no excitement*!

# Lucy in the Sky

"So, Jamila," asked Maggie, continuing the previous conversation regarding the appearance of meteorites in Moonlight, "how have things changed since the meteorite hit?"

"Since Moonlight appears to be at the focus of the strike," Jamila said, "we've been inundated with treasure-hunters—some legitimate, as most meteorite collectors are, but some not so much—nefarious would not be too strong a word. The fact is, there really are diamonds to be found—some very small, microdiamonds, or even nanodiamonds, they're called—though there may be even larger, gem quality stones embedded in bigger pieces. And it's not just diamonds—other, even more desirable minerals are found in meteorites. But diamonds, in any case, are close to becoming commodities in the gem market. Synthetic diamonds are not only as good as real diamonds, they're also becoming more desirable, because they are marketed as being the ethical choice. People don't want so-called 'blood diamonds' anymore, despite the even more intense marketing still surrounding natural diamonds."

"There is still a lot of interest in real diamonds, though," Fuentes said, "but from less controversial sources. A guy found a huge diamond in Crater of Diamonds State Park in Arkansas recently; nine carats, the size of a large marble. I think they said it was worth about a million bucks."

"The same thing for meteoric diamonds," said Jamila. "Even

though the market is small, given their uniqueness, they still command a relatively high price. The result is that since the strike the situation here has become very unpredictable. The consensus is that a large piece of it landed around here somewhere, and a lot of people are coming into the area who want it, and want it badly."

"You think some of these treasure hunters are dangerous?" asked A.C.

"Well, let's just say there have been some disturbing incidents," said Fuentes. "Not just simple trespassing, which is rife, but several more serious confrontations: threats exchanged, vehicles vandalized, that sort of thing. There have been a sufficient number of such incidents that Moonlight Security has really clamped down on access. Not just Jack Creek Road, which as you know, being private, has always been something of an access issue. They've not only stepped up patrols, but have also implemented a registration system for all of Moonlight Basin—checkpoints at every access point, and severe restrictions on guest passes. It's really playing hell with construction and service access, and it's nearly impossible to get a guest pass these days. Fortunately, you and Maggie—and Big Frank—were already in the database, so as repeat visitors getting a pass for you was not impossible. Difficult, but not impossible."

"What's going to happen next, do you think?" asked Maggie.

"Hard to say. I thought it would have calmed down some by now. I suppose the treasure hunting isn't going to die down much until someone finds the primary body, what's left of the big one that created the fireball and exploded. Oh, people will still want to find small pieces; that will probably go on at some level for a long time. But the hysteria will die down once the big one is found. At least I hope so." He paused, reflecting. "But it's also true people are finding small diamonds all over the place. A friend of ours, Monte Johnsen, found one in the Chopper's Pub parking lot in Big Sky."

"There's a rumor going around that the meteorite was *all* diamond," Jamila said, "a chunk of a white dwarf star called 'Lucy in the Sky.'"

"*Lucy in the sky…*," Maggie began to sing in a rich contralto.

"*With diamonds*," finished A.C., in a scratchy, not so rich, off-key baritone.

"Yes, exactly," Jamila went on. "The astronomical name of the star is BPM 37093. It's theorized its core has crystallized, and since white dwarfs are mainly carbon and some oxygen, the core could be solid diamond. Trillions of carats! Of course, it's just not possible for a meteorite to be thrown out of a star—they either cool down and eventually die, or blow up, leaving nothing behind but an ionized clod of gas and dust—but people out here are ready to believe just about anything."

"It's hard to imagine it can get any weirder," said Fuentes. "Last week a couple of guys climbed down the side of Lone Peak to a small lake there—around here it's called 'Lost Lake' but it's actually unnamed on the USGS charts—I've started calling it Lone Lake, which makes more sense, especially since we've already got some 'lost lakes' up behind the seventh hole at the Reserve—but anyway, these guys carried in scuba gear in order to search the lake for the meteorite. Other meteorite hunters have set up elaborate base camps and are conducting extensive grid searches, using meteorological data to try to pinpoint the location of the main strike."

"But even if it has tiny diamonds in it, or whatever, can it really be that valuable?" asked Maggie. "I thought a meteorite was almost all iron."

"Most do contain a large percentage of iron—that's why they're so heavy," said Jamila.

"And can usually be found with a metal detector," added Fuentes."

"Meteorites in general are very collectable," continued Jamila, "and are typically worth thousands of dollars, or even more."

"You mentioned other desirable minerals," said Maggie. "What else in a meteorite could be valuable?"

"Olivine," replied Jamila. "Actually, olivine crystals. Which, if large enough and pure enough, are cut and faceted to make a light-green gemstone called peridot. So far, only some preliminary tests have been completed, and the one that hit here doesn't appear to be that type of meteorite. Although one report I read—again, very preliminary, and based on who knows what—hinted at the presence of an even rarer component, something called pallavine. It's crystalline like olivine, but has a richer color, a deep spring green. I've had several desperate inquiries from colleagues in Germany asking whether this could be a pallasite, that is, a meteorite containing olivine or pallavine. It was a German meteorite collector who obtained an extremely large piece of a pallavine meteorite, several years ago. It's the only source of pallavine in the world right now. If the Moonlight meteorite does prove to be pallavine, and not olivine, it's very rare indeed. But there's no indication it's either one, based on what's been found so far. The present mania is nothing to what you'd see in that case. But the chances are very slim."

"Does Frank know about pallavine?" asked A.C. anxiously. "All this sounds as intriguing as hell, but in my experience, intrigue often leads to endangerment of some kind. I'm afraid if it gets out of hand, Frank will end up like the old prospector in *Treasure of the Sierra Madre*—dancing a jig on top of his lost fortune."

Fuentes frowned. "Well, I, for one, will be glad when it all dies down. But I'm involved in it, regardless. Which reminds me— I won't be able to guide you on any prospecting tours right away. My friend Mandy, the manager at the Wilson Hotel, wants me to meet her there tomorrow afternoon. She recently met a woman who's been asking around about a meteorite hunter—her brother— who went missing last fall. She asked Mandy if she knew anyone who could give her information about the area. Mandy naturally thought of me."

"How on earth does it involve you?" asked Maggie.

"I'm not sure; Mandy said her friend is particularly interested in searching the areas in and around Moonlight. I told her I'd be glad to help any way I can. But there's something about this missing person Mandy doesn't know about. I don't know if I should…" His voice trailed off

"Well?" asked A.C, following an exasperated pause.

Fuentes hesitated. "I shouldn't have brought it up."

"Oh, no, mister," said Jamila archly. "Now that you *did* bring it up, you have to tell them."

"I may have found his bones."

# A Really Poor Bedside Manner

Fuentes was not disappointed at the opportunity to visit the new Wilson Hotel bar. It was rivaled, in his opinion, only by the bar at Michelangelo's Restaurant, both, however, being second to the Moonlight Tavern. The long, sleek, white marble bar had an incredible view, but in the current social-distancing environment due to the pandemic, it was not open. Like the Moonlight Tavern, the bar stools had been removed, and only very limited seating was available in the equally elegant main dining room. Fortunately, the Wilson had an exquisite outdoor patio, with multiple firepits and spacious seating arrangements. That's where he and Jamila met up with Mandy.

"Mandy!" Fuentes greeted his hostess enthusiastically as they entered the hotel lobby, where she'd been waiting.

"Doc, thanks for coming down. Jamila, so good to see you! It's been a while." She gestured at their masked faces and laughed. "Well, *sort of* see you, anyway. But we can unmask as soon as we get outside."

"You said we'd be meeting your friend here?" Fuentes asked.

"Yes, Abigail MacLeod," said Mandy. "A very nice girl, Doc—bright, vivacious, just delightful." She paused. "And very determined to find out what happened to her brother."

Fuentes nodded slowly. "That's what you said when you

asked me to meet with her. And exactly what I'm afraid of—her wanting too many answers."

"Oh, I don't think that will be a problem; she seems very level-headed." Mandy paused. "But determined." She turned and pointed in the direction of the outdoor patio. "Come on out to the patio; I've got a space reserved. Abigail should be here any minute."

Jamila leaned close to Fuentes as they made their way through the lobby, whispering, "What are you getting involved in now?"

"Don't worry," he whispered back. "Nothing is going to come of this."

***

Just as they'd settled in on the patio and ordered drinks, Abigail came through the door from the lobby, pulling her mask off as she walked towards them. Mandy stood up and waved. "Over here, Abber," she called.

Fuentes stood up as Abigail came towards them, watching her approach with some trepidation. His assurances to Jamila had sounded hollow, even to him. But now that he saw her, he began to relax. She was young—very young by his increasingly elderly standards—perhaps about twenty-three or twenty-four, of slight build and moderate height, with long, silky brown hair framing a gorgeous heart-shaped face.

"Abigail," Mandy said, "this is Dr. Fuentes, more commonly known as Doc, and Dr. Jamila Sayvetz."

"I'm very glad to meet you, Dr. Fuentes, Dr. Sayvetz," Abigail said as she moved to the other side of the low table separating the four large wicker chairs arranged around it. "It's so kind of you to take the trouble to meet with me. I was afraid I would be imposing, but Mandy assured me you would very graciously agree to hear my story. Of course, I have no intention of placing you under any obligation, Dr. Fuentes. I'm just looking for anything that will help me find Stony—my brother, Dan—his nickname is Stony. That's what all his friends at the magazine call him. Seems a bit silly, I know, but we're all used to it, now. . .we *were* used to it..."

25

She trailed off as if uncertain where she was going with this, and slightly embarrassed at her rambling, but perhaps more evidently upset by the reminder of why she was telling the story. But then she straightened her shoulders and continued, quickly back in control. "I am interested in anything, anything at all, you might know that can help me locate him."

"Tell me a little more about him," said Fuentes. "You mentioned he's a geologist, but you also mentioned something about a magazine?"

"Oh, yes. Well, Stony, as I said, is a geologist, a very good geologist, but he has this romantic streak. I used to tease him about being the 'Indiana Jones' of geology, always looking for the next great geological adventure. Well, he's made some fantastic finds in the past, even if there were no crystal skulls involved, and he *does* have quite a good reputation. This led to a gig with the Smithsonian museum, and the magazine. They love that kind of stuff— scientifically sound, but exciting to the lay reader, you know? Stony is very good at that. He sorta likes being an Indiana Jones kind of character, but it's just in fun. He doesn't take himself too seriously." After a short, reflective pause, she added, "Even though he is one of the premier meteoric geologists in the field."

"I wouldn't think geology was all that adventuresome an occupation," commented Fuentes, "or all that exciting to the Smithsonian, unless it also involved paleontology or something like that."

"Yes, that's what you would think, isn't it? But when it comes to geology, Stony doesn't limit himself to normal, everyday, down-to-earth geology. Oh, no, his interests are more, well, cosmic. The real reason he got the nickname 'Stony' is not just because he's a geologist and geologists are interested in rocks, but because he is interested in very unusual rocks. Meteorites. There are two types of meteorites called 'stony,' the most common ones, and 'stony-iron' meteorites, which are rarer. There are also some even rarer types, but, well, they're very hard to come by, obviously; that's why they're so rare." She gave a rather forced laugh. "Sorry. I'm rambling again."

Fuentes waved his hand. "No, you're giving us a very vivid

picture of your brother. You seem to know quite a bit about meteorites, as well."

"I guess I've become a meteorite hunter, too," she replied. "I started helping Stony with his work by being his back-office support. Editing his magazine articles, keeping up with his banking, arranging his travel issues on the fly, keeping him informed of the latest meteor events, arranging potential buyers or jewelers for his finds, and best of all, occasionally searching with him for interstellar treasures. I telexed him at his hotel in N'Djamena, Chad, with the news of the Moonlight Basin meteorite strike. He had been in Chad for three weeks—there had been rumors of a fireball and a nearby strike, but it wasn't panning out—in any case, moving on to Moonlight was an easy decision for him, and he left Chad almost immediately after my report. I met up with him here last September. He was here for almost a month before I arrived, and then we searched together for several weeks. When I left to go back to Washington D.C. to catch up on my office work, the weather was already turning cold. Heavy early snows." She paused and looked down at the table. "That's the last time I saw him."

Then she looked up at the three of them with determination. "But I'm sure there's a reasonable explanation for his disappearance. I really expect to find him off in the wilderness somewhere, in a neat little camp, completely out of sight, out of cell range, totally absorbed in the hunt. He gets like that, sometimes. A couple of years ago he went missing in the deserts of Mali for over a month, then suddenly reappeared in Marrakesh, carrying a large olivine meteorite he found in a relatively unexplored region close to a known find from 2009."

"Mali! Isn't that a very dangerous place?" remarked Jamila.

"Yes, very. But Stony is nothing if not resourceful." She paused. "If I can do anything to help him out in the meantime, before we find him, I want to do it. But finding Stony is the important thing. That's where you come in, Dr. Fuentes."

Fuentes leaned forward. "Why do you think I can help?" he asked. "And call me Doc, please."

"Okay, Doc it is. And you can call me Abber." Fuentes smiled in agreement. "Well, Mandy tells me as a full-time resident of Moonlight, you know a lot more about who comes and goes than the part-time residents, and you are very 'in' with Moonlight Security. I was hoping—and I know this is very presumptuous—you could get me into Moonlight. Mandy says it's practically under lockdown due to the meteorite strike. I mean, even more than the pandemic lockdown."

"That's true. We've had some trouble. Some, well, very shady-looking types have been coming into the area. Moonlight is just trying to keep things under control. As a private community, they have a responsibility to their members to maintain a safe environment. Which is now being threatened."

At this moment, he happened to look over at two men sitting at the table nearby. One of them looked back, but as soon as he made eye contact, the man turned away quickly, leaning toward his companion, whispering. The man was dressed rather shabbily in a brown suit, very thin, with an even thinner face which made his bulbous eyes stand out ominously. He had a ragged look about him, and fidgeted in his chair constantly, shifting his drink from one hand to the other. The second man was much heavier, dressed in work clothes—dungarees, plaid shirt, lumberjack jacket—with a round, pink face with narrow set eyes, and with the same ragged look as the first man. He looked over at Fuentes briefly, then bent down and began furiously texting on his cell phone, fat fingers flying.

Fuentes leaned over towards Mandy. "Any idea who those guys are?" he asked, tilting his head slightly in their direction.

Mandy shook her head. "Just part of the new crowd. It's like the Klondike gold rush around here lately. They ran out of 4-wheel-drive rental vehicles at the Bozeman airport about three weeks ago. REI sold out of about ninety-percent of their backcountry gear in the last month. Everybody and his dog think they're going to make their fortunes in Moonlight. And they all think they know exactly where to look."

"That's something Jamila might know something about," said Fuentes, earning a sharp glance. "What I mean," he artfully hedged, "is she has her own theories about where the strike occurred, just like everyone else." He gave Jamila a sidelong look, nodding slightly in recognition of his slip. He looked around, anxious to change the subject.

Thankfully, Mandy went on talking about the two men at the other table. "They booked into the hotel three weeks ago," she said. "Separate but adjoining rooms. They pay in cash day-to-day. The place is full of them, either staying here or meeting up in the lobby at night, then gathering out here where they can drink. They're loud, obnoxious, maybe even dangerous, by the look of some of them. Not the kind of business I want, but they were here first and are taking up all the available rooms. I'm turning away families, retirees, young couples, all looking for a getaway from the city—I hate it. But what can I do?"

As Mandy was describing her clientele woes, another man walked out of the hotel lobby and over to the two men. Jamila had by this time also been watching them, and when the third man walked over, she gave an audible gasp. He was hideous. He was tall and heavily built—heavier even than the pink-faced man—not in an obese way, but more like a stereotypical stevedore, or bricklayer, or even a heavyweight boxer. Substantial, but carrying his obvious strength with ease. His face was abnormally asymmetric, starting from a forehead sloping disconcertingly off to the right, as if he'd been dropped sideways on his head as a small child. One eyelid drooped, covering about half of his right eye, and seemed frozen in place. Thin lips stretched crookedly under a large misbegotten nose which only drew attention to the skewed position of his eyes.

The man leaned over to the thin man at the table. "I'm here, just checked in. Let's go somewhere private where we can talk about our prospects." This almost seemed aimed at Fuentes. His next gesture was not as ambiguous—he leaned over in their direction, and staring directly at Abigail, winked. Not a friendly wink, but a leering, oleaginous wink. Abigail turned her head. Then the three of them left the patio and went back into the hotel.

"What a creepy guy!" said Jamila, to no one in particular. Then turning to Abigail, she said, "I guess you get a lot of 'pretty girl' winks, but I don't think that was one of them."

"You're right," Abigail said with a dismal note in her voice.

Jamila sensed Abigail was holding something back. "Who is he?"

"His name is Orvis Mooney," Abigail said, her voice muted, as if Mooney could still overhear. "Stony often warned me about him. A claim jumper. He always steered clear of him." She put her hands to her forehead. "And now he's turned up here."

This cast a pall over the group, and they sat there in silence for a minute or two before Fuentes tried to get things back on track. "Abigail, um, Abber...before we go on," he said, "I've been meaning to tell you ever since you sat down, I've been admiring your ring. The stone, especially—it's very unusual. Beautiful."

Abigail sat back slightly, somewhat surprised, and held up her hand, and Fuentes took a closer look. The ring was silver, perhaps platinum—he couldn't be sure—with a bright, light yellow-green stone set in the center of a circle of small diamonds. "Why, thank you, Doc," said Abigail, demurely. "Yes, the ring is rather special. It was a present from Stony, so it means a lot to me." She tilted her hand back and forth slowly, causing the gem to flash white, green and yellow.

Fuentes leaned forward as Abigail held out her hand. "May I take a closer look?" he asked. She nodded her assent, and he took her hand in his, holding it gently. Her fingers were slender, light and pink, well-manicured. The stone glittered brightly in the light of the flickering firepit. He had a sudden vision of the same stone glowing green under a thin dusting of snow. The finger which had held the other ring had been light as well, but more than slender, more than light: desiccated and bone-white. He looked up.

"Abigail, your brother is dead."

***

With a loud gasp, Abigail jerked her hand back. *First Mooney, and now this?* She looked at Fuentes with an intense look of—despair? Shock? Or could it be fright? She suddenly held her hands up to her face and began sobbing spasmodically.

Jamila leaned close to Fuentes and hissed, "You don't know it was her brother!"

He held his hand up and replied out of the side of his mouth, in an urgent, low tone: "But the ring!"

Suddenly Abigail was on her feet, turning back and forth, as if in confusion as to where to go. Mandy stood and took her by the arm and led her into the hotel lobby, and from there to the lady's room.

Fuentes and Jamila sat in uncomfortable silence while Mandy and Abigail were away, scarcely daring to look at one another. Jamila swirled the ice in her drink, a little too vigorously, Fuentes thought, by the look on his face. He motioned to the waitress.

"Another floater, please?"

"I'm sorry, what is a floater?" She had replaced the waitress who'd originally served them and wasn't familiar with his special version of scotch and water.

"A glass of ice, spring water up to just below the rim, with a splash of Famous Grouse floated on top."

"Okay, perfect! I'll have it right out to you."

"Thanks."

After a few minutes, Abigail and Mandy returned to the table, Abigail composed and calm, Mandy looking somewhat bewildered. She sat down with an accusatory glance at Fuentes. He gave a slight shrug.

"I'm so sorry, "said Abigail, as she settled back into her chair. "I just wasn't expecting that." She stiffened a bit. "And I don't believe you. I know Stony is out in the wilderness somewhere, searching for the meteorite. I just need your help to find him."

"But no one has reported seeing him all winter," said Fuentes, in what he hoped was a placating manner. "What has he been living on for six months? Why hasn't anyone reported seeing him? Found his camp?"

"You don't know Stony. I told you he's very resourceful."

"But six months? No, more like seven, by now."

Abigail set her jaw, straightened her shoulders, and leaned forward like a determined candidate in a particularly heated political debate. "I refuse to believe he's dead! I have no reason to believe he's dead. I know Stony. I know what he's capable of, even though you seem to want to believe the worst. I need to get into Moonlight! Just get me access. Just let me prove to you how wrong you are."

31

She thrust her face forward defiantly.

Fuentes squared his shoulders to match Abigail's determined posture, began to say something, and then suddenly slumped back into his chair, as if relinquishing the fight. He raised his head in an anguished tilt and looked up at Abigail, eyes averted.

"Abigail, your brother was murdered."

***

This was too much.

Abigail let out a strangled shriek and clapped her hands to her face once again. Mandy reached over, and while glaring pointedly at Fuentes, lifted Abigail up by the shoulders. "Come on, Abber," she said softly, and once again escorted her back into the hotel.

Once they were alone, Jamila set her drink onto the table with a deliberately loud thump. "Doc! How could you! Even if it was him, you don't know it was murder! It's been ruled a backcountry misadventure, that's all! They haven't even found any more remains."

"But I've explained this all to you. No one has followed up on my suggestion about the spiral fracture of the ring finger. It's been completely ignored, even with me pressing them."

"It's very thin, Doc. The arm was detached. It was ravaged by bears. Wolves. Whatever."

"Yeah, the whatever, that's the thing. It's only the ring finger that was fractured like that!" he hissed determinedly, keeping his voice low to avoid any more attention being drawn to them. "That type of fracture is very uncommon. It takes a lot of torque to twist a bone like that. Wolves rip and tear. Gnaw. Bears bite right through bones. They don't twist."

Jamila turned away, hoping this conversation could just be over, but Fuentes persisted.

"You know it's what I've been thinking all along. Regardless of what the medical examiner says. Regardless of what you might think. I'm telling you, a fracture like that takes a concerted effort. Exactly as if someone were trying to violently twist a ring off."

"You have no proof!"

"Maybe not." He looked up as he saw Mandy and Abigail returning from the lobby. "But she's wearing the same kind of stone!"

"You can't even be sure of that much!"

Fuentes had no opportunity to reply to that. Mandy and Abigail had returned. He half stood as Mandy and Abigail seated themselves, in a sort of bow. He looked over at Jamila. She stared straight ahead.

"I apologize for being so blunt, Abigail," he said. "Perhaps I'm jumping to unwarranted conclusions. I occasionally get a bit carried away, especially when it's something as unusual as what I discovered up on Lone Peak."

"Doc!" Jamila's eyes glared at him, and not with the reflected glow of the fire pit next to them.

"What do you mean?" Abigail's lower lip was quivering.

"Sorry. It's nothing to do with your brother, I'm sure. Forget I said anything."

"But if you know something…" She seemed again to be on the verge of tears.

"No, nothing, really. And I'm sure," he said soothingly, glancing again at Jamila, "I'm sure you'll find your brother. If there's anything I can do to help in the search, just let me know, and I'll do everything I can to help."

"If I can just get access to Moonlight," Abigail replied, her voice steady, with what seemed to be a new determination. "Moonlight. That's where I really need to start looking."

"I'll arrange a pass for you first thing tomorrow."

"Oh, Doc, thank you!" She leaned forward. "With your help, I can't fail!"

***

As they drove out of the hotel parking lot twenty minutes later, Jamila couldn't help but ask, disgruntled, yet with some concern, "How did you ever succeed as a doctor with such a lousy bedside manner?"

33

"I'm an anesthesiologist. All my patients were unconscious. What would they know of bedside manner?"

"Not funny."

"I'll have you know I was often complimented on my bedside manner," he retorted. "By both doctors and patients." He sighed. "Oh, I don't know. Guess I've lost my touch."

"Well, lose the crazy murder theory while you're at it."

The trip home proceeded in silence.

# Finders Keepers?

They had started out on the Moonlight Reserve golf course playing Best Ball, with Fuentes and A.C. on one team, Frank and Maggie on the other, each team using the lowest score of the two team members for that hole. Jamila, who normally walked along with Fuentes looking for lost golf balls (his and others, and there were always plenty of each), had stayed at home working on her computer, analyzing the imaging data from the night of the strike.

After the fourth hole, struggling mightily to maintain even double bogey scores, they declared discretion to be the better part of valor and switched to straight Scramble. The Scramble format had the advantage of still using the best ball of each player every time, and it also gave them more opportunity to chat, since they all converged on the same spot and dropped their ball for the next stroke.

"Bad luck!" Fuentes called out to the others as they retrieved their errant shots. "Our best ball is sitting right behind a pretty good-sized example of bear scat."

Maggie came up behind him and looked over his shoulder. "No! Really? Bear?"

"Oh, yeah," said Fuentes. "See all the berries?"

She looked around quickly in all directions. "Is he still here?"

He laughed. "No, long gone. But anyway, we automatically

get relief." He stooped and picked up the ball, then dropped it a couple of feet away. "Club rules," he explained. "Bear, elk, deer—natural hazards. You should see what an elk can do to a well-manicured green," he added.

"Oh, do you think we'll see an elk?" asked Maggie, her voice rising in excitement.

"You never know. Last week I saw a bear on nine, and a bobcat on twelve. Elk and moose are a dime-a-dozen, hardly even worth mentioning. And not long ago," he continued, "I was trailed for several minutes by a pair of wolves."

"How big were they?" asked Frank.

"See the path that's been cut through the high grass over there?" Fuentes asked, pointing up the hill. "When the wolves that were following me took off, they went through that path. Their backs stuck up above the top level of the grass, so at least two feet tall. And I'd say they were between five and six feet long."

"That big?" Maggie squeaked.

"Oh, yeah," said Fuentes. "One of them up on his hind legs could look you right in the eye!"

"Oh, stop it now!" she cried. "But there were only two, right? So not really dangerous?" she asked.

"I saw just two that day. They were probably part of the local Fan Mountain pack."

"How big is a pack?"

"It depends on the area. A pack might number as few as three, or almost forty. I think the Fan Mountain pack has around twenty wolves."

Maggie's tone shifted from excitement to anxiety. "Could we be attacked? I mean, right here, on the golf course?"

"Very unlikely," Fuentes answered. "Wolves hunt at night."

"Well, that's a relief. But I'd still like to see one. An elk or a moose, I mean," she quickly clarified. "No bobcats or bears." She shivered theatrically. "And certainly not any wolves!"

By this time, Frank and A.C. had caught up with them, bringing their less well-placed shots with them. "Or lions, or tigers, oh, my," said A.C., chuckling as they walked up behind them.

"Oh, be quiet. You'd like to see one, too."

"Here's our drop area," said Fuentes, pointing at his ball. "Now, from here," he said, pointing down the hill, "just remember everything is trying to follow the natural drainage. Away from the mountain. So, whatever you do, aim left."

"This is the only course I've ever played where my chronic hook is an advantage," commented Frank.

"It's served you well, today," agreed A.C., dropping his ball. "Let's hope it works here. The area over to the right looks pretty wild."

"Oh, yeah," agreed Fuentes. "Once it rolls off the edge over there, it's gone for good. Even Jamila won't go down there alone."

True to form, Frank hit a long draw, and it worked perfectly. The ball hit the left edge of the fairway, rounded the corner, cleared a slight rise, and rolled down to a level area in line with the green.

"Good job, Frank," said Fuentes, as they gathered at his ball. "I think we have a shot at par."

"Not the way I pitch," said A.C., looking up the hill at the elevated green, now about sixty yards away. "Nicklaus sure knows how to challenge you, that's for sure."

"Yes, but remember, all you have to do is get within about six feet of the cup; then you've always got a pretty level putt. Jack doesn't believe in being too tricky close in. He's ensured the greens are challenging enough as it is without adding unnecessary bumps and lumps close to the hole."

"If you say so," he grumbled.

Fuentes had mentioned earlier the local developer had been floating the idea of a new golf course, to be located south of the Reserve course, between Horseshoe ski run and the cart repair barn. "One of the wildest and untrammeled areas in Moonlight," he'd called it. Not ironically, he'd said it "should be a challenging course."

"Doc," said Frank as he placed his ball, "I don't understand why, with a course as beautiful as this,"—he gestured at the surrounding mountains—"why on earth would anyone want to build another golf course in Moonlight?"

"Several reasons. One of the biggest being the necessity of getting rid of sewage effluent. You've seen the construction going on around here—with full homesite build-out, new condos and townhomes, and this year with a wet spring and early summer, we can barely manage to get rid of it. Since we have a short summer season and a high elevation, evaporation won't do it."

"Why not dump it into Jack Creek?" asked A.C.

"Oh, no. Even if proven to be safe, which it is, it would never be allowed. You're from New York. Remember Love Canal? That's what everyone would say. No, can't just dump it."

"How about building a pipeline, sending down to the ranchers down below in Ennis, to irrigate their alfalfa?"

"Not a bad idea, and one that was floated. But what if in the future, Ennis decides they don't need it anymore, or even worse, want to start charging Moonlight to take it?"

"How about snow-making?" Maggie asked. "Don't they do that all over the place out here?"

"Sure—Colorado, Idaho, Wyoming—they're all using effluent to make snow. But the Montana DEQ—Department of Environmental Quality—has said no. Not just no, but hell, no. The Yellowstone Club, the resort area over the hill there, spent more than a million dollars on a pilot program, proving it was perfectly safe— no bacteria, no toxins, no pollution of any kind—but the DEQ still said no. They're trying again to get approval, and maybe they'll have better luck this time, but no guarantees. With the membership at Moonlight growing like mad, and with our short golf season, another course is starting to look like a very good idea."

"Just so it's easier than this one," said Frank as he watched his ball sail off into the wild on the downhill side of the green.

"Don't worry, Frank," said A.C., after making a perfect pitch onto the green, the ball landing just a few feet from the pin, belying his earlier comment. "I'll save this hole."

Frank just glared.

***

They'd gotten back home in time for cocktails and were sitting out on the deck when the head of Moonlight Security, Geno, stopped by on his way home.

A.C. got up to greet him—they'd become acquainted on his previous visit to Moonlight. "Geno! Good to see you again!" A.C. automatically reached out for a handshake as Geno came out onto the deck, then realized his faux pas. "Oops, sorry. Without masks, it's hard to remember the rules." They wore masks whenever necessary, but with adequate distancing out in the fresh air, they were considered a hindrance. Besides, you couldn't drink with one on.

"Great to see you, too, A.C.," Geno replied with a wave, then settled himself into a deck chair. "It's been a while since our big adventure out here. Been in any Liberty Valance shoot-outs since you were here last?"

It had been over two years since A.C. had become involved in a murder investigation in Moonlight; Geno had been instrumental in providing surveillance. The gunfight Geno was referring to had taken place in the Moonlight Tavern, and had ended with a twist even an out-of-work TV script writer would be embarrassed to pitch.

"No, thankfully," A.C. replied, laughing. "Almost shot myself in the foot last time. No, sir, I know when to quit."

"Oh, you'll never quit, not if there's a mystery to be solved," said Jamila, who had come out onto the deck midway during the conversation.

"I suppose you're right," A.C. admitted. "It's good things are so quiet here."

"Other than the fact that Doc thinks there's been another murder."

Fuentes jumped up from his chair at the far end of the deck. "No need to get into that. I'm probably wrong, anyway."

"Then why did you—?" Jamila began to say.

Fuentes shook his head and flashed a pleading glance at Jamila. "Not now, okay?"

"I guess you're right," she conceded, not sounding too certain. "Probably nothing." She turned to Geno. "You'll excuse me? Dinner in forty minutes, Doc." He nodded, and Jamila went back into the house.

"So, Geno, are things settling down at all?" Fuentes asked.

"Getting worse," he answered, accepting the Famous Grouse

floater Fuentes brought over to him. "Everyone seems to be getting in on it. The other night, I found Paul and Paula—"

"Paul and Paula Farrell," Fuentes explained to A.C. in an aside. "You'll meet them soon."

"—out on the golf course at midnight," Geno went on, "both with big, fancy metal detectors. I asked them what they were doing out there, and they acted like, what a dumb question! 'Meteorites,' they said. 'Diamonds, you know?" They said they use the detectors to locate a meteorite, then focus their headlamps on it to see if anything 'shiny' shows up. I asked them if they'd found anything, and they both started stammering out evasive answers, so I dropped it. But I did ask them how often they were out there. 'Every night,' they said, as if, of course they should be out there every night. 'But do you think it's safe being out here in the middle of the night?' I asked. Their answer was, 'two cans of bear spray each.'"

"What if they do find something out there," asked A.C., "a meteorite full of diamonds, say. If they find it on Moonlight property, can they keep it?"

"Good question. Nobody knows for sure. Matt Kidd, the managing director of Lone Mountain Land Company, has been trying to get the board's permission to issue a ban on treasure hunting in all of Moonlight, not just on the golf course. It apparently dates to the early railroads, who received the mining rights when tracks were first laid down. These rights passed to the timber companies the railroads formed and today onto LMLC here in Moonlight. When the land was sold off to individual investors, LMLC kept the mining rights—but does it apply to something found on the surface, something that isn't underground, isn't even part of the land, something that wasn't there before it fell out of the sky?"

"If it's located on private property," insisted A.C., "surely it belongs to the property owner."

"Maybe, maybe not," said Geno. "I've been told even on public lands, like national forest, there can be disagreement on whether or not a found meteorite belongs to the finder or to the government. In any case, I'm sure the law is going to get a thorough test in Moonlight, with everything that's going on. But in the meantime, Moonlight Security is enforcing a strict no trespassing order for anyone not an owner or member. But it's been hard to keep everyone out. And there are some suspect types trying to get in, let me tell you."

"I, for one, would certainly be worried about the legality," said A.C. darkly.

"Oh, come on, A.C.," said Fuentes. "You know the old saying about forgiveness and permission."

"When it comes to a rock full of diamonds," he replied, "I'm not sure forgiveness would enter into it."

# Check Out My Blog

Fuentes and Jamila had planned a reconnaissance trip to Lone Lake, in part to scout out possible strike areas—Jamila's analysis, while still preliminary, pointed to the general area—and partially out of curiosity. There were reports of unusual activity on this side of the mountain, and Fuentes had promised Abigail he'd begin to look around for any evidence of her brother Stony's whereabouts.

That promise had come about with some reluctance on his part. Jamila had forgiven him, barely, for his bluntness with Abigail. He had to admit he had very little to go on. And Abigail had been very persuasive. She seemed to generate energy—just standing next to her would charge your cell phone, Frank joked one day. But the fact was she had very quickly inveigled herself into the group, as Fuentes described it. Inveigled was too strong a word, Jamila had insisted, but still—it had happened very fast.

So fast Frank's head was still spinning. Somehow, he'd agreed to let her move in with him, into the Silvertip house he was renting. It was a large, four-bedroom house, and, he was first to admit, had more space than he needed, so there was plenty of room for her to semi-isolate. They were both gone a lot, Frank to his sluice boxes and Abigail on her quest to find Stony. But he couldn't quite remember exactly how it had come about that he'd offered her a place to stay. There had been a discussion of the Wilson's rates and the inconvenience of being all the way down the mountain. This had taken place over drinks out on the Wilson patio, that's true. But in addition to being an extremely level-headed type (he'd had to be in his career—which three-letter agency he'd last worked for, Fuentes had never been able to discern), he could really hold his liquor. His capacity should surely outclass five-foot-something, hundred and ten-pound Abigail. But she more than held her own, and that's when Frank invited her to move in. Who would have thought?

Now there she was first thing every day, in the kitchen making her Chai, her perpetually sunny disposition rivalling the early morning light slanting in through the kitchen windows.

***

The trail to Lone Lake began on Moonlight property where the road ended at a large galvanized steel gate. A small shed—a sort of guard shack—sat off to the side of the gate. It was normally unmanned, but after finding the padlock on the gate cut one morning, Geno arranged for someone to man the gate during daylight hours. At night, surveillance cameras—repurposed infrared wildlife cams—streamed images back to the security office.

Past the gate, the road quickly petered out and the trail started, now on National Forest Service land. The trail, originally marked as a ski patrol path, allowed emergency evacuation by sled from the bowls below Lone Peak. Initially quite moderate, the trail steepened significantly on the approach to the lake. The final stretch required the traversal of some rather large rock formations, where the lake spills into a narrow stream. At the bottom of this section, they stopped to take a picture of the small waterfall marking the edge of the final ascent to the lake, when they were startled by the noise of someone coming up behind them.

"Geno!" called Fuentes, as he turned to see the security officer rounding a bend below them, "What are you doing up here?"

Geno stopped and waved, then continued up close to where they were standing but keeping his distance since none of them were wearing masks. "Doc, Jamila. How's it going?"

"We're fine, out enjoying the day," Fuentes answered, "But

43

what are you doing so far from Moonlight property?"

"Well, I could ask you the same question," said Geno, a bit defensively. "You're usually not this far out of bounds either. Don't tell me you're up here treasure hunting?"

The quick glance Fuentes and Jamila exchanged nearly gave them away, but Geno had already turned his head, looking up at the rocky slope in front of them. "Tough hike. Have you been up here before?"

"Only once, last year," answered Fuentes.

"Okay, so you know we're almost there." Geno set out again, Fuentes and Jamila following a bit behind.

As they made their way up alongside the stream, Geno looked back over his shoulder occasionally to explain his motives. "We're trying to get an idea of how vulnerable we are to interlopers coming in from this side of Moonlight. Pretty rugged country, but we're getting reports of a lot of activity up here, of all kinds: well-provisioned gem hunters armed with hi-tech equipment, drones, elaborate metal detection gear; complete amateurs armed with nothing but sunblock; even heard there were some scuba divers up here."

"We heard the same thing," said Jamila. "Crazy."

"We weren't really prepared for this, well, call it an invasion. But we're catching up quickly. This is not the first time I've been up here recently, by the way. After the lock was cut off the gate, I've been making the trip up here about twice a week. Giving the old quads a workout, I'll tell you. A lot of the folks I run into up here," he said, waving his hand around, "aren't very talkative. They'll nod and smile, but don't stop to talk. Quite a few of the ones who do talk are asking directions. I make a note of what they're wearing in case we get a missing person report, but so far we've been lucky."

"What's attracting them to this area in particular?" Jamila asked.

"It's being fueled—as usual—by social media. Everyone thinks they know right where the big one hit. It's all over Instagram, Facebook, whatever; all claim to have figured out, based on visual reports, a few lucky videos which caught part of the fireball, and general run of the mouth, where to look. A lot of wild guesses masquerading as inside information. Anything to get the blog click-rate up."

"Has anybody you've talked to found anything?"

"Nada. Oh, a few of them claim to have found some diamond encrusted fragments, or small pieces embedded with flecks of green crystal. And a lot of interesting looking shiny stuff. Something like what used to be called fool's gold in these parts, which is iron pyrite. It's the most common thing mistaken for a meteorite."

"Nothing bigger is being found?" asked Fuentes.

"Not that I've heard. Just the rumors of finding small stuff, real or not, is enough to feed the madness."

After a few minutes of hard climbing, they reached the lake. It was a typical high-mountain tarn, a bowl scooped out by glacial activity which had filled with water ages ago. From where they stood on the bank on the lower side, they looked up at an impressive wall of rock, the west side of Lone Peak. A large scree field bordered the lake from the bottom edge of the cliff down to the water. Fuentes and Jamila sat together on a large rock; Geno remained standing on a small hummock nearby.

"How did scuba divers get their stuff up here?" asked Jamila.

"They rappelled down the cliff face. Gold fever," said Geno. "No, meteorite fever. Ever see those pictures of the miners during the Alaska gold rush climbing the White Pass Trail? Pure madness."

They sat on the hillside overlooking the lake in silence, enjoying the stillness, the clear air, the somehow calming mass of the mountain looming above them.

"What's that noise?" Jamila suddenly asked. "Sounded like rocks tumbling."

"I heard it, too" answered Fuentes. "I think it was just a small rockslide. As the rocks heat up in the sun, they expand, and sometimes something gets dislodged."

"Hmmm."

A minute later, they heard it again.

"I think it's mountain goats!" said Jamila. "Give me the binoculars." She scanned the rocky hill on the other side of the lake.

"Anything?" asked Geno.

"Just a sec." She handed the binoculars back to Fuentes.

"Look for a large outcropping, about a quarter of the way up, by a bunch of white flowery bushes." Fuentes started searching for the spot she described. "Mountain goats!"

A minute later, he handed the binoculars back to her. "I'll be damned, Geno, she's right. Mountain goats, two of them, crossing over the grassy area by those two large rocks. A big one and a small one."

"I see them."

"Hot rocks, indeed," said Jamila.

They watched the goats for a few more minutes, then Geno started towards the trail. "I'll leave you two alone." Jamila laughed and waved. "See you soon, Geno." He was soon out of sight.

"Look at the color of the water!" said Fuentes. He'd noticed it on the way up, as soon as they'd crested the last rise below the lake. Unlike the bright blue they typically saw at Ulery's, Lone Lake was green.

"Yeah, very pretty, almost emerald." She stood up and hitched her fanny pack up a little higher, took a swig of water, and pointed to the shallow edge of the lake. "Green lakes are sometimes caused by algae, but typically at lower elevations. This water is nice and clear. In this case, the color is probably due to a small amount of glacial silt suspended in the water. Sometimes it's called rock flour, very fine particles, micrometer sized, or smaller. Water filters out the long spectrum light—red and yellow—and the rock flour absorbs the shorter wavelengths, purple and indigo. What gets reflected is what's left—green."

Fuentes looked over at her with a look of admiration tinged with reproach. "Do you have a scientific explanation for everything? You probably can't even look at a rainbow without analyzing it. Doesn't that take away from the beauty?"

Jamila shook her head. "Exactly the opposite. The deeper the understanding of something, the more open it is to a fuller appreciation. The more elegant the explanation, the more beautiful the phenomenon."

"Is this your own theory of aesthetics?"

"I had some help from the Professor" she said. Professor Tamos Szabó had meant a lot to them, when they were living in New

York. A close friend of A.C.'s, he'd been killed in what became the most significant case in A.C.'s career, on or off the force. Both she and Fuentes had been intimately involved in that case, on a personal level, and Jamila had been an invaluable technical resource. Her expertise had led to the recovery of the principal evidence that led to the killer. "Speaking of unusual colors for things," she went on, "did you see the pink snow on the way up, in the shaded area? There's also a patch of it on the mountain over there, across the lake, in a small couloir."

"Yeah, I see it. What's special about dirty snow?"

"A perfect example of what I've been talking about. Once you know something about it, it's much more than just funny-colored snow."

"I'll admit it looks unusual, but beautiful?"

"In its own way. It's called 'watermelon snow.' Both for the color, and for the fragrance."

"It smells?"

Jamila laughed. "Some people say it smells like fresh watermelon, yes."

"I suspect it's not just red dirt making it pink."

"Nope. Although in the eighteen-hundreds they thought it was 'meteoric iron deposits,' believe it or not."

"Appropriate."

"But not true. It was finally determined the coloration, and the odor, comes from a type of red algae. The red color is a carotenoid; it's what gives pink flamingos their color, among other things."

Fuentes stood up and moved over to her, slipping his arm around her waist, which she imitated, looping her arm under his. "Okay, I don't know how you know all of this stuff, but you've convinced me." He motioned over the lake. "Nice up here, isn't it?"

"Very. Let's stand here and enjoy the silence for a minute."

The silence Jamila wanted to listen to was a pure Montana silence—the silence of the trees brushing the breeze; the small whisking sound of the blowing grass at their feet; the sudden crack of a goat-footed rock landing at the bottom of the ravine across the lake; the snickering of a marmot, the distant tap-tap-tap of a nuthatch, or a flicker, or a lazy woodpecker. It was why Fuentes had settled in Moonlight, and a big part of why she was here, to share it with him.

A quick squeeze, a tilt of the head. "Okay, I'm ready; let's head back."

They'd only gone about fifty yards along the edge of the lake when Jamila stopped. "What is that?" she exclaimed, pointing across the lake to something glinting in the afternoon sun.

"Not sure," said Fuentes. He pulled the binoculars from his pack. "Oh, my God."

"What is it?"

He passed the binoculars to Jamila. She looked over across the lake, then lowered them, turning to him, perplexed. "I still don't know what it is," she complained.

He laughed. "Scuba tanks."

Jamila took another look. "Lazy bastards," she said. "They managed to get the tanks all the way in here, but they couldn't be bothered to pack them the rest of the way out?"

"I suppose the forest service will have to take care of it." He gestured back down the hill. "The craziness will end soon."

"Not soon enough."

***

Downhill, as Fuentes had known, was harder than up, but they made good time. About ten minutes from the gate, they heard someone call out to them from below the trail. "Doc? Jamila?"

It was Abigail. She seemed to be everywhere these days.

"Hey, Abber!" called Fuentes, a bit awkwardly. (She'd recently told them "Abber" was what Stony always called her, and she'd like them to call her that as well—it helped to make him feel a little less lost, she'd said.)

Abigail climbed up the steep slope to the trail, bright-eyed and bushy-tailed, Fuentes could not help thinking, no sign of being at all out of breath, as he was. "What are you two doing out here?" she asked.

"Just out for the day," said Fuentes, cautiously. "And you?"

Abigail's features clouded over briefly, a quick squall. "Just out looking for Stony," she said. "But no luck," she continued. "Not yet." Then she brightened. "But it's early innings, right?"

"Why up here, Abigail?" He couldn't manage another "Abber."

"I'm pretty sure this is where Stony was searching."

"But what makes you think he would be looking here, in particular?" insisted Jamila.

Abigail hesitated. "Well, I guess I can tell you. He emailed me last fall. He said this would be the best place to look."

*And just a mile or so above us*, thought Fuentes, *I found his arm*.

# Pennies from Heaven

Frank and Abigail hosted dinner that night. It was a casual affair, held out on the expansive Silvertip deck with ample social spacing between several small tables and chairs. Frank made his famous baked ziti, one of his specialties when he'd been chief cook and bottle washer at the 1850 House in Oswego. He'd also worked with A.C. on more than one unofficial investigation after the restaurant had closed, but didn't see much chance of that happening again.

"How are you and Abigail getting along together?" asked Fuentes, as Frank puttered in the kitchen. A.C. stood nearby at the kitchen bar in case the need for kibitzing arose. (As members of a "safe pod," interactions among themselves could be somewhat more relaxed than with strangers).

"Great. Of course, we don't really see one another too much—I'm usually down at my sluices early, before she heads out on her daily quest. She leaves a little later in the morning, for better light, she tells me. We exchange 'good mornings' and that's about it. At night, she pretty much stays in her room. Even takes her dinner—usually something microwaved—up with her. So, yeah, it's working okay, and I'm glad to help her out."

"Has she said where she's been going?"

"Not exactly. I just know it's out in the relatively unchartered territory; she doesn't stay on Moonlight property. I'm a little worried about that—she's mentioned running into some scary types out in the wilderness. I guess she's gotten wind of my past to some extent; she asked me if I could teach her any self-defense tricks."

"And did you?"

"For now, only one or two defensive moves. There's no time, and besides, she only weighs about a hundred pounds. I asked her if she knew how to handle a gun, and if she had one."

"You think that's wise?" asked A.C., "encouraging her? That kind of thing could end up getting her in more trouble."

"Well, after some discussion, she admitted to having a gun, but claimed she never carries it. She also said it was pretty old and couldn't remember the last time it was used. I told her to clean it— I'd help if needed—and keep it handy. And to keep it loaded with a round chambered. I also said if I get a chance, there are a few things—defensive techniques, military police tactics, mostly—I could show her to give her an edge in a fight."

"Abigail with a gun," said A.C., skeptically, "and keeping a round chambered? I don't think that's such a good idea."

"Yeah, well, *you'd* better not keep one chambered or you might shoot off a finger."

"Like I damned near did last time we were here, you mean. Very funny, Frank."

"Got to keep you on your toes—until you shoot them off, that is."

A.C. moved towards the kitchen, as menacingly as a seventy-six-year-old man with arthritis, glasses and thinning gray hair could. "If you weren't busy cooking dinner, we'd have a lively discussion, and I don't mean talking. It's just a good thing I'm hungry."

Fuentes motioned with his hands. "Okay, separate corners." They all laughed as A.C. took his place back at the bar. "Back to Abigail. Frank, did she tell you she saw us on the Lone Lake trail today?"

"No. What time was that?"

"About two. We were on our way down and had almost reached the gate when she popped up out of nowhere. We asked her why she was looking up there, and she said she'd been in touch with Stony by email, after she'd returned home to D.C. She said it was right before he disappeared, and he'd told her to look in that particular area."

"She say why?"

"Nope. Just that's where she should be looking. She also said she hadn't found anything. And that the terrain is rougher than she expected."

"But I thought they were out here together, last fall." He shook his head in exasperation. "Too many diamonds, too many secrets…but in any case, she should already have known where to look."

"That's what I thought, too."

"Did you ask her about it?"

"No, didn't even cross my mind until later."

They turned as Abigail came into the kitchen. "Frank, have we got any ice?" she asked.

"Sure." He opened the freezer door and pulled out the lower bin. "Help yourself."

"Thanks." She scooped some cubes into her glass. "What are you two up to? Scheming on how to locate the main strike?"

"Not me," said Frank. "I've got more than enough work with my sluices. They're really paying out, too. I don't need to look any farther. Here. Let me show you what I dredged today."

He went into the living room and picked up a small wooden box. "Come take a look," Frank said, holding up the box and flipping open the lid.

Fuentes and Abigail leaned over and saw what Frank considered doing well. On a piece of purple velvet (cut from a Crown Royale bag, Fuentes guessed), he had arranged three rough diamonds, not extremely large, but still a good fraction of a carat apiece; some flecks of gold; and a very small, misshapen piece of greenish crystal.

"Nice, Frank," said Fuentes, pretending enthusiasm.

Abigail leaned closer. "What's that green stone?"

"Not sure," said Frank. "But it looked interesting, so I saved it."

"Are you seeing a lot of it?" Abigail's tone had shifted subtly, from mere curiosity to clear interest.

"No, why? Do you know what it is?"

Abigail straightened up and flicked her hand at the display, as if suddenly disinterested. "Oh, not really. But like you said, it is interesting." She looked around distractedly. "I should get back out on the deck, I guess." She turned and walked away, glancing once over her shoulder at the box as Frank closed the lid.

"Bring it out and show the others, Frank," said Fuentes. "A.C. has been very skeptical about the sluices, I have to tell you. This will prove to him you know what you're doing."

"Maybe he'll change his mind, come out and help shovel the unclassified material I've collected into the sluice."

"Sure, can't hurt to ask him. Maybe he's getting bored sitting around the house."

***

Back out on the deck, as the group passed Frank's findings box around, he explained that, sure, this was just small stuff, so far, but there are a lot of folks out there who think something big is going to be uncovered soon. "They're calling it 'Lucy,'" he said.

"We've heard," said Maggie, who began to sing the line, only to be hushed by A.C., who was drawing his finger across his throat in the universal signal for "nip it."

"As I've tried to explain to several people around here," said Jamila, "it can't possibly be pieces of a star. I mean, really. And that's only one of the crazy theories being spread around. Every time someone sees an article in USA Today or on Space.com about something exotic in space, they think they've found a new Holy Grail. The facts are ignored. An exo-planet called 55 Cancri A, a so-called 'super-planet,' was originally thought to be primarily diamonds; then they revised their theories and said, no, not diamond, but maybe sapphire, or ruby. Every time one of these things is reported in a scientific journal, the pop media publishes another story about something of fantastic worth flying around up there, just waiting to fall to earth so some lucky devil can find it and become fabulously wealthy overnight. The ultimate treasure hunter's

53

dream.”

“But there are meteoric diamonds being found,” objected Frank. “All over Moonlight.”

“Sure,” said Jamila, “and most even smaller than what you’ve just shown us.”

“But there could be larger stones out there. In fact, there are larger ones; people have already found them. And gold,” said Frank.

“I suppose. But realistically, the chances of finding something significant are very small. Most meteorites are just rock—the ‘stony’ meteorites. Some are nickel-iron amalgams, and sometimes don’t contain much iron. Contrary to popular belief, you can’t always tell a meteorite from a rock by using a magnet. Some aren’t magnetic at all. They come from a variety of extraterrestrial sources—some are from asteroids, some are comet dust, some are pieces of Mars that got knocked off by something larger. Some of the Martian meteorites even contain signs of four-billion-year-old water.”

“But there could be some pieces out in the forest which contain significant gemstones. Diamonds, for sure, and maybe even some large pieces of that green crystal,” insisted Frank.

“Very unlikely,” said Jamila. “Incompatible types. But I must admit, this one does appear to be quite unusual. Maybe even extraordinary.”

“Jamila,” interrupted A.C., “how is it you know so much about meteorites? I thought your doctorate was in electro-mechanical engineering, not astronomy.”

“New hobby.”

“And knowing you, you have gone into it full throttle.”

“No more than usual,” said Fuentes

“Well, I for one am not going to spend every waking hour looking for it,” Jamila said emphatically. She nodded at Fuentes. “That’s his job.”

“And it’s your job to tell me where to look,” he responded.

Abigail sat up and pointed at Fuentes. “So, that’s why you were up at Lost Lake today!”

“You mean ‘Lone Lake.’ Lost Lakes are up behind the golf course.”

"Whatever. What do you know, Jamila?" Abigail asked.

"Nothing that everyone else up here doesn't already know, I'm sure." Jamila turned to Frank. "Do you really think there's going to be a market for this stuff?" she asked, subtly changing the subject.

"There's already a market. The local jewelers in Big Sky and Bozeman are buying whatever they can get. It's not small potatoes, either. They're paying real money for anything of interest. Of course, they're managing the transactions so there's never anything over ten-thousand dollars exchanged. Bank reporting," he clarified, at Jamila's quizzical look. "Keeps it under the radar. Don't know how long that's going to work, though. Some major players are getting involved as well. Reps from De Beers have been making the rounds, drumming up business. Guess they need to find an alternative to blood-diamonds. Sorry, not editorializing, just what's happening in the market." He held his finger to his lips. "Don't quote me on this," he said melodramatically, "but I've heard there's a private hangar at the Bozeman airport that's been the center of *a lot* of activity."

"What kind of activity?" asked A.C.

"Can't say," said Frank, shaking his head. "But my sources are reliable."

A.C. knew Frank knew more than he was saying. "Local sheriff involved, Frank?" he asked. "Sounds like criminal activity, to me."

"My lips are sealed." He gave the slightest of nods, and A.C. understood more information would be forthcoming, at the appropriate time.

"Doc, you said there may be legal issues related to any finds on Moonlight property. Something about old railroad deeds?"

"Yeah, I was talking with Geno about that. He says LMLC, the outfit that owns Moonlight, wants to shut down all unauthorized prospecting on Moonlight property. They've filed multiple complaints regarding illegal mining activity with the Montana Bureau of Land Management and the state Board of Land Commissioners, and anyone else they think would care, but so far, no response. Their complaints are based on the old railroad law I told you about, which said the railroads owned everything under the soil; the mining rights, in effect. Those rights transferred to LMLC. However, like most laws, even if on the surface it looks comprehensive, someone is always looking for a loophole.”

“What does the regulation say, specifically?”

“I looked it up. I’m not sure I’m reciting it verbatim, but it states there shall be ‘no prospecting, mining, quarrying, tunneling, excavating, or drilling for any substance in the earth.’ Then it lists the things you can’t dig up: oil, gas, minerals, hydrocarbons, gravels, rocks, even sand.”

“So, Doc,” said Frank, “according to LMLC’s interpretation of this old regulation, taken to its logical extreme, that covers everyone’s property! You can’t rake your lawn, kick a stone off a bike trail, trench for a gas line, or dig a basement. Even Doc’s Rock might not be yours.”

“That’s the problem. How far can they take it? Are they going to stop Jamila from picking up lost golf balls?”

A.C. raised his hand, index finger pointing up, an old habit acquired during his years as a detective, when asking a pertinent question. “How enforceable is this law, as it stands today? What’s the position of the sheriff?”

“He’s not sure there has been an actual crime that can be prosecuted,” said Fuentes. “Until LMLC gets some sort of ruling from the state, he can’t do much. Fortunately, most of the activity so far has been in national forest land. That doesn’t alleviate the issue of access through Moonlight; and the prospecting could spread, as the fervor spreads. Even LMLC is getting into it. One of Geno’s new duties—an unwelcome duty, he told me—is safeguarding the operation of a big, new sluice LMLC just built on Lone Creek. They won’t say much about it, but Geno’s heard they are finding quite a bit of valuable stuff—the same thing you’re finding in your sluice, Frank—diamonds, gold, and the green crystals.”

“Where is this sluice, exactly?” asked Abigail.

“Lone Creek comes down from Lone Peak,” Fuentes answered. “On Moonlight property it’s accessible from where the creek dives under the South Road, near the Six Shooter ski lift. You should have seen it when you were up there.”

"Oh, I didn't come in that way; I started up much farther south. Anyway, why do they think that's a particularly good area to be looking? Do they have some data on the location of the strike?"

Fuentes looked over at Jamila. "That's your area of expertise," he said. "Have you heard anything?"

"I don't know what information they might have," she replied. "But according to the image processing I've been doing, indications are the strike was inside the boundaries of Moonlight, not up by Lone Lake."

"Are you getting caught up in this after all, Jamila?" asked A.C. with a smile. "Or is it just scientific curiosity?"

"That's all it was at first, curiosity, and the challenge of making a discovery, perhaps even something I could publish. I was very skeptical of all the frenzied hunting going on. But now, after seeing the kinds of meteoric treasures everyone is finding, I'm wondering, why should I miss out? Why shouldn't Doc and I cash in on this, too? So, when the snow started melting, I got busy. I've got the AI program running full time, and I'm spending every spare minute sifting through the results. I can hardly wait to see the final data points! If I'm right about what I'm seeing so far, I should be able to pinpoint it within a day or two."

She looked over at Fuentes. "I've already started thinking about what to do with my share of the fortune, Doc; some charity first, of course, and definitely something for the Safe Haven Holocaust Refugee museum in Fort Ontario in Oswego—and then? Well, I guess I don't know for sure, but like they say—the sky's the limit!"

Even as well as he knew her, he wasn't quite sure if she was being serious or not.

# Mending a Wall

Jamila had just finished spreading some wildflower seeds down by the stream—below Frank's sluices, which she had been firmly set against from the beginning, but which he had agreed to build at a discreet location in the woods above the house. He was well away from the part of the lot they'd taken to calling the wildlife viewing area—fox, moose, elk, the occasional bear, they all gravitated to this one spot, not far from the house, directly behind the rear deck. One day not long before, a moose had spent practically the entire afternoon there, grazing, resting, chewing his cud. It was like having a live National Geographic channel in the front yard.

Once she'd finished sowing the wildflowers, she returned to her latest project, building a small natural rock wall along the edge of the house, below the drive, using the rocks scattered about the area. It was not that the wall was completely necessary, but it would look nice and was a wonderful outlet for the repressed energy she had stored up, especially during the past few weeks, as the prospecting activity around Moonlight continued to increase. She was starting to grow weary of it all, even Frank's sluices. But he was having such a good time with it she'd eased back on her complaints.

Even the distraction of working outside had not completely cleared her mind of a nagging problem; the image processing had stalled again. She'd spent an hour that morning trying to resolve the latest issue—the AI program was matching sections of the sky that appeared to be completely unrelated, producing data containing impossibly correlated images.

She bent down and pulled a rather large rock out of the soil, evaluating its size and shape, calculating where it would best fit in the section of the wall she was currently working on. She held it up and viewed it against the partial wall standing a few feet away. She angled it several different ways, dark side facing her, straight edge up, pointed edge up. It looked like it would fit the best in a section of the wall about a foot behind where she'd stopped. She really didn't want to rebuild that section of the wall; it had seemed perfect. She looked away for a second, distracted by the sound of one of the sluices—it sounded like he'd just shoveled in a particularly large batch of what he called "unclassified material." As if anything Frank ever did was "unclassified," she thought.

She turned the rock over and held it up again, this time looking at the lighter side. She moved it back and forth across the face of the wall. As she held it up against the section of wall where it had seemed to fit best a minute ago, she thought again it really did belong there, despite having to rebuild that section. Then she realized it was fitting into a slightly different spot on the wall, slightly above and to the left of the area she'd thought perfect before.

She turned the rock over and refocused. It still fitted perfectly into the area she'd decided on earlier. She turned it back around, refocusing. Now it appeared exactly right for the new location. How it fit depended on whether she was looking at the light or dark side of the rock. Both were perfect, but one way it was by looking at the rock as the foreground, the other way by looking at it as the background. She blinked and looked again at each configuration. Both worked equally well. Figure and ground.

She dropped the rock and almost ran back into the house. She suddenly knew how to fix her AI program.

# Figure and Ground

"One of your nefarious characters has shown up in the area," said Frank, as Fuentes brought drinks out to the deck.

A.C. was leaning on the rail, admiring the Spanish Peaks range stretched out on the other side of the valley, looking like a Bierstadt painting. "Doc," he said, "has anyone ever climbed up to the top of that peak?"

"Which one?"

"The tall, rugged-looking one, above the ridge."

"Beehive Peak. Sure. I've been up there, just below it, actually; there's a very nice trail up to the base. But I could never climb the peak itself; it's a technical climb—you need ropes, bolts, slings, all the hardware, what climbers call 'a full rack.'"

"I can imagine. Looks impossible."

"I was trying to talk to Doc about something important, A.C.," interrupted Frank, mildly.

"Sorry. Get carried away by the scenery here. Majestic. You were saying?"

"This is something you should hear, too, A.C.," continued Frank. He never took A.C.'s little digressions personally; it was something you had to get used to, especially in the last year or so. He tended to lose focus. "There's apparently some kind of a crazy bastard roaming around the area," he went on, "harassing the other prospectors. Geno had a run-in with him last week, up by the

Moonlight sluice. He apparently came out of nowhere, threatening to shut it down. Geno said he was practically raving."

"But that sluice is on Moonlight property."

"That's what Geno told him. So, then he said he's going to build a dam up on Lone Creek, on national forest land, build his own sluice, and cut off water down below."

"How does he think he can get away with that?"

"Did I mention he's obviously a crazy bastard? But that's not all. He's been threatening people with a gun, telling them he has prior claim to the strike area."

"Has the sheriff been called?"

"First thing Geno did."

"What have they done about it?" asked A.C., who had left the railing and come over to sit down with the other two. "They could get him on trespassing, criminal threatening, intimidation, brandishing—probably more."

"That's true, A.C., if they could. But he's being cagey, pushing it just so far, and then backing off. I think he's representing other interests and keeping random treasure hunters away. Even trying to keep LMLC out of their own property. That way his clients have a clearer shot at getting what they want."

"That's it, then? They're not going to do anything?" asked Fuentes.

"What can they do? Unless he's caught in the act, it's all hearsay." A.C. took his drink and turned back to the view. "Beautiful," he said, "just beautiful."

Jamila and Maggie came out onto the deck. "Where's Abigail tonight, Frank?" asked Jamila. "Still out searching? It's getting late."

"She said she'd be back by now, "said Frank, glancing at his watch. "I expect she'll be along shortly."

Before he even finished his sentence, they heard Abigail calling from the patio down below. "Hey, up there!" She waved. "Can I come up?"

"Front door's open," called back Fuentes, looking down to where she was standing, next to Doc's Rock.

"Be right there!"

Frank suddenly leaned forward. "Doc, about this crazy guy. Geno said his name is Orvis Mooney. Know anything about him?"

"Only that Stony warned Abigail about him last fall. She said he's known as a claim jumper."

Frank looked up as Abigail came out onto the deck, his eyes narrowing in concern. "Abigail! You know this Mooney character?" he asked her abruptly. "The one who's been causing so much trouble around here?"

Abigail stopped in her tracks. "I only know him from what Stony told me," she said defensively. "Jamila," she said in an aside, "he's the creep who winked at me at the Wilson." She looked back at Frank. "What's this about?"

"He's causing trouble. According to Geno," Frank continued, "the sheriff's office ran a make on him. He's been in and out of trouble more times than you can count, from here to Timbuktu. He was even held for a time on suspicion of murder somewhere, Ethiopia, I think Geno said." He looked over at Abigail. "And you know him?"

"No, not really. Stony warned me he can be unpredictable."

"Not just unpredictable," said Frank, flatly. "In fact, more like very predictable. As in, likely to be dangerous."

"I guess you're right," said Abigail, thoughtfully. "What Geno said is true; Stony told me once he thinks Mooney killed someone over a meteorite find, in Africa."

"My God, Abigail, why didn't you tell us this the night we saw him at the Wilson?" asked Fuentes incredulously.

Abigail looked down sheepishly. "Well, I *did* say Stony warned me about him. I don't know why I didn't say any more. Maybe I'm just trying to avoid the truth."

Frank spoke up again. "Abigail, do you think he was here with your brother last September? Maybe he knows something."

"Or more likely," said A.C., "he was involved in Stony's disappearance."

Abigail blanched at that. "You mean…he might have killed Stony?"

A.C. looked at Abigail and spoke somberly. "Let's say he's just moved beyond being a person of interest to my prime suspect."

***

The group broke up, Maggie going back into the house to prepare dinner, the others splitting off into two groups: Frank and A.C. standing at one end of the deck in deep conversation, Fuentes and Jamila at the table. Abigail came over and sat down next to Jamila and leaned in. "Do you have anything new about the main strike? I think that's where I'm going to find Stony."

Jamila hesitated, then answered carefully, "It's too early to say."

"But you should know pretty soon, right?"

"Well, there's some sort of data anomaly I can't explain."

"What seems to be the problem?" asked Fuentes.

"It's hard to explain. Are you familiar with the concept of 'figure and ground' perception?"

"You mean where an image looks like one thing if you focus on what looks like the main object, but like something else when you focus on the background?" Fuentes asked. Abigail frowned in perplexity, as if this were getting much more technical than she had anticipated.

"Yes, exactly," said Jamila. "The standard example is a black and white graphic of two identical profiles facing one another, two faces, if seen as foreground, with a white background. But when the black profiles are perceived as the background, the remaining central, white image—now the foreground—looks like a chalice, or a fancy vase. What you see depends on whether you focus on the black background profiles or on the central white image, the vase. There seems to be something in the meteor imagery acting in the same manner. Like there's something hidden in the data, and I'm just not seeing it correctly. I've just modified the processing software to look specifically for something to explain the anomaly."

"You still haven't said exactly what you are seeing, or think you're seeing," said Fuentes.

Jamila shook her head in frustration. "Well, it's impossible, but it looks like there are two distinct fireballs, arriving at the same time."

"But what's the problem with that?" he asked. "The meteor

broke up in the atmosphere, didn't it? So, there would be more than one piece, and so more than one meteor trail."

"That's the problem. The second large fireball is traveling in a different direction. As if it were a completely different meteor. But that can't be right. I'm missing something, I know. But there *is* something odd showing up in the data, and I don't believe it's spurious. There's something there, if I can just tease it out."

"But you know where the main strike is?" asked Abigail.

"I don't want to say too much until I've analyzed the data completely. It may be close by, maybe not. I'm almost done, but we'll just have to wait and see."

"Please let me know as soon as you've got something definite," Abigail said. "That could be huge." Jamila nodded noncommittally. Abigail straightened her shoulders and took a sip of her martini. "Anyway, the important thing is finding where Stony is hiding out. So, the area up by the lake is where I'm heading again tomorrow."

"But what about Mooney?" asked Fuentes. "Isn't he going to be out there, too? We know he's dangerous."

"I'll be careful."

***

"How close are you, Jamila?" Fuentes asked after everyone had gone, leaving them alone on the couch. "I could tell you were hedging. Do you have a definite fix on the second fireball?"

Jamila sighed. "I'm this close," she said, holding two up two fingers about a millimeter apart. "I modified the AI image processor to factor in the problem I described, that is, the perceptual shift I think I'm seeing. My first crack at it produced what looked like an intriguing set of data points, but when I plotted it, it didn't make any sense."

"But you're close, right?"

"Oh, definitely. I tweaked the AI again this afternoon, adding combinatorial optimization—oh, I'm sorry, I'm getting geeky again."

"No, please, go on. I love it when you talk techie."

64

She smiled. "It's something called the 'ant colony' algorithm. It improves image segmentation. I've also added code related to the **obliquity of the ecliptic, used in calculating the heliocentric coordinates of a meteor.** Geeky enough?"

"For now. Maybe later, in bed…?"

"Stop it."

"Sorry. Please continue."

"Oh, nothing more to say, I guess. But I expect this new algorithm will be a big improvement. It's custom-made for what I'm trying to get out of this weird data."

"So, you're close. That's exciting. You'll tell me if you need me to run anything, kick off a processing run?"

"I will. And thank you."

He leaned over and kissed her. She responded amorously, putting her hands around his neck. The kiss went on for quite some time. As they pulled apart, he patted her on the head affectionately. "Let's go to bed, geek."

She stood up, then turned and reached out to him. Taking his hands, she pulled him up off the couch. Hand in hand, they walked silently to the bedroom.

There were no more technical discussions for the rest of the night.

# "9-1-1. What is your emergency?"

"Someone is hurt! Please, send an ambulance!"

"Is the victim breathing?"

"I don't know. I didn't go in the house."

"But someone is hurt, is that right?"

"Yes. Just inside the house. Not moving."

"Who's calling?"

"This is Chris. From UPS."

"What is the address?"

"Mountain View. 12 Mountain View. In Moonlight."

"12 Mountain View, in Moonlight Basin, is that right?"

"Yes. Please send help!"

"An ambulance is on the way. But I need more information."

"Okay."

"Chris, can you go in and check on the victim for me?"

"Oh, man, I don't know!"

"It's very important. Please just go in and tell me what you see. Will you do that for me?"

"Okay. Okay. I'm going in. Oh, my God."

"Don't worry, Chris, you'll be fine. Is the victim breathing?"

"I don't think so. Just a minute. No. No, she's not breathing."

"Do you see any blood?"

"No, no blood."

"Is the body warm?"

"Oh, my God. Just give me a minute."

"That's fine, Chris."

"I think she might be dead. Oh, my God."

"Chris, do you know CPR?"

"No, no. I can't do that."

"Okay, don't worry. Now, Chris, do you see any weapons?"

"No, nothing. I'm sorry, can I go back outside?"

"Sure, Chris. Just a few more questions."

"Okay."

"When you first got there, what exactly did you do?"

"Well, I was delivering a package, and I brought it to the front door."

"Yes, go ahead."

"The door was open a little, so I called 'hello' through the crack in the door."

"And then what, Chris?"

"There was no answer."

"Did you go in?"

"No. I just put the package down next to the door."

"Is that when you saw the victim?"

"Yes, that's when I saw her lying there. Through the crack in the door."

"Okay, Chris. You said you didn't go into the house, didn't touch anything?"

"No, I just ran back to my truck and called 9-1-1."

"Did you see anyone in the area, inside or outside?"

"No, no one. Oh, I hear a siren!"

# A Special Gift

Geno at Moonlight Security had picked up the call on the radio. A deputy sheriff was standing outside the front door of the house when he arrived a few minutes later.

"What's going on?" Geno called as he jumped out of his vehicle.

The deputy sauntered in Geno's direction, thumbs hitched in his belt loops. "Looks like a nasty one." He stopped as Geno approached.

"What do you mean? What's happened? Has there been an accident?"

The deputy motioned for Geno to follow him to the house. "No accident," he said, as he pushed open the front door.

Geno stopped so suddenly he almost fell over. A woman was lying in the foyer, her head twisted at an odd angle, long hair fanned out smoothly on the floor beside her. She was not moving. The deputy was rattling on about something. Geno forced himself to look away and focus on what the deputy was saying.

"Sheriff is on the way," the deputy said. "It's got to be the meteorite in the patio," he went on confidently. "It's been busted up. They must have heard of it, and it was her bad luck to be here when they came for it."

Geno tilted his head, not quite sure what he was hearing. "What are you talking about?"

"What else could it be? These crazy prospectors around here, according to the sheriff, they're out of control. And Dr. Fuentes, as I understand it, was none too careful about keeping his private meteorite a secret. Anything but. It was almost a tourist attraction. He sort of brought it on himself. I think he of all people should have known better."

"The meteorite? It's busted up?" Geno looked around confusedly.

"Yeah. Oh, not much. Looks like they tried to get it out but it's stuck in the concrete."

Out of the corner of his eye, Geno could still see her lying there. He turned and looked away from the house. "What did you say, he should have known better?"

"You know what I mean. Maybe if he'd kept it quiet, or had the thing removed, it wouldn't have attracted so much attention. But as it is, everyone knew about it, and thought it must be something special. Just a crime of opportunity."

"Sure."

"Very poorly planned."

Geno could see this deputy was good at jumping to conclusions. He looked up the hill towards the main road. "When is the sheriff due?"

"Oh, any minute. I might be new on the force, but I'm pretty good at these things. I'm sure he'll agree."

***

Frank heard the sirens from inside the house and went out onto the deck to see what was up. He saw the sheriff's car in the driveway down below, lights flashing. He rushed back into the house and pulled on his boots, then sprinted out the front door. He scrambled down the hillside and ran towards the house. By the time he got across the road and down the driveway, Geno was there to meet him.

"Frank, stop," Geno said, holding up a hand.

"Geno, what the hell?" Frank tried to brush past him, but Geno blocked him with a shoulder. "Frank, just hold on."

69

Frank sensed something was very wrong. "Geno…?"

"It's bad." Frank again tried to push past him, but Geno grabbed him around the shoulders. "Listen to me, Frank. She's dead."

Frank stood and stared. "Dead? Who?"

Geno's voice broke as he forced it out. "Jamila."

***

"Does Doc know?" Frank asked immediately.

"I tried calling, but it went straight to message."

"Yeah. He and Maggie went to Ennis on a shopping excursion this morning. Whiskey from Willie's Distillery and groceries from Madison Foods." *Damn.*

"Well, with no cell signal on most of Jack Creek Road, it might be a couple of hours before we can reach them. Where's A.C.?"

"He's at the golf course. Lunch, some time on the driving range, and a lesson with Austin, one of the pros." *Double damn.*

Frank took over from Geno as the primary contact. He was sitting in front seat of the sheriff's the patrol car in shock, but coping. It was a job he was well suited for—while never having revealed which clandestine government agency (or agencies) he'd been associated with during his post-military career, he'd proven to be invaluable in prior situations. Calm even under intense pressure. None of his previous experiences, however, had been quite this fraught with personal feelings.

Sheriff Moreland looked exactly like what Frank imagined a Montana Sheriff should look like—broad-shouldered, tan shirt taut across a torso only recently tending to flab, a well-weathered face that would look good on a crime-prevention poster, dark eyebrows locked in a permanently skeptical attitude, and an off-color, unkempt mustache.

They'd already covered Frank's situation—why he was here, what he'd been doing, how he knew Dr. Fuentes and Jamila. Frank told him Fuentes was currently on Jack Creek Road somewhere, on his way back from Ennis, but still out of cell phone range. The

70

sheriff made some cursory notes.

"What about this meteorite?" the sheriff then asked. "There's quite a large piece of it embedded in the patio downstairs. Or what used to be a large piece."

"Yes. Doc—Dr. Fuentes—and Jamila were out on their deck when it hit. They made it the centerpiece of the patio."

"Must have been quite a shock. Lucky no one was hurt."

Frank nodded in agreement, thinking of the odds of being killed by a meteorite. Or hit by lightning. Or murdered. "I suppose so, yes."

"Has anyone shown any particular interest in the meteorite lately, anyone unknown to you or the family?"

"No, not that I know of."

"It's pretty valuable, though, as I understand it."

"It could be."

"Any reason for you to think Ms. Sayvetz was in any danger? Any recent threats? Any disagreements with anyone?"

"No, nothing."

"Then it appears the theft of the meteorite—since it was damaged in a failed attempt to dislodge it—is the likely motive. She was probably killed as soon as she opened the door. Then whoever it was went downstairs and tried to get the meteorite out of the patio, failed, and ran off. Unfortunately, we don't have much to go on, given the current situation. Since nothing appears to be missing, there's probably nothing we can trace."

"What about this guy who's been harassing people around here lately, Mooney? Do you have anything on him?"

"Don't worry, we'll investigate all possible suspects."

"Just put him at the top of your list."

Moreland checked his notes, as if looking for something Frank had said that could incriminate him. "Anyone else have access to the house, Mr. Ivanovich? Other than yourself?"

"Dr. Fuentes has house guests here now, old friends from New York."

"Names?"

"A.C. and Maggie LaFleur."

Moreland frowned. "A.C. LaFleur. Isn't he the one who was

here a couple of years ago and—"

"Yes, that's him."

"You were here too, as I recall."

"Yes, that's right."

The sheriff nodded and wrote something in his notebook. "Where are they now?"

"A.C. is at the golf course. Geno went to get him and bring him back here. Maggie is with Dr. Fuentes. They went shopping together."

"Okay. We'll want to talk to them both, of course. Is there anyone else? Neighbors, other friends?"

Frank hesitated. "There is a woman staying with me, Abigail MacLeod. She's here with us occasionally for dinner, that kind of thing."

"Know her well?"

"No. Just acquainted."

"She's living with you? And you say you're just acquainted?" Moreland managed to convey quite a bit of disdain in his question.

"Look, Sheriff, you've got the wrong idea," Frank said calmly. "She's a house guest, nothing more, staying with me as a favor to a friend of Doc's. A friend of Dr. Fuentes, that is. She has an upstairs room in a rather large house." He craned his neck. "The big house, right up there," he said, pointing up the hill. "I hardly know she's there."

"Is she at home now?"

"No"

"Do you know where she is?"

"No."

"When you see her please tell her to expect a call. We'll need to talk with her."

"Of course."

It appeared the sheriff had all he wanted for the moment. "Okay, Mr. Ivanovich, thank you very much." He pointed at the passenger door handle. "That's all for now."

***

72

In the meantime, Geno was on his way back from the golf course with A.C., who had been surprised to see him. Immediately suspicious, he asked, "Geno, what the hell is the matter?"

"An emergency at the house. Get your things together and let's go. I'll explain on the way there."

It wasn't until they were half-way back to Moonlight that he finally told A.C. exactly what had happened. Like Frank, A.C. had some pretty good defense mechanisms, after all his years as a detective in Oswego. But also like Frank, it had never been this personal. As Geno negotiated the curves on the golf course road a bit faster than usual, he filled A.C. in on what he'd heard of the sheriff's initial theories on the crime. But A.C. was only half listening.

"I can't believe it was because of the meteorite, can you?" Geno said.

"I'm sorry, what?"

"That's what they're saying, it must have been a robbery gone bad. Trying to bust the meteorite out of the patio and she surprised them."

A.C. shook his head, already skeptical, but not trusting himself to speak at this point.

***

"Hello, Mr. LaFleur," Moreland said as Geno brought A.C. to the front door. "You understand this is none of your business? Especially after the near-fiasco you engineered the last time you were here."

"It didn't turn out all that badly, given the final outcome."

"You were lucky you had the Feds on your side," Moreland replied. "I'd advise you to stay out of this one. And I mean *out*." He shook his head slightly. "You seem to have a special gift when it comes to getting yourself involved in things that don't concern you."

"I prefer to think of it as a special ability," A.C. said mildly. He leaned to one side, trying to look past Moreland into the house, where the door stood open. "Are they done in there?"

"I believe they're about finished, but—"

73

"If you'll excuse me?" He strode forcefully into the house.

The shock of seeing Jamila's body lying on the floor was nearly his undoing. Her face was turned up at an unnatural angle, her black eyes shining but vacant. One shoe was missing. He gasped, steps faltering. The sheriff's voice came to him as if from a great distance.

"Mr. LaFleur. Don't touch anything!"

Not bothering to respond, A.C. stepped gingerly past the body, trying to concentrate, and failing. *Oh, Jamila.*

"Excuse me." A deputy elbowed his way past A.C. to get a better camera angle. As the deputy took several photos, A.C. stepped back, momentarily disoriented, again almost stumbling as the flash hit his eyes like distant bursts of lightning. He quickly regained his composure and began to move forward, intending to order the deputy out of the way.

It was then that the two-man ambulance crew moved in, brusquely pushing him aside. They began to bag the body. As they rather awkwardly maneuvered her into position, Jamila's shirt rolled up her back several inches.

A.C. bent down, staring intently.

"Mr. LaFleur."

A.C. looked up.

"Please step away," Sheriff Moreland said, not politely. In fact, scowling rather pointedly, as if he were about to arrest LaFleur for the crime, or at least interference, tampering, something, anything.

"Of course, Sheriff. My apologies."

***

Fuentes and Maggie arrived home late, having spent some unplanned time in Ennis at a couple of additional shops, including more than an hour spent at a friend's wood-carving studio, buying keepsakes for A.C. and Maggie to take home with them. They were met at the garage door by A.C., who by his haggard look alerted them to the fact that something was very wrong. He shepherded them immediately into the bar downstairs.

It had never come easy to him, informing loved ones of tragedy; he all too often took a personal stake, invested a bit too much of himself into every case. It was a failing of which he was proud.

But this time…he had good reason to break down before even uttering a word. Thankfully that helped, in a small way, to prepare Fuentes for the news.

# The Boy in the Bubble

An invisible bubble enveloped the deck chair at the far corner of the deck, a force field composed of sorrow, regret, and incomprehension. Fuentes sat encased in the bubble, violated only reluctantly and briefly by funeral guests attempting to express their condolences. He responded politely to his visitors to the extent necessary, but otherwise remained engaged in somberly studying the silent peaks standing across the valley, shining in the afternoon's slanting sunlight. The nearby hole in the floor made by the meteorite that had apparently led to Jamila's death had been roughly patched, the patched area until recently covered by a small throw rug of Jamila's choice: forest green with a border of tan antlers. Fuentes kept tripping over it, and told her to remove it. He'd come out onto the deck at four A.M. that morning and carefully replaced it.

Maggie hovered nearby, her nursing instincts dialed up to high, trying unsuccessfully to get him to eat something. She didn't think it advisable he have anything to drink, other than Pellegrino, knowing his depression was deep enough without adding alcohol. In any case, he hadn't accepted anything, not even Pellegrino, but she'd insisted, and he finally took a small plate of food she'd made up from the provisions sent over by Jorge, the chef at the Moonlight Tavern. The bar man from the tavern, Ryan, had set up at the downstairs bar, but so far had not even been able to mix a floater for "the Doc."

The cremation had taken place earlier in Bozeman, attended only by Fuentes and A.C.; Jamila had no relations back in New York, save two or three cousins she didn't really know, and who had not yet been notified of her death. The reception—Fuentes refused to call it a wake, not being Irish and seeing nothing to celebrate—had been scheduled for that afternoon at the house. The guests were now milling absently about the house as funeral guests do, chatting with one another in forced amiability, conversation in this case made much more difficult due to the unspoken circumstances. When they did mention it, it was often in oblique terms of what it might mean for themselves—*What has happened to our community? Are any of us safe?*

Abigail sat in the opposite corner of the deck, away from Fuentes, occasionally weeping but for the most part composed. She'd not approached him yet, fearing she might bring on more distress. Frank and A.C. were sitting close by, talking in low tones.

Maggie was standing by the front window talking to a very fit-looking, attractive young woman with ginger hair wearing a bright green dress. She motioned to A.C. to come over.

As he approached, he recognized the woman she was with as Emily, one of the hostesses at Michelangelo's, a very popular restaurant in Big Sky. "Emily, good to see you!" he said. "How are things at the restaurant these days?"

"Busier than ever! Thank goodness we were able to stay open all summer, even at reduced capacity. You two should come down when you get a chance."

"We'll try, thanks." He gestured out to the deck. "Have you talked to Doc?"

"Yes, a few minutes ago. He's holding up well, don't you think?"

"Better than I would," A.C. replied, giving Maggie a long, affectionate look, which she returned. "Better than I would."

After an awkward pause, Emily shifted her stance away from them, towards the deck. "You know, I couldn't say anything to Doc about this, but maybe I can ask you…"

A.C. waited for her to continue.

Emily finally turned back to them. "Mr. LaFleur, I remember

what you did the last time you were here, those Pappy van Winkle bourbon murders? Is this like that? Are you going to investigate?"

"Well, Emily, that was a completely different situation. And as much as I hate to admit it, I was extremely lucky back then. No, this time we just have to let the sheriff do his job."

Emily firmed her stance, straightened her shoulders, not to be put off. "But if you *were* to investigate, where would you start? With the meteorite, like they're saying? The diamonds?"

A.C. gave Maggie a discreet eye roll. He didn't like the way the conversation was going. "I really don't know, Emily. I suppose I would start there. Although I don't know much about the jewelry business, to be honest.

"You must have some ideas about what happened, though."

"Well, yes, I do. But that doesn't mean I'm investigating anything."

"Mr. LaFleur, you know me from Michelangelo's, but I also used to work for a jeweler in town, Warsheim's. One of the best. I know a lot about what's been going on around here lately. I have contacts. I have an inside track. I can tell you everything you need to know about Montana jewelry."

"She may have something there, A.C.," Maggie said. "It couldn't hurt to learn about it."

He couldn't disagree. She was more often right than wrong when it came to these things. "Okay, Emily," he said. "I guess my first question would be, how profitable could these Moonlight diamonds be? So far all I've seen are what I would call diamond flakes. Outside of a few somewhat larger stones, admittedly, but, really, nothing all that large. What makes these Moonlight diamonds desirable?"

"We're seeing for the first time that diamonds are not 'forever,' as the famous De Beers marketing campaign claims," said Emily, warming to her role as advisor. "Diamonds have lost their luster, their mystique. First it was the reaction against conflict, or blood diamonds, and then it was the increasingly high quality of artificial diamonds, which used to be good only for industrial use, but as techniques improved, so did the size and quality of the diamonds. They've become just another commodity. To really impress a girl, you'd better come up with something better than a synthetic diamond. Like the ones being found here."

"I didn't realize it had gotten to quite that point," said A.C.

Maggie chuckled. "Oh, you've *always* thought 'diamonds are forever' is only the title of a James Bond novel."

"Wasn't it a movie?" Emily asked.

"I'm sure," said A.C. "What you're saying," he continued, "is since these diamonds are meteoric, from an exotic source, they are more valuable than any other diamonds on the market."

"Exactly! Millions, billions of years old, and from outer space! Pretty cool. My old boss can't get enough of the stuff. That's one reason De Beers is out here trying to buy everything up—they don't want the competition."

"Besides De Beers, do you know of any other large players operating in the area?"

"Well, there's the Farrells, but I guess they're not exactly professionals."

"Not from what I've heard."

"No. But there are some pretty well-established gemstone mines in Montana—a garnet mine in Madison County, and the Yogo sapphire mines up in Granite County. You could start there." She paused. "If you're interested, that is."

***

As Matt Kidd left the house after saying goodbye to Fuentes, he spotted Kevin Germain, VP of Moonlight Development, starting up the drive ahead of him. "Kevin! A word!" he called. Kevin stopped and turned, giving Matt a quick wave. Matt caught up with him and they continued up the hill together.

"Hello, Matt."

"Kevin."

Matt gestured back at the house. "It was very thoughtful of you, arranging for Chef Jorge to cater the food, and have Ryan at the bar. They did a nice job."

"Thanks. Seemed like the least I could do. They were glad to do it, of course."

"I'm sure Doc appreciated it."

"Yes, I'm sure. Say, Matt, while I've got you here, there's something I've been wanting to discuss with you."

"Sure, what is it?"

"I'm getting worried about the LMLC stance concerning mining rights on owners' properties. Particularly after this horrific murder. Are things getting out of control? What does LMLC think about all this prospecting, this treasure hunting, back at the home office in Boston?"

"Don't worry, they're on board with it. The corporate attorney used the analogy of finding lost golf balls to demonstrate how confusing the issue has become, and how that could apply to meteorite fragments. I'm sure they'll get it worked out soon; with a clear legal ruling, things should calm down."

"What's going on with the sluice up on Lone Creek, by the south road?"

"Believe it or not, it's become wildly profitable. One of the principals even suggested—tongue in cheek, I presume—that we consider becoming strictly a mining company."

"They've come down with gold fever, have they?"

"Indeed, they have. In fact, two of the principals are at the sluice today going through the concentrates themselves. They're like kids on an Easter egg hunt. 'Never had so much fun making money,' they said. One of them even said he's thinking about looking into buying the local garnet mine."

"The one out past Virginia City?"

"That's the one. Maybe even the Yogo sapphire mine near Lewiston."

"Why on earth are they so interested in this all of a sudden? Just because they're finding some stuff in meteorite fragments?"

"Southwest Montana jewelry is hot as can be right now. They want to get in on it. Imagine—they say—Moonlight meteoric diamonds with Montana garnets and sapphires. Maybe even the other gemstone, peridot, I think it is. There's another gem they find in meteorites sometimes—can't think of the name offhand."

"Incredible."

They stopped at the top of the hill. "Have you heard anything about a jewel operation working out of an empty hangar at the airport in Bozeman?" Matt asked.

"Just vague whispers, nothing substantial. Wait—the principals think there's already competition?"

Matt shrugged noncommittally. "Let's just say I've been charged with keeping a very close eye on things."

"Keep me informed?"

"Will do."

***

As several of Doc's friends came out onto the deck, hesitantly edging towards the bubble, A.C. motioned to Frank to come back inside. He led Frank up to an upper story loft, well away from the increasing crush of visitors. Doc had been not just well-known, but well-liked, and Jamila possibly even more so. Everyone said she'd become the perfect complement to his studied sociability; pert, intelligent, and unassuming, she'd quickly found herself at the center of the Moonlight community.

A.C. ushered Frank to a chair in the loft. "Well, what do you think, Frank?" he asked.

Frank was not quite sure what A.C. was getting at, even after knowing him all these years. A.C. had a way of sneaking up on you, coming in from left field. "How do you mean?"

"The sheriff is saying Doc led the killers here, by leaving the meteorite embedded in the patio. What do you think?"

"Well, I didn't hear your conversation with the sheriff. You're saying that's their firm position? That it's Doc's fault?"

"So far, that's their position."

"But you don't think so." One of Frank's favorite ploys, asking a question with a statement.

"I'm starting to have my doubts."

Frank waited patiently for an explanation; he recognized one of A.C.'s equally famous ploys, making the other party lead the discussion. He continued to wait.

"Okay, Frank. Here it is," A.C. finally said. He looked out over the loft railing towards the deck where Fuentes was sitting, still

81

valiantly trying to accommodate his guests' discomfort at being there. "Jamila was killed by asphyxiation, by choking. I saw the signs: discoloration, bruising, swelling. There were no obvious signs of a struggle, so she was probably taken by surprise, maybe while sitting at her desk. It would have happened quickly—loss of consciousness within about thirty seconds, making it easy for the killer to continue pressure, leading to death within minutes."

"What about that doesn't fit the sheriff's M.O.?"

"Let's start with what happens as a person dies. Doctors understand this almost instinctively, after all their training. Doc has seen it a thousand times. Respiratory failure, renal failure, the result of whatever illness or injury killed them. Of course, in the end everyone dies of heart failure. I don't claim to know much about the medical details of the *process* of death, the clinical causes. But I do know quite a bit about what happens *after* death."

"I'm not sure I'm following you. What does that tell us about Jamila?"

"Everyone's heard of *rigor mortis*, right?" Frank nodded. "But there are actually four stages of the postmortem process," A.C. continued, "the four stages of death, you might say. The first stage is *pallor mortis*. That's the paleness of the skin, which happens anywhere from fifteen to one-hundred-and-twenty minutes after death. Along with this is the gradual reduction in body temperature, *algor mortis*, which is a steady decline of about one-and-a-half degrees per hour. That's why temperature is so useful in determining time of death. The third stage is *rigor mortis*, which everyone knows is the stiffening of the body. This generally begins about four hours after death, and has its own stages, but we can ignore that for now.

"The first three stages are fairly well-known, even if some of the Latin terms are unfamiliar—loss of color, gradual cooling, and finally *rigor mortis*. But there's another, lesser known, 'mortis—' *mortis* is Latin for 'death,' by the way—something called *livor mortis*, *livor* meaning bluish in color. This is also referred to as postmortem lividity, *livid* being the Latin root, meaning lead colored, or bluish, of course."

"I appreciate the language lesson, A.C., I really do, but can you get to the point?"

"Just let me finish. *Livor mortis* starts as soon as twenty minutes after death, but is often very hard to detect, as other bodily changes take place. More than two hours after death, it's very difficult to see, unless you look hard for it."

"You still haven't explained exactly what it is, or why it's relevant."

"It's caused by blood pooling into those parts of the body that are dependent, meaning situated at the lowest point. That is why I doubt the sheriff's somewhat pat version of the murder motive."

"You saw something. Something they didn't see."

"Yes. As the ambulance attendants moved the body, which had been lying on its side at the door, I noticed some *livor mortis* on the lower side of her torso. But I also saw a region of *livor* on her back, a darker blue."

"I'm not following."

"Also, one of her shoes—the left—was missing. I saw it just outside the door of her office."

"Which means…"

"She was not killed at the front door, as the sheriff assumes. She was killed somewhere else in the house, and sometime later, within twenty minutes or so, she was moved to the foyer. That's what the *livor mortis* tells me, and the missing shoe—which must have fallen off as she was dragged through the house—confirms it. If I can figure out why she was moved, and from where, I'll be able to find the killer."

"Are you serious? There were no fingerprints—we've all been printed and excluded—and there was nothing stolen, other than a few fragments of the meteorite, possibly."

"But thanks to Abigail we have a good suspect."

"You mean Orvis Mooney."

"Exactly."

Frank nodded slowly. "Well, you find out who did it, whoever it is, and maybe I can take care of the rest."

"What do you mean?"

"I've heard you say 'justice is where you find it.'"

"On occasion. Depends on the circumstances."

"And the circumstances here lead me to believe we will not

see the justice Jamila deserves." He paused. "There's no heaven waiting for me. No family. Nothing to stop me."

A.C. cocked his head. "What the hell are you getting at, Frank?"

"You find out who did it—and if it's Mooney, so much the better—and I'll enjoy dispensing justice. Real justice. I don't think she's going to get it any other way."

After a moment, A.C. looked up, staring Frank in the eye. "Frank, I wish I could disagree. But I'm afraid you're right." He took a deep breath, let it out noisily. "Since it's Jamila—this time I might join you."

# PART TWO: FIELD TRIP

"Just can't wait to get on the road again…"
—Willie Nelson

# The Garnet Gallery

After considering Emily of Michelangelo's advice on gathering information at local sources of gemstones, A.C. commandeered a car and early the next day headed down Jack Creek Road.

His first planned stop was the Alder Gulch Red Rock Mine and Garnet Gallery. The route took him through Jeffers, Ennis, Virginia City, and then finally to Alder—coincidentally, the site of Chick's Restaurant and Bar. A.C. had been there once before, on his previous visit Montana, while tracking down the killers of a young woman Fuentes had met at the Bozeman airport. It was always something with Doc, he often said. In any case, he'd spent some time at Chick's and had (not altogether intentionally) lost some money there. And not just in the poker game he sat in on one night trying to get information. They had this betting game going on that involved pushing toy cars around the long, curved bar—well, you had to be there.

He missed the Gem Gallery the first time by and had to turn around and go back. It was off to one side of Highway 287, an unassuming red building with a white roof and an open area covered by a slanting tin roof. Next to the building were several round tables—cable spools turned on end, some of them. As he got closer, he could see some of the tables were covered with dirt. Alder Creek ran alongside the road to the left. To the right were several piles of what A.C. would soon learn were tailings piles, the equivalent of Frank's unclassified material.

As he pulled into the parking lot, he narrowly avoided hitting a man carrying what looked like very heavy cloth bags over to the area with the round tables. He got out of his car, and seeing another bag lying on the ground next to the building, he picked it up and carried it over to where the other man was dumping one of the bags onto a table. The man looked up in surprise.

"Hey, thanks, fella. Usually on my own here."

"Glad to help." A.C. looked around. "I gather this is the garnet mine?"

"If you're looking for the Red Rock Mine, then, yes, this is it. But I'm sorry—I'm not open for business yet today."

"Should I come back later?"

"Oh, no, you're fine. I'm usually open by now; it's just that I was robbed last night. Would shake hands, but you know…"

"Oh, hell. I'm sorry," said A.C., backing off a bit. "Forgot my mask again."

"Oh, no problem. Out here in the open, we're probably fine."

A.C. looked around. *Robbed?* "Excuse me for asking, but you said you were robbed? Of what?"

"Cleared the whole display table. Even took two bags of unsifted gravel. Must have thought there was something special about them. At the end of the day, after carting this stuff around, I'm too stiff and sore to bother moving any of it inside. Still, it was a real surprise to come out and see the stuff gone. Things are really getting crazy around here lately."

"Lately? How lately?"

"Since the meteor strike over in Big Sky last August. Good thing winter came on early, kept things tamped down. But this summer it got crazy. Who knows? Maybe it'll be like back in the eighteen-hundreds. Claim-jumping. Vigilantes." He looked over at A.C. with a look of half suspicion, half hopeful expectation. "I suppose you're here looking to get lucky and find a few garnets?"

"Sorry, no. No sifting and concentrating for me today. No, I'm just looking for some information."

"Oh. Well, then." Relief and disappointment often come in

pairs in this world, Al had found. He stood back and took a sideways look at A.C., a studied, inquisitive look. "I've seen you before."

A.C. pulled his head back, expressing doubt. "I don't know how that could be. I'm from New York. Just here visiting."

"I've got a gift for faces. I know I've seen you before."

"Like I said…"

"Chick's"

"What?"

"I think I played poker with you at Chick's. Couple of years ago, maybe."

"Are you sure? You're right, though; I was at Chick's, but only that one time. How do you—?"

Al interrupted again, confidently now. "Yeah, it was you. I made you for a detective then, and now you're back here asking for information. It was you." He looked at A.C. with a new comprehension. "You're the one who blew up the Pony crime ring!"

A.C. looked at the ground, then back up at Al. "Okay, you've got me there. Well done. My name's A.C. LaFleur."

"That's right, I recognize the name, now. I'm Al. Al Carlton. Glad to meet you—again. You're a lousy poker player, by the way," Al said jokingly. "I recall taking you for quite a bit that night."

"I don't think it was so much. In my defense, let me say there were extenuating circumstances. I was preoccupied at the time."

Al appeared to accept this as a reasonable explanation, one that did not reflect badly on their relative skills at poker. "What really happened up there at Pony, anyway? It was all hushed up, like there'd been UFOs up there, or Russian spies, or something."

"Something like that. But I'm here now on something new. A murder in Moonlight."

"Oh, no. The poor woman they found murdered?"

"Yes, that's right."

Al shook his head in dismay. "Bad. Bad all around. The sheriff was here the other day, asking if I'd seen anyone showing any unusual interest in things, if I'd had any trouble here, with the garnets and such. Before last night the answer was no."

"Did the sheriff say anything else? Anything related to the murder?"

"Not at first; not until I asked him why he was nosing around. Then he told me about the murder. Said it looked like a 'crime of opportunity,' is what he called it. I guess the guy who lives there has a meteor in his house, one that hit right next to him, almost killed him, I guess. Great big thing, from what I've heard. He just left it there, stuck in the side of his house. Right in plain sight. And it's worth a lot of money."

"You heard about the meteorite that hit the house, even out here?"

"Oh, yeah. That's what brought it on, according to the sheriff. 'Hubris,' was the word he used. Like the guy was showing off. But what with all this going on, this gold fever—meteor fever— he should have known better."

"Should have known, what, exactly?"

"That he should have been more careful. The sheriff said it's pretty clear, method and opportunity—grab and go. The lady just got in the way."

"He told you that?"

"Yeah, that's what they're thinking—drifters, outsiders, treasure hunters looking for an easy score. No planning, just grab and go. Too bad that lady got in the way." He paused. "You know, the sheriff said they were probably long gone already. But now, after last night, maybe not gone far enough." He paused again, looking at A.C. with what seemed to be a new interest. "You think so too, don't you? They're still around?"

"Too early to say. The sheriff might have it right."

Al brushed his hands vigorously on his faded jeans, sending small clouds of dust into the air. "You mentioned you are looking for information."

"Maybe you can start with garnets."

"You've come to the right place!" said Al, motioning A.C. over to a bench under the covered area. "Sit right over there. Social distancing. Seems to be the only thing that makes sense, getting this thing stopped. Anyway, like I said, you've come to the right place. I'm pretty much the garnet expert around here, and a member in good standing of the local historical society. So, where to start…okay, this old earth got started about four and a half billion years ago. Nothing much happened, garnet-wise, until about two billion years ago. That's when the mineral deposits in southwestern Montana were created. Of course, Montana wasn't where it is now, back then, but that's a different story. So, mountain building and erosion going full blast. Silt and sand flowing like mad down into the early oceans, and over time compressed into shale and sandstone. Then more compression. Things heat up. The minerals in the shale layers transform, change into gold, copper, other things. Garnets. Everything gets shaken around, and then the uplifting of these layers brings it to the surface, where it settles out, into rivers, or higher up, where it gets washed down. Of course, some of it stays deep underground, in pockets or seams." Al leaned back and took a deep breath.

A.C. took this opportunity to ask a question, hoping to advance the timeline a few eons. "When did gold fever hit Alder Gulch?"

"Mid-eighteen-hundreds," Al replied. "First the explorers, then the prospectors. They found gold just lying around in the streams, and the rush started." He pointed to his left, across the parking lot. "Gold was first discovered in Alder Creek in 1863, right across the road there. Started out with hand-panning, then sluice boxes—high-speed panning, I guess you could call it. This was followed not long after by large scale hydraulic mining—blasting away at the gravel with high-powered water hoses. This started in about 1867. Good idea, really, the more water, the more you could process. Even the Romans used water for mining. But even though hydraulic mining uncovered a lot more material, they still didn't have enough to process. That's when they brought in the floating bucket dredges. First ones came in here, oh, 1898, I think."

"Floating dredges?"

"Oh, yeah. Big barge with a bucket line in front, floating right out in the river, pulling up the riverbed and dumping it into huge sluices at the back. Really tore up the rivers, I'll tell you, even more destructive than the high-pressure hoses. But they were after the gold; nothing else mattered."

"They get a lot of gold?"

"In just the first three years, they pulled out over thirty

million dollars' worth." He lowered his eyes and gave A.C. a significant look. "Two billion, in today's money."

A.C. whistled. "That's a lot of gold."

"It was a big business. Thousands of people lived here, all along Alder Gulch. It must have been crazy. All that money, no law to speak of, so plenty of crime. Not sure I'd want to have lived here, back then."

"What's the population of Alder now?"

"Besides the tourists usually crowding into Chick's, in a good year, anyway? A hundred and fifteen, give or take."

"But today, it's mostly garnets?" A.C. asked, once more trying to get Al back on track. He still hadn't come to the pressing issue of what was happening in the area now that the meteorite strike had resurrected something like the old gold fever.

"All these tailings piles around here, all the way from Virginia City to Alder—"

"I saw them on the way out."

"Full of garnets. The old-timers, they wanted gold. Their sluices were filled with gold, sure, but also with dark red almandine."

"Almandine?"

"Garnets. It was just discarded. These tailings piles are full of it."

"That's what you're doing here, right? Sifting garnets out of the tailings."

"Yeah, but on a small scale. My neighbors down the road, Garnet USA, they're not even interested in the tailings. They're doing open pit mining, recovering garnets from the host schist way below stream level. But you can still find garnets aboveground, along the streams around here, and at Ruby Reservoir."

"Rubies! They're a lot more valuable than garnets, aren't they?"

"Bad news. Even though we've got the Ruby Valley, Ruby Creek, and Ruby Reservoir, we have damned few rubies. A few, sure, but nothing worth mentioning. The names probably came about very early on, when someone thought they had found rubies when all they had were garnets."

A.C. began mentally kicking himself for allowing Al to draw him this far into the history of Alder Gulch garnet mining, but was not sure how to extricate himself. Although it might prove—eventually—to be useful. "How can you tell the difference? Between rubies and garnets?"

"Ah, well, the eye of the beholder, in a way. Comes down to the refractive index of each, the way light gets from the stone to your eye. Rubies are a much more brilliant red, and made up of a different mineral, corundum. Same mineral group as sapphire, by the way. Anyway, a ruby is also more brilliant because a garnet is typically not as pure. There will be flecks of orange or other earth-toned minerals. Hold a garnet up to the light, and in its spectrum, you'll see a piece of a rainbow—yellow and green bands. Rubies absorb yellow and green light, so there are no refractive bands for those colors. So, they are redder."

"I have come to the expert, obviously."

"Oh, well, I've been doing this all my life, after all. But I'm not sure I've been any help to you. Garnets are pretty, but when it comes down to it, just a January birthstone. Not worth as much as what they're finding in Moonlight. That's the problem. That's what's feeding the frenzy up there. But it's really nothing compared to what went on back then."

"You think so? So, what was going on here, back in the day?"

"Let me digress."

A.C., again wondering what was coming next, and how far afield it might be, calmed himself as Al enthusiastically continued his history lesson.

"The gold rush, as I think I mentioned, started in 1863, the middle of the Civil War. Well, as you may or may not know, the early years of the Civil War did not go well for Lincoln and the Union. Out here in Montana, a lot of folks were sympathetic to the aims of the Confederacy. Many of the residents had come from parts associated with the Confederacy, and regardless of where their thoughts lie regarding slavery, they felt a sort of kinship. It was a nationalistic thing. Virginia City in those days was called Verona City. It was named after the wife of Jefferson Davis, Varina.

Unfortunately, they misspelled her name. No matter, they were loosely allied with the Confederacy. In 1864, Lincoln had a memo cross his desk that must have alarmed him—over six hundred thousand dollars a week's worth of gold was coming out of Virginia City, in 1864 dollars. Thirty-three million today. War is expensive. And six-hundred thousand a week was a hell of a lot of money. Lincoln wanted the gold to stay in Union banks. Montana was, at the time of the start of the war, in a sort of limbo, part of an unsupervised area called the Dakota Territory. Very quickly, Montana was included in a new, federally governed area called the Idaho Territory. This didn't last long, though, and soon after, Montana became its own Territory, and that's when the Union was able to move in. The Confederacy lost control of the gold."

"You said what was going on then was worse than what we're seeing now. How, exactly?"

"Vigilantes. The Feds were a long way away, after all. No trials, no need for evidence, and no mercy. There were twenty-two hangings in Virginia City in the space of a few months. One group of criminals, calling themselves the Henry Plummer Gang, rampaged all over the Gulch. Vigilantes hanged them. Not that they probably didn't deserve it. Of course, some accounts say it was the Confederate sympathizers who were the target. But there were a lot of hangings."

"That sounds incredible."

"You can still see the hanging beams in Virginia City, sort of a tourist attraction. And then, of course, all the gold the Confederacy held eventually became worthless Confederate dollars. The Union dollars kept their value."

"The gold fever led to all of this?"

"Yep. If it gets this bad up there in Moonlight…well, with luck, history won't repeat itself."

"So far it's under control."

"Just as long as the money doesn't get any bigger."

"What do you mean?"

"The more it spreads, the harder it is to follow. That's something you should keep in mind. As you're interested in local garnets, if you're looking to follow the money related to Montana jewelry, you need to check out Yogo sapphires."

"Where do those come from?"

"A couple of different places, some fairly remote, but a good place to start is a shop called the Gem Gallery, over in Bozeman. Friends of mine."

"Then I'm sure it will be worth a visit. MSU is in Bozeman, right?"

"Yep. Go Wildcats. Great school. Started in 1893 as a land grant school, an agricultural college. Of course, all the gold money in those days went back east. Harvard University operated bucket dredges on Alder Creek, which led to the largest university endowment in the country."

"Doesn't seem fair."

"All's fair in love and gold. And garnets."

A.C. stood up and brushed the seat of his pants. "Al, I can't thank you enough for your time and trouble. You've been very helpful. But before I go, is there anything else you can tell me about recent activity around the area that might be useful? Anything at all."

"Well, now that you mention it, maybe a couple of things. Might not be anything, I don't know. I got a call from some fella who said he wanted to buy me out. Property, inventory, the little bit of equipment I've got, everything. Now, I wouldn't think there would be any interest in a place like this—it's just a sideline for me, almost a hobby—my regular business is a tree service. Anyway, I told him no. Called me back the next day wanting to know if I'd sell my production for the next year, in advance. I'm not sure what to make of it."

"Somebody really wants a lot of garnets, I guess. You said a couple of things. What else?"

"I got an anonymous email asking if I had found anything particularly interesting since the meteor hit. I ignored it; I think they call it phishing."

"Were they asking about anything specific?"

"Yeah, something called pallavine. I had to look it up."

A.C. turned his head and stared out across Alder Creek for a moment, as recognition hit him. "Someone was telling me about pallavine just the other day," he said, more to himself than to Al. He turned back, nodded, and held up his hand in a virtual high-five. "Al, you've been a tremendous help. Thanks again!"

"Glad to have the company."

It was about an hour to Bozeman from Alder, A.C. figured, plenty of time to try to digest everything Al had told him, try to make some sense of it.

And too much time, he thought sadly as he pulled out onto the highway, too much time to think about the emptiness newly settled at the heart of Doc's house.

# The Gem Gallery

Just after noon, A.C. parked his car in the middle of Main Street, Bozeman, across from the Gem Gallery. He could see from across the street that it was quite a nice storefront—Al had apparently not led him astray.

He pulled open the front door, then stopped and backed up after seeing the "Masks Required" sign on the door. "Damn." He reached into his back pocket and pulled out his mask. After securing it, grumbling even while accepting the necessity, he went back to the door and entered the shop.

He was immediately struck by the sheer size of the place and impressed by the finely finished interior. Wood paneling and dark wood floors added a warmth to the river rock walls and bright glass display cases, decorated and filled with jewelry of all types, many featuring bright blue or red stones.

Looking around—he was the only one in the place at the moment—he soon spied an attractive young woman approaching him from the rear of the store. She was dressed in what A.C. had come to call "cowgirl chic:" western-style shirt with pearl snaps, stylish jeans, and artfully patterned boots. The long blonde hair hanging down past her shoulders framed an undeniably beautiful face, fresh and wholesome as a field of Montana wildflowers, which sadly disappeared behind a mask as she came closer.

"Hi, welcome to the Gem Gallery. I'm Bingo Brennaman."

Her voice, softened but not muffled by the mask, was exactly what A.C. had expected, bright and hopeful, carrying all the joy of youth. "What can I help you with today?"

A.C. nodded a slight greeting. "My name's LaFleur, Ms. Brennaman, A.C. LaFleur. I was told by Al over at the garnet mine in Alder you might be able to help me with something."

"Oh, well, if Al sent you, you must be okay. I'll sure try to answer any questions you have. And please call me Bingo."

"Okay, Bingo, I like the sound of that! But I have to ask, how did you get a name like 'Bingo?'"

"Well, my given name is Brenda, but I hate it. Bingo was the name of my first horse when I was just a kid. I just loved him, and spent every waking hour with him, darn near. Somehow the name stuck to me, too."

"So, Bingo was your first. How many horses have you had?"

"Oh, quite a few. I've been ropin' and ridin' for a long time. But right now, I'm in my senior year as a geology major at MSU, on a rodeo scholarship."

"A rodeo scholarship! Never heard of such a thing. What kind of rodeo stuff—I'll admit I'm a real novice here—what is involved with that, jumping fences and such?"

"Oh, no, that's quite a different thing, called show jumping, or stadium jumping. Much more formal. You've heard of dressage?"

"Yes, fancy walking, different gaits, that kind of thing?"

"Exactly. That's also done along with the kind of jumping you're thinking about. The rodeo events I compete in are breakaway roping, barrel racing, and goat tying."

"Wow. I wish my wife were here to meet you; I know she'd be fascinated."

"Well, since she's not here, why don't we pick out some jewelry for her?"

A.C. looked around at the wide expanse of jewelry counters and wall displays. "Oh, I don't know. I wouldn't know where to begin."

"That's what I'm here for."

"So, you're a rodeo expert and a jeweler, too?"

"Well, my parents own a jewelry store in Helena, and as I

mentioned, I'm a geology major, so working here part-time is perfect for me."

"Actually," A.C. replied, "I'm here hoping to learn something; maybe jewelry shopping can come later?"

"Of course! It's a slow day. Well, every day has been pretty slow with this COVID thing, so I have time to answer any questions you might have." She motioned to a small table and chairs set up between two huge wooden beams, in front of a large rock fireplace. "Let's sit over there, shall we?"

"I really appreciate this," A.C. said as he settled into his chair. "I'll get right to the point. I'm a police detective, retired for some years now, out here visiting a close friend in Moonlight. I'm investigating—unofficially, I should say—a murder that took place there recently."

"I just saw something on the Explore Big Sky newsfeed about a murder up there. A robbery attempt gone bad, they said. Something about a jewel-encrusted meteorite stuck in the house?"

"In the patio, but yes, that's what I'm working on."

"How are you involved?"

"Let's just say it's personal."

Bingo could tell this was a sensitive area and silently nodded her understanding.

A.C. continued. "Since the crime could be related to the meteorite, and the gems embedded in it—at least, according to the sheriff's department—I thought I should start by getting a good overview of the local gem industry, and the current level of activity. I started over in Alder with garnets, and was told this is the place to get a handle on Montana sapphires. It appears I've found the expert I need."

"Where should I start? I mean, how much do you want to know?"

"Give me everything. I've found it's almost impossible to know in advance what's going to turn out to be important."

"Education and perspective. Okay. I'll start with something that's been in the news lately, a big find in Sri Lanka. A fourteen-hundred-and-four carat blue star sapphire. That's so big it would practically fill the palm of my hand. It's valued at over three hundred million. And now is just the right time for it."

"How so?"

"There's been a recent surge in the demand for sapphires, worldwide. A lot of interest related to wedding engagements. Diana started it all with her twelve-carat sapphire ring; that's the one Kate Middleton has now, as her engagement ring."

"Whatever happened to 'diamonds are a girl's best friend?' Not anymore?"

"No, exactly. Diamonds have fallen out of favor and sapphires have taken their place."

"How do Montana sapphires fit in?"

"That's a great story." Bingo leaned in a bit from her end of the table, visibly animated, even behind the mask. She had very expressive eyes. "Almost all North American sapphires are sourced right here in Montana. Sapphires are classified mineralogically as corundum, the same mineral which makes up rubies, interestingly enough—brother and sister gems, I call them. But to get back to sapphires—the finest in Montana, and probably the world, are Yogo sapphires. They're found in an area in the Little Belt Mountains called Yogo Gulch."

"Where did the name 'Yogo' come from?" asked A.C., knowing he was getting off track but unable to resist—what a strange name!

"I'm not sure anyone really knows," said Bingo, her eyes perplexed. "Maybe an Indian name?"

"No matter. Sorry I interrupted."

"I'll look it up later. Anyway, Yogo sapphires are a beautiful cornflower blue; that's due to traces of iron and titanium. They're very difficult to mine, because they typically occur only in vertically resistive igneous dikes—uh oh, your eyes are glazing over," she said, chuckling. "Too much geology makes Jill a dull girl."

A.C. couldn't help laughing out loud at this and smacked the table with his palm. "Bingo, you're a treasure! Please, go on."

"Well, it means the excavations have to be deep and narrow. And dangerous. A miner died in a mine collapse in 2012."

"How did sapphire mining get started in Montana?" He felt sure this was a relevant question, rewarded by what he felt sure was a bright smile behind the mask, followed by another torrent of information.

"It started with a gold rush, but not as wild as Virginia City, and Alder Gulch, where you were this morning. In 1865, no, 1866, they found gold in Yogo Creek. There were reports of "blue pebbles" in the stream by about 1878, but it wasn't until 1894 that they were identified as sapphires. A rancher named Jake Hoover gave a cigar box full of these pebbles to an assay office, who sent them to Tiffany's in New York, asking if they had any value. The Tiffany's appraiser called them the "finest precious gemstones ever found in the United States.' Well, this really started things up, as you can imagine." She paused. "You're familiar with the artist Charles M. Russell, of course."

"Sure," he replied. "Famous western artist."

"He was one of Hoover's cowhands."

"Interesting." He stretched his arms behind his back. "All this talk of deep rock mining is making my back stiff," he said. "Can I suggest a short break?" He added, a bit self-consciously, "Do you have a restroom?"

"Of course! In back, to the right." She pointed the way.

A few minutes later, they reconvened at the table, at least one of them much refreshed.

"Thanks for that," A.C. said. "Now, you were telling me about cigar boxes full of precious gems, cowboy artists, and vertical igneous dikes. But I was wondering—if these Yogo sapphires are so rare and valuable, why aren't there any famous Montana sapphire mines?"

"Because they're so difficult to mine. A lot of companies have tried and failed. British conglomerates, Citibank—in the end, that effort came down to a big pile of gravel-filled bags, bought at auction by a local jeweler."

"What happened then? Did it all just die out?"

"Not entirely. In 1969, a developer had the idea of selling off Yogo Gulch sapphire rights along with homesites—it was called Sapphire Village."

"Do any good?"

"Oh, the homeowners there still find a few, but nothing

significant."

"Anything outside of Yogo Gulch?"

"Not much. There are other areas of Montana where sapphires are found, but they aren't the same quality—they're heat-treated to enhance the color, like sapphires everywhere else in the world. Yogos are unique. That's why we stock them exclusively."

A.C. stood up and walked over to a nearby display case. "These are Yogos?" he asked, pointing at some rings set with brilliant blue gems.

"Absolutely. In fact, the owner of the Gem Gallery just reopened a mine in Yogo Gulch. He thinks the demand is going to keep growing."

A.C. walked back over to the table and sat down. "What's next for you? You really seem to love geology; is there a career path there for you?"

"That's the plan. I love geology. Kicking around in the dirt. Maybe that's why I love rodeo. Getting down in the dirt, with the goats." She shook her head, laughing at her own joke. Then she sobered, eyebrows knitted, the scowl visible even through her mask. "But I have to say, this year has been very disappointing. I should be attending senior seminars on the future of geology, meeting with professors, pursuing an advanced degree. COVID sucks." She glanced up, embarrassed by her momentary lapse into self-pity. "There's so much to be done, not just here on Earth, but in planetary, even interstellar geology."

"Interstellar?"

"You've seen an example of at least planetary, and perhaps even interstellar geology, right there in Moonlight. Who knows where that meteorite came from?"

A.C. had a sudden vision of the meteorite sitting in the concrete pad of Doc's patio, surrounded by accent lights, the glittering, beautiful, obscene thing that had brought on so much sorrow, so much unwarranted distress. With a will he had to draw down deep to find, he brought himself back to the present, back to the reason he was here. It was time to wrap it up.

"Anything else you can think of that might be useful?"

"Well, I don't know if this is important, but the owner

recently got an anonymous offer to buy his entire inventory, along with everything produced at the mine. He was very suspicious. He's upgrading the security here, better cameras and additional gem safes."

"I can't blame him, from what I've seen in Moonlight. But as for you—what will you do now?" he asked in a solicitous tone.

"I graduate in the spring. Geological career prospects are uncertain. And I don't really want to sign up for the women's PBR."

"PBR?"

"Professional bull riding. I'm not sure I would even want to get into the regular rodeo circuit, even as much as I enjoy it as an amateur. For one thing, I'd have to start paying my own way. For another, too often the commercial interest in us gals comes down to tank tops, tight jeans, and gaudy boots. Ugh."

"I think I understand." He stood up slowly and looked over at Bingo with an expression of respect commingled with commiseration. "I can't thank you enough for your help. I wish you all the best in the future. If you talk to Al, be sure and thank him for sending me here. It's been delightful as well as informative."

"Oh, Al! We all love old Al. An authentic Montana character."

As Bingo walked A.C. towards the door she broke protocol, pulled her mask down, and put her hand on his shoulder. "You know, Mr. LaFleur, everything we've been talking about, the garnets, the Yogo sapphires—they're all of this world. What you're dealing with is something else entirely."

"You mean because of the meteorite. Because it's off-world."

"Yes. And I think there's only one place to go."

"And that is?"

"The gem and mineral division of the Smithsonian."

"In D.C.?"

"Yes. They'll have the expertise and the resources you need."

"It's odd you should mention it. There appears to be a rather strong connection to the Smithsonian already." Her quizzical look told him he'd perhaps said too much. "In any case, I'll certainly consider it.”

As he opened the door to leave, she caught his shoulder once more. “One more thing,” she said as he was halfway out the door. “Since we’re talking off-world?”

He stopped, head down, waiting.

“If it turns out this has anything to do with pallavine?”

A.C. jerked his head up and looked over at her in surprise. *I never mentioned that…*

“Be careful,” she said as the door closed behind him.

# The Wild West

Frank had made instant friends with the group of kids who roamed the neighborhood on their bikes. They ranged in age from about six to twelve. Normally they stopped by to visit him at the sluices for a while, then would pass by two or three hours later on their way home.

Today, however, about an hour after they'd been there, they all came roaring back down the hill, jumped off their bikes and rushed up to Frank, breathless and agitated.

"Frank! Frank!" "You've got to help us, Frank!" "He tried to kill us!" The two youngest hung back, wordlessly sobbing.

"Whoa! What's going on?" They crowded around him, still chattering, obviously upset.

"He tried to kill us!" one of them repeated, while the others talked over him.

"Calm down, guys. I don't understand what you're talking about. One at a time."

One of the oldest, a girl named Ella, stepped forward. The others immediately quieted down—she was obviously their spokesperson.

"He pointed a gun at us, Frank, and screamed like he was going to shoot us. And we weren't doing anything, just riding around!"

"So, we took off out of there!" added Ethan, one of the older boys. The others began shouting their agreement.

"Okay, okay. Who did this?" Do you know him?"

"The scary-looking guy who's been hanging around," said Ella.

Frank looked down at the ground for a moment. "Scary-looking guy. You mean Orvis Mooney?"

"Yes, that's right, Mooney," they all chimed in.

"Where?"

"Up by Horseshoe."

Frank threw down his shovel. "You kids get home. Don't stop for anything." The kids scattered to their bicycles and tore off down the road.

Five minutes later, Frank pulled his pickup off to the side of the road. He saw Mooney fooling around with something by the sluice. Mooney didn't see him until he was almost on him.

"What the hell do you want?" Mooney said, looking up.

Frank kept walking.

Mooney pulled out his big revolver and pointed it straight at Frank's chest. "Stop right there!"

Still without saying a word, Frank kept walking. Less than a second later he was standing right in front of Mooney. In the next fraction of a second, Mooney's pistol was in Frank's hand, and in the fractional second after that, Frank clubbed him in the side of the head with it. Mooney grunted and went down.

As Mooney lay on his back groaning, conscious but immobilized, Frank flipped open the revolver and removed the bullets. He dropped the empty gun onto Mooney's chest. It thumped like a wet drum.

"First and last warning, Mooney."

Mooney glared as Frank walked back to his truck. He didn't even try to get up until Frank was long out of sight.

# Off to see the Docent

"This looks great!" A.C. walked up to the kitchen bar where Maggie was laying out a buffet. "I'm famished!"

"Everything will be ready in a few minutes. It does look good, doesn't it? It's all thanks to Chef Jorge and the neighbors. Jorge brought over an elk ragout I can't wait to try. Paul and Paula brought over a mac & cheese they said is to die for."

A.C. looked around the living room. "Where's Doc?"

"In his bedroom, cleaning up."

"How's he doing?"

"Better. Making eye contact, and initiating conversations at times. He even seems to be interested in dinner, thank heavens."

"Glad to hear it."

"What did you learn today? Figure anything out?"

"Only how crazy gold fever—and gem fever—can get. Worse in the old days, but everyone I talked to seems to think that's where we're heading." He turned and looked out through the large window that opened onto the rear deck. Frank was out there pacing back and forth from one end of the deck to the other, head down. "What's Frank upset about?"

"I'm not sure. Something happened, but he didn't want to talk about it. Now that you're here, we'll probably find out. I'm afraid it's something related to—" She broke off and looked over as Fuentes came in.

"Doc!" said A.C., coming around the bar. "Good to see you up and about. Would you like a floater?" Maggie coughed into her hand and scowled at him. A.C. held up his hands as if to ask, *what now?*

"No thanks, A.C.," Fuentes replied to Maggie's relief. "Maybe later. I don't know."

Frank came bursting in from the deck. "A.C., welcome home. Hi Doc. You're looking good. Fresh clothes? Looks like you could use a floater."

"No, thanks, not just now."

"Well, I could use one. Or two. As a matter of fact," he said, raising his voice, "I'm going to make mine a reverse floater—Grouse with just the tiniest drop water on top. How about you, A.C.? Maggie?"

Maggie shook her head. "I've got a glass of wine around here somewhere."

A.C., however, responded enthusiastically. "Just what the doctor ordered." He glanced sheepishly over at Maggie. "I mean, yes, thanks, Frank."

Frank walked over to the end of the bar and grabbed a couple of glasses. As he filled them with ice, A.C. edged a little closer, and in a low voice said, "Frank, you seem a bit agitated."

Frank jammed a couple of more cubes of ice into the glasses, then unscrewed the cap off the Grouse. "Agitated? Damn right, I'm agitated. No, not agitated. I'm mad as hell." He tilted the bottle and poured Grouse liberally over the ice, splashing some onto the counter. He picked up a napkin, wiped it up, then grabbed the bottle and poured some more, splashing the counter again. This time he left it. "Mad as hell." He looked up at A.C. and pushed a drink over to him. "What did you find out today, A.C.? Anything about Mooney? Please tell me you found out Mooney is behind it. I'm ready for him. More than ready. Right now!" He picked up his drink and downed half of it in one swallow.

Maggie backed away from the bar, gave them both a significant look and stalked off. "I'm going to go look for my glass of wine."

A.C. waved distractedly, took a sip of Grouse, then took a

napkin from the bar and carefully wiped down the sides and bottom of his glass. He looked at Frank over the top of his glasses. "Let's move out into the foyer; more private." He then looked over his shoulder at Fuentes, sitting placidly at the dining table. Frank nodded in understanding.

Once away from the dining room, A.C. asked, "What happened?"

Frank took a deep breath, and using a napkin to clean off his own glass, visibly tried to calm himself. He wadded the napkin up and threw it in the direction of the kitchen. "You know the neighborhood kids? The group riding their bikes around together, like a posse?"

"No, haven't noticed. How many kids?"

Frank held up his hand and counted them off. "Ella. Ethan. Jack. Lola. Peyton. Carter." He blinked, then held up a seventh finger. "Oh, and Caeden. Can't forget little Caeden. My new best friends."

"You know all of their names? How did you get to know them?"

"They've been stopping at the sluices every day while they're out riding around. I've been letting them pick through the concentrates, letting them take whatever they want. They're great kids, always chattering away about one thing or another. I've been learning a lot about what the kids are up to, and how they've adjusted to social distancing."

"And how is that?"

"Oh, they ignore it. No harm in that. But I've also learned a lot about what goes on around here. Sometimes the adults are not so careful about what they say; never heard the old saying, I guess, 'little pitchers have big ears.'"

"Did they say something today that's got you so worked up?"

"Nah, it's nothing the kids did, or heard. It's what happened to them. And me." He took a large gulp of his drink, nearly finishing it off, started to reach for the bottle, stopped himself, and went on. "When they pulled up, they were all excited and out of breath. Then Ella and Ethan told me the story while the others backed them up.

They were up on the south road by the Horseshoe ski run when someone came running out of the woods screaming at them. Said he yelled at them, 'Get out of here and never come back!' That was enough to frighten them, at least the younger ones, and they slowly started to turn around; but then he pulled out a gun and started waving it at them, yelling threats at the top of his lungs. The kids were afraid to repeat some of what he'd yelled at them. The two youngest, Carter and Caeden, started shaking and sort of sobbing while Ethan was telling me this, and then Caeden started crying." He took a sip of his drink. "It was Mooney."

A.C. leaned in close to Frank. "But the kids are all okay? He didn't touch any of them, did he?"

"No, just scared them to death. They're all okay."

"You didn't leave it at that, did you?"

"No." He finished off his drink while A.C. waited for an explanation. "I tracked him down and pistol whipped him with his own gun."

A.C. couldn't help smiling, even if a bit grimly. "Ah, the old skills—and instincts—never leave us." He finished his own drink in one long swallow. "You think he got the message?"

"Oh, yeah. He understands now what he's up against. In fact..."

Just as Frank was about to go into more detail, the front door opened. It was Abigail.

"The door was unlocked," she said cheerily. "Where's Doc?"

Frank stood back as A.C. ushered her into the dining room. As soon as she saw Fuentes at the table, she rushed over, put her hands on his shoulders, and leaned over and kissed him on the forehead. "Doc! You look so much better! How do you feel?"

He drew back slightly as she continued to hover. "I'm doing okay, I guess." He shifted a bit in his chair, creating a little more space. "How about you?"

"I'm great! I widened my search today. I got all the way over to the edge of the Moonlight ski area—Horseshoe, I think it is? Quite a way west of there. It's very rough terrain, heavily forested..." She trailed off when she saw Frank come back in to the room. "Wow,

Frank! I saw what you did to Mooney.”

Frank’s head jerked up. “You saw that?”

“Yeah. It was awesome. I couldn’t even see your hands move. Is that going to be my next lesson?”

Frank ignored the question and went into the living room and found a chair by a window. Abigail watched him go with a bland expression on her face, not saying anything.

Fuentes straightened up and turned to A.C., who had been watching the exchange between Abigail and Frank with interest. “A.C., how is the investigation going?” Seeing A.C. hesitate, he gave a quick smile and said, “It’s okay to talk about it. I want to know.”

“The sheriff’s theory of grab and go with the house meteorite, but gone bad, appears to be the consensus,” he said carefully. “Jamila got in the way.”

“Oh,” said Fuentes. “I overheard some of the talk at the memorial. ‘Doc’s Rock,’ that’s what they’re calling it. And that’s what drew them here.”

Abigail stepped forward and took him by the hand. “None of this is your fault. It’s just awful…just awful thieves would do something like this.”

Maggie had come over when she saw Abigail standing next to Fuentes. *Holding his hand.* “You aren’t convinced by the sheriff’s theory, are you, A.C.?”

“They may have it right this time. Probably have it right.” He didn’t make it sound too convincing.

“But?”

“I’ll admit I’m a bit uneasy about it. Something I saw. Or thought I saw.”

“So, you’re not done yet?” Fuentes said with a note of distress in his voice.

“No, Doc, I’m not done. I guess I’d have to say I’m still warming up.” He turned to Frank. “Maybe we could talk privately?”

Fuentes shook his head. “No! I want to hear what you’re doing. Maybe I can even help.”

“No need for that, Doc. Frank, I’d like to talk with someone at the Smithsonian, someone who knew—knows—Stony. Someone with connections, if you get my drift. Could any of your three-letter agency pals get me in? It's closed up tight with this virus thing."

Frank gave A.C. one of his Cheshire cat grins. "Give me a few minutes." He started towards his loft room, then turned back. "Forgot my floater."

"Oh, that's what you're calling a floater these days?" asked Fuentes.

"Sign of the times." He grabbed his drink and left.

Maggie started for the kitchen, saying the buffet was ready, don't let it get cold. Then she stopped and faced A.C., a frown settling onto her face, a frown A.C. recognized as stormy times ahead. "A.C., are you sure about this? We're in the middle of a pandemic and D.C. is close to the epicenter. Are you ready to deal with all the complications of airline restrictions, hotels, risk of quarantine? You think this is necessary?"

"Hey. Since we're in Montana, let me use a western cliché: this is not my first rodeo. Hong Kong flu, Summer of Love, 1968; then Obama's pandemic, the H1N1 influenza in 2009. This is my third, and I'm still standing."

"A.C., you've aged since then. Our immune systems weaken over time. You're at much higher risk now."

Fuentes looked up at Abigail as he gingerly pulled his hand away from her ever-tightening grip. "I think Maggie is right, A.C.— there's been enough sadness around here. Why not sit this one out? At least wait for the vaccine."

"How soon is that going to happen? Six months? A year? I know they're working like mad on it, but I don't want to wait; I can feel the trail going cold already. What little trail I have. I want to leave as soon as possible, providing Frank can hook me up."

"What can you do there you can't do from here? Everyone's working from home."

"Not my style. You know that. I need information, insight, understanding. I need to *talk* to someone, even if it's through a damned mask." He took off his glasses and rubbed his eyes with a fist. "I need a breakthrough, and I don't see that happening unless I can get a better handle on what's going on here. If a trip to D.C. is what it takes, that's what I aim to do."

That night, Frank arranged two meetings for him. A.C. left for Washington the next morning.

# Hope Springs Eternal

Delta Airlines was still spacing passengers to ensure an empty middle seat, a requirement Maggie had insisted upon. The connections were good, as well—Bozeman to Minneapolis to Ronald Reagan. (A.C. didn't like to call it "National" out of a vaguely held respect for presidential names, and Reagan in particular.)

Maggie had booked the JW Marriot for him, right next to the White House, and which was within walking distance of the National Mall. The Smithsonian National Museum of Natural History, with its imposing Romanesque columns, stands directly on the Mall. Somehow A.C. walked right past it, probably because the entrance was hidden by scaffolding and construction mesh. Circling back with the Washington Monument as a landmark (*now, there was a President*), he finally located the front entrance. His contact, senior docent Huguette Martine, was waiting on the steps for him. Trim and of medium height, about his age, with coppery-gray hair cut in a neat bob, she was dressed in a stylish tweed business suit and carrying a small brown leather valise. A.C. was immediately impressed with her demeanor. She greeted him warmly, her voice low and welcoming, furthering his good impression.

"Mr. LaFleur, I presume? It's an honor to welcome you—my first guest in months!"

"Hello. I'd shake hands, but, well…" He reached up and

self-consciously adjusted his mask, which was threatening to creep down below his nose. "Thank you for allowing this visit; I know it's unusual."

"Yes, it is. You have a very influential friend!" She paused, as if afraid she may have offended him. "But given the circumstances," she continued, in a more subdued manner, "we're more than glad to assist you any way we can. Especially as you've had to come quite a long distance, from Big Sky, Montana, I think the General said."

"Nearby; an area called Moonlight Basin. We're staying with Doc out there, that is, Dr. Fuentes..." He trailed off.

Huguette frowned sympathetically under her mask. "Yes, we're so sorry." She straightened her shoulders and turned towards the front entrance. "Well, Mr. LaFleur, shall we get started?"

"Lead on. Oh, and please call me A.C."

"And A.C. is short for…?"

"Alonzo Carlton. Two uncles I never met. But no one has called me by that name for as long as I can remember."

"Well, I think it's a nice name; but A.C. *is* much easier to say." She stopped at the museum entrance before showing him in. "I meant to tell you earlier—unfortunately General Dunway has been held up, perhaps for an hour or so. But he asked me to show you around, and to give you some background on what you'll be talking about when you meet. We thought you might appreciate an overview of the museum's history, to begin with—is that all right with you?"

"Certainly, but I don't want to impose too much, given the health risks, and all."

"Oh, don't worry; we'll keep our masks on, of course, but in fact, I've already had my bout with the virus; mild, thank goodness. I picked it up at Sun Valley. It was the first large breakout at a ski resort, just my luck. In any case, don't worry."

She ushered him in through the large front door, locked it behind her, and led him towards a large hallway. "On the way to the gem and mineral gallery, which I know is your real interest, I'll give you a bit of Smithsonian history. I'll start with James Smithson, one of the most, if not *the* most, fascinating tales on the Mall."

"Well, you have me there; I know nothing about him."

"James Smithson was born in France in 1765 and christened James Lewis Macie. He was the illegitimate son of Elizabeth Hungerford Keate Macie and Hugh Smithson, the Duke of Northumberland. The pregnancy, as well as delivery, remained well hidden in France. His mother changed his name to Smithson and made him a British citizen when he was ten. When he was seventeen, he enrolled in Pemberton College, Oxford, and graduated four years later. In the late 1700s, chemistry and its use in studying minerals was the new up and coming science. James by this time had developed quite a reputation. He loved going into the field collecting minerals and ores throughout Scotland and Europe. He was very tenacious, apparently going out in all weather and terrain."

She paused, indicating a stairway. "The gem and mineral section is on the second floor. Are stairs okay, or...?"

"I'm fine. Lead on."

As they went up the stairs, she continued her history lesson. "Within a year after graduating, James was accepted into the Royal Society of London, nominated by Henry Cavendish, the discoverer of hydrogen. James was to later study zinc carbonate, which became known as Smithsonite. That makes quite a nice connection to the mineral exhibits, don't you think? In the meantime, he became quite wealthy."

They reached the top of the stairs, and A.C. stepped aside, breathing a bit heavily.

"Are you okay?"

A.C. smiled and said, "Guess I can't take the big drop in elevation from Montana."

She smiled. "Shall I finish up with the history before we go on to the exhibits?"

"Good idea."

"Well, Smithson died in Genoa, Italy, in 1829. He left his fortune to his nephew, but stipulated that should his nephew die without heirs, the entire fortune would go to establish a national educational institution in the United States. Why an English scientist of such renown should bequeath his fortune to found an American institution is uncertain. In any case, the nephew died in 1835, without heirs, and Andrew Jackson's administration became the beneficiary."

"Quite a story. And that's how it ended?"

"Not quite. A quarry expansion in the Genoa cemetery in 1904 necessitated removing Smithson's body. They decided to bring him to Washington DC.; Alexander Graham Bell accompanied the corpse the entire way. He's interred in the original building. That was the first time James Smithson ever entered the United States."

"Wow; who knew?"

"Shall we continue on to the exhibits?"

"Lead on."

The gem and mineral galleries were almost overwhelming. They walked through the first section as Huguette went on with her lecture—she was enjoying having an attentive guest after rattling around the empty halls for so many months. "We have over thirty-five thousand mineral specimens, and at least ten thousand gems. Many were from Smithson's own collections, which came back with his body, with Bell."

"What's the difference between a gem and a mineral?"

"A mineral occurs naturally and has a characteristic chemical composition and crystalline structure. A gem is a piece of mineral crystal that's been cut and polished. Some are more desirable than others, of course, depending on rarity and quality."

"Why is jewelry so important, in general, do you think?"

"Humans started inventing things around ninety thousand years ago. Jewelry came along—as far as we know—about seventy-seven thousand years ago."

"Sounds like you've got it pretty well nailed down."

"The dates could change with more research. That estimate is based on current archaeological knowledge. But it already predates the bow and arrow by several thousand years. Obviously, it was an important cultural development. Jewelry transcends all aspects of civilization: politics, royalty, finance, crime—and romance. Maybe especially romance. It almost defines what it means to be human."

Huguette stopped at a large exhibit. "The Hope Diamond," she said.

A.C. tried not to look dazzled.

"The faint bluish color is due to trace amounts of boron," she went on. "The history of ownership goes back four centuries to India, where it was found. And it is cursed."

"Cursed?"

"As are many famous jewels."

"What's it worth? Not to be too crass about it," he amended.

"Oh, three hundred and fifty million, give or take."

"You trust me standing next to it?"

"Since you're the only visitor in months, it wouldn't be too hard to track you down if it went missing."

"I was recently told of a large star sapphire found in Sri Lanka. Would that be comparable?"

'Yes, quite similar in value. It's called the Star of Adam, after a Muslim belief that Adam was sent to Sri Lanka after being expelled from the Garden of Eden. There is a mountain there called Adam's Peak—very striking. Pilgrims climb it to watch the shadow at sunrise as it descends the mountainside. It's also home to a footprint of Buddha."

"Very ecumenical of them. Would that sapphire be a candidate for the Smithsonian's collection?"

"Possibly—but we already have the Star of Asia—five hundred and sixty-three carats, almost perfect clarity. But that reminds me, speaking of sapphires—we have quite a few Yogo sapphires from Montana."

"I was just at a sapphire gallery, in Bozeman."

"They're lovely gems. And since we're in Washington, D.C., I can't help mentioning the presidential connections."

"Really? What would those be?"

"Florence Harding, the wife of president Warren G. Harding, owned a ring made of Montana gold and Yogo sapphires; and President Truman, his wife Bess, and daughter Margaret, all had a collection of Yogo sapphires." She motioned they should finish up. "The General will be here soon."

"Okay, thanks. But before my time with you runs out, can I show you something?"

"Certainly."

A.C. reached into an inside pocket and pulled out a small jeweler's box. Holding it carefully in front of him, he flipped open the lid.

***

Huguette's reaction when she saw the ring was immediate and somewhat unexpected. "Oh! I recognize that ring! It was made here for a young man we know, by one of our local jewelers! May I?" she asked, reaching towards the box.

"Of course." A.C. extracted the ring from its cushion and handed it to her.

"Look," she said, pointing to the underside of the ring, "you'll see a jeweler's mark, just there."

A.C. looked closely at the spot she was pointing out. "Yes, I see it," he said. "You said you know who it was made for, a young man?"

"Oh, yes. It was made for Stony."

"Stony MacLeod?"

"Yes." She looked at A.C. with a new comprehension. "That's why you're here!"

"I'm afraid so."

"Is there any news?"

"I'm sorry, no, he hasn't been located yet." *Not all of him, anyway.*

She handed the ring back to A.C., and it went back into the box and back into his pocket. Huguette ushered him out of the gallery, past the Hope Diamond and back into the circular balcony surrounding the rotunda, their footsteps echoing hollowly. They walked over to the ornate railing and leaned out, looking down at "Henry," the African elephant presiding over the large empty expanse. He appeared to be striding purposefully across his raised platform, away from them, as if late for a meeting.

"Stony was working as a consultant for the Smithsonian, is that right?" A.C. asked.

"Yes, but he was so much more to us than just another consultant. You see, he was adopted by one of our docent couples.

119

He and his sister, along with the other staff children, played here among the exhibits, had birthday parties here. Many of them, like Stony, worked in various parts of the building during summer vacations. But Stony was a standout; so enthusiastic, and with such a joyful, playful personality. Even when he was little, he wanted to be a geologist. He always had his backpack with him, with his play pick and shovel, and later, his rock collection; you know, the kind of collection kids have at that age, iron pyrite and quartz crystals, striped rocks. He even had a small geode. You never saw him without his backpack."

"That's when he developed his Indiana Jones persona?"

"That's right. We all played along, and later he enjoyed keeping it up. But he became a very serious geologist, all the same. After he graduated from the Colorado School of Mines—one of the premier geological schools in the country—he worked as a private field investigator for several years, but always had time for visits back here to the Smithsonian. I would ask him—jokingly—to bring me something special from the field, a ruby, or a sapphire, but he always said, 'only if it falls from the sky.' By that time, he had specialized in astrogeology."

"That's when he came back to work at the Smithsonian?"

"Yes, in the geological research division. He's also written several excellent articles for the Smithsonian magazine."

A.C. turned away from the railing and leaned back against it. Huguette did the same, as A.C. reached into his pocket and brought out the ring again. He removed it from the case and held it up to the light. "What can you tell me about this stone?"

"Well, I don't recall Stony ever said, but knowing his interests, I always assumed it is peridot. Rather large, but it's not unheard of for a peridot to be that size."

"Peridot can be meteoric, can't it?"

"Yes; it's composed of the mineral olivine, and is sometimes found in meteorites."

"Anything else it could be?"

"No, not really—well, there is another stone that looks very similar, almost the same color, but it's very unlikely that's what this is. It's called pallavine. Mineralogically very close to olivine, but with a different crystalline structure."

"Why is it unlikely?"

"There is only one source of pallavine, worldwide, a small company in Germany. They own what is known as the Jepara meteorite, named for the place it was found, in Indonesia, I think. It is not at all like Stony to buy a gem, or even the raw crystal—he is very proud of the fact that every item of jewelry he wears, or gives as a gift, for that matter, is from something he's found himself. Jepara pallavine is too rare and too valuable." She paused, looking over at him intently. "You're going to think this is very unscientific of me."

"I'm not known to be judgmental."

"Stony would never wear Jepara pallavine." A.C. waited patiently for the explanation he thought was forthcoming. "It's cursed. Like the Hope Diamond."

"Whoa. That I was not expecting." He put the ring away. "Should I be worried, carrying this thing around?"

"Oh, I don't know. I guess it is rather silly; I'm not sure Stony really believed it." Her phone trilled. "It's a text from General Dunway. He'll be here in five minutes; you can meet him down in the rotunda, and he'll take you to one of the offices in the staff wing on the first floor. I have a Zoom meeting coming up so must run, but please stop by my office on your way out. The General can direct you."

"I'll be sure to come by when we're finished."

She put her phone away and started to reach out to put her hand on A.C.'s shoulder, but stopped herself. She took a deep breath. "You're holding something back, aren't you, A.C.? The fact that you have his ring…well, it can't be good, surely."

"There's been nothing definite."

"But you have reason to believe—can you tell me how you happen to have it?"

"I'd rather not go into it in detail. As I said, nothing definite, but yes, we have reason to believe he became lost in the wilderness over the winter. 'Backcountry misadventure' is the current status with the sheriff's department. But Abber hasn't given up. She's still hoping to find him alive."

"Oh, I wasn't even aware she was out there."

"Yes, she's in Moonlight now, has been for a couple of weeks. We've all become very well acquainted with her in a short time. She's staying with a friend of ours, close to where Doc lives. I can't get used to calling her Abber, though; it's such an odd nickname. I usually call her Abigail."

"We *always* knew her as Abber, not Abigail." She looked puzzled. "I may be wrong, but I don't think—oh, my, it's getting so hard to remember things."

"Don't I know it!" said A.C., laughing. "Maggie—my wife—tells me I'd forget my own name if I didn't go by something as simple as A.C.!"

Huguette laughed along with him, then gave him a thoughtful look. "You know, I haven't seen Abber, or heard from her, for that matter, for quite some time. I should look her up after she returns home."

"Yes, I'm sure she would like that."

# The General

While waiting for General Dunway, A.C. looked at the electronic displays in the lobby—they were still up and running, even in the absence of patrons—showing the wide range of exhibits offered. As he stood there deeply regretting this was his first visit, he heard footsteps. He looked over toward the front entrance and saw a short, stocky man in uniform striding across the rotunda floor. He immediately saw a resemblance to the pose Henry the elephant displayed—someone who knew where he was going and was impatient to get there. He would come to learn General Dunway was one of those increasingly rare men in the military who damn well knew his job and what's more knew how to do it.

"Mr. LaFleur," the general called out as he approached, stopping about ten feet away. "I'm glad you made it. Sorry for the delay."

"No problem at all, General Dunway; I've just had quite an education."

"Ah, yes, Huguette certainly knows her stuff. You got the short version, unfortunately, since I was on my way here."

"She packed a lot of information into a short time."

"Pull down that mask so I can see what you look like," said Dunway brusquely, pulling his own mask down. "Can't judge a man without seeing more than the whites of his eyes!"

Once the general's mask was down, A.C. had an even

stronger feeling of confidence that he'd not made the trip in vain. Dunway seemed to simply radiate competence. Bright steel-blue eyes looked out from a square, pink-hued, no-nonsense face, seeming to take in A.C.'s entire being with one look. Heavy blond eyebrows accented a short military-style haircut, which showed only the slightest touch of gray at the temples. A.C. could not help but imagine the stub of an unlit cigar sticking out of the corner of the general's mouth—had there been a cigar, the general would have made a perfect World War Two-era Life magazine cover.

Pulling down his own mask, A.C. felt suddenly self-conscious, a rare feeling. But the next words from the general put him completely at ease.

"Mr. LaFleur, you look to be the kind of man who knows exactly what he's doing. I can't wait to get to know you. And my condolences, by the way—I understand you were a close friend of the victim."

"I appreciate that, thank you."

With that, Dunway pulled his mask back up and walked over to A.C., gesturing as he came in the direction they were to go. "I have a room prepared in the research wing. This way." A.C. adjusted his own mask as they walked down the hall.

"Thank you for meeting me on such short notice, General Dunway."

"Well, to begin with," said Dunway, looking over at A.C. with those steely eyes, "call me Caleb."

"Thanks, Caleb. I'm usually known as A.C. Again, I can't thank you enough for agreeing to see me, especially given the difficult circumstances."

"The reason I agreed to meet with you, as you know, is due entirely to Frank Ivanovich. We owe quite a lot to Frank. Of course, he can't tell you why; suffice it to say we are extremely indebted to him. That's what got your foot in the door. But when I realized who you were, well, I couldn't resist meeting you."

"General, uh, Caleb, really, I—"

"No, what you did is held in very high regard in the circles I travel in. I don't know how you pulled it off. That business stretched out over eighty years, and yet you exposed every well-hidden detail."

"It was touch and go. We got lucky at the end."

"From where I sit, I would say luck had very little to do with it. Toppling that bastard and the rest of the knaves associated with him—well, a lot of us knew there was something pretty goddam hinky about those defense department connections, but no one really knew how far back it went."

Once again, A.C. thought of the Professor, and how his death had led to the exposure of years of war profiteering by a family-held consortium that went all the way back to World War Two. In avenging the Professor's murder, A.C., Fuentes, and Jamila had brought down not only one of the largest defense contractors in the country, but had also destroyed the political careers of some of those involved, which had gone to the highest levels of government.

"Your contributions to the justice meted out to those responsible for the unnecessary and callous loss of so many military lives over the years rings loudly in the halls of the armed forces." He stopped suddenly and turned to A.C. "Sir, I salute you."

A.C. reddened, looked down at the floor, and stammered a muted thanks. It was all he could muster.

They continued down the hall. "Here's our office," said Dunway, opening an unmarked door for A.C. "I believe there are refreshments," he said, following A.C. in. "Ah, yes. Not as sumptuous as in times past, but adequate." A.C. looked over to see a table loaded with a variety of pre-packaged snacks, water—still and sparkling—and a coffee urn, red light glowing.

"Nice to see some things never change," said A.C.

The conference table was about ten feet long, with only two chairs, one at each end. "I had them set it up so we can remove our masks—this wing has an extremely good air filtration and circulation system, so we will be perfectly safe spaced apart like this." He placed his briefcase on the table. "Help yourself to snacks, water, whatever, then we'll get down to business."

As they arranged themselves at the table, each with their chosen selection of goodies, Dunway wasted no time. "Well, you saw the Hope Diamond." Not waiting for a response, he continued. "Fascinating, romantic, impressive, but also relevant to our current situation. We're sitting now in one of the research wings." He waved his hand around. "The wing responsible for gem and mineral research, to which I have been attached for over a decade. I'm going to do a sort of 'show and tell,' well, mostly tell, of what goes on here. A lot of, but not all, of what we do here is classified." He lowered his head and looked at A.C. under his impressive eyebrows. "No current security clearance, I assume?"

A.C. shook his head.

"No matter. What you are interested in learning is not classified. It relates to the government's efforts—by way of the Smithsonian—to own and display the most important gems in the world."

"How does that connect to my investigation?"

"Let's back up a skosh. State ownership of major gems— and I mean, Hope Diamond major—projects a certain level of political might and resolve; 'cultural standing' in the parlance of the diplomats. But as always, the competition is fierce. In the West— Great Britain, Europe, the U.S.—we've fallen behind."

"Behind whom, exactly?"

"China, of course, but also Saudi Arabia."

"Ah."

"What's more, the Moonlight meteorite strike has engendered an unprecedented amount of interest, particularly among the two parties I just mentioned. Local banks are being inundated with funds from clandestine sources, sources we've nonetheless identified as primarily Chinese and Saudi. Oh, the Swiss are there too, but then, when aren't the Swiss involved?"

"To what purpose?"

"They're setting themselves up to be able to buy up whatever comes along, on the spot. The non-amateur hunters will be ready to deal and won't care with whom. They'll be looking for the highest bidder; there won't be any preference given to an institution like ours, as was the case when we had Stony working with us. If things progress the way they have in other parts of the world, the competition is likely to get nasty, leading to an increase in violent crime."

"We've already seen some evidence of this."

"I don't doubt it. But it gets worse; there's much more at stake than what I've just outlined."

"As bad as the days of the gold rush in Virginia City?"

"Not comparable. It's much more complicated." He opened his briefcase and pulled out a folder. "Some background before I get to the juicy details. Planetary geology is becoming increasingly important as we look beyond Earth for resources. Something like fifty universities now offer degrees in planetary geology, astrogeology, exogeology, along with the standard astrophysical degrees. The first major conference related to extraterrestrial mining was held in Australia in 2013."

A.C. slowly opened a bag of sour cream and onion potato chips, a thoughtful look on his face. "You said a minute ago there is a lot at stake here, beyond the situation in Moonlight. What, exactly?"

"Nothing less than the future, and who controls it." Before A.C. could react to this, Dunway went on, while shuffling through the folder he'd put on the table. "An asteroid known as 16 Psyche was discovered by an Italian astronomer in 1852. It's big, even as asteroids go, about the size of West Virginia. Most asteroids are made up of ice and rock. Recent detailed investigations of Psyche from Earth-based instruments, using wavelengths from visible to infrared to radar, indicate it is likely to be almost pure nickel-iron. Now, putting a monetary value on that much metal is somewhat of an intellectual exercise, but based on current prices, it's worth something like one thousand trillion dollars. A ridiculously large sum, but one that plays well in the tabloids."

"But still, you're saying it's extremely valuable, no matter how it gets sensationalized."

"Exactly."

"How does that relate to what's happening in Moonlight?"

"Patience, A.C.; I'll get to that. Now, NASA hasn't been able to get back to the moon in the last fifty years, and the way they're going they probably won't get to Mars on their own either, but they're hell on wheels when it comes to unmanned solar system exploration, and they know where to go to get the job done. They've just contracted with SpaceX to launch a probe using their Falcon

Heavy vehicle. It's scheduled to launch in 2022, to arrive at Psyche early in 2026." Dunway found what he was looking for in the folder and passed it to A.C. "Here's an artist's conception of what it looks like." He slid the picture down the table.

"A small moon, craters and all."

"One of my jobs is to prepare to harvest the metals from Psyche in the future, and from whatever else of equal value that happens to pass by, or even hit Earth; as in, say, the Moonlight meteorite."

"There's enough material out there to make that kind of effort worthwhile?"

"Oh, yes. It's estimated over sixteen thousand kilograms hits the Earth every year, mostly small objects of fifty grams or less. That's one reason the Moonlight strike is significant; it could be well over the average amount of interstellar debris that impacts the entire Earth in a year."

A.C. stood and went to the table to retrieve a bottle of Perrier. "But it seems like there would be enough nickel and iron already on Earth without having to rely on meteorites." As he returned to his chair, Dunway slid another sheet of paper down to his end of the table.

"For now. But here's some information on some of the other things we're interested in. Do you know the acronym REE?"

"Another three-letter agency of the type Frank used to work for?"

Dunway chuckled. "No, it stands for Rare Earth Element. Heavy metals. Scandium, Yttrium, Neodymium; there are about seventeen altogether. They're extremely important elements used in electronics, electric car batteries, electric motors, cell phones, cruise missiles…"

A.C. picked up the paper and scanned it while Dunway continued. "Though relatively abundant on Earth, most of the supply now comes from China. But they are occasionally found in meteorites."

"Diamonds, gold, exotic gems, and now rare earth elements. I had no idea I'd be getting into something this complex as a result of a murder investigation."

"I haven't told you one of the most fascinating, and potentially most important part of my job."

A.C. looked up expectantly.

"New elements and mineralogical compounds never before seen on Earth. For example, there's something called Wassonite, named after planetary geologist John Wasson, found in a meteorite in Antarctica. It's a combination of titanium and sulfur with a unique crystalline structure. There are others. The potential uses for compounds like these are just beginning to be explored—everything from structural materials to vehicle components to $CO_2$ capture and storage. Who knows where it could lead?"

"Along with military applications, I assume?"

"Of course."

"Well, you've certainly given me a lot to think about; I have a totally new perspective on the importance of meteoric elements." Despite the mannerisms and appearance of a throwback to an earlier era, A.C. now realized Dunway was a man of the future. "That brings me back to the real reason I'm here," he continued. "The murder. Frank led me to believe there has been some official interest not only in locating the meteorite, but regarding the crime."

"That's right, A.C.; several agencies have been involved in monitoring the situation in Moonlight since early last fall, immediately following the strike. Since then, of course, we've been looking at both the murder of your friend and Stony's disappearance." He shuffled the papers on the table distractedly for a moment. "While we're on the subject of Stony, do you mind if I ask you for your professional opinion?"

"Of course not."

"Will he be found alive?"

"I'm sorry to say, based on what I know now; no, he will not be found alive. There's every reason to believe certain remains found on a Moonlight Basin ski slope last winter are his." He paused, then continued. "That has not been confirmed by local authorities, through no lack of trying. But Dr. Fuentes and I are convinced—for several reasons—that it is Stony MacLeod."

"Thank you for your candor. It's what I expected to hear. We're going to miss him around here. And not just on a personal level, but professionally as well. He was a very valuable asset to the Smithsonian."

It was A.C.'s turn to hesitate. "May I make a suggestion regarding that?" he asked.

"I'd be much obliged."

"I've recently become acquainted with a young woman in Montana whom I think may be a good candidate for a replacement. Oh, I don't mean to say…well, I'm sure you know what I mean." Dunway nodded. "Her name is Bingo Brennaman—an unusual nickname, but no more than 'Stony,' perhaps? In any case, she is graduating from MSU with a degree in geology, and is a remarkably energetic and capable young woman."

"She sounds very promising. Please send me her details and let her know I'll be in touch."

"I will."

"Thanks. Now—I'm sorry for the digression—regarding the murder of Jamila Sayvetz. In that case, we agree with the local sheriff's position, but only to the extent we believe it was brought on by the exhibition of the large fragment of meteorite that hit Doc's—Dr. Fuentes's—house. We disagree, however, that it was an unplanned, opportunistic robbery attempt gone bad. We think it was a professional operation, perpetrated by a party or parties still in the area."

"Frank had hinted the government is interested in Doc's meteorite. Is that true?"

"Yes. We've already authorized payment, should he agree to sell it. But it's not just us—the foreign governments I mentioned earlier, as well as freelancers, some unscrupulous, are also going after it, in addition to searching for the major strike location. By the way, we do have some concern some of the local amateurs are getting in over their heads."

"Anyone in particular I should be aware of?"

"There's one couple we're quite concerned about—the Farrells. Like Dr. Fuentes and his so-called 'house meteorite,' they are making quite a public show of things. They could be in danger. Do you know them?"

"I've been introduced. I'll talk to them."

"Good. There's also the operation at the Bozeman airport. We're keeping a close eye on it." He picked up his folder and replaced it in the briefcase. A.C. began to push the papers Dunway had given him back down the table, but Dunway waved him off. Please, keep those." He started to slide his chair back, but stopped abruptly. "There's one other thing. I've been procrastinating telling you this, I'm afraid. It concerns Frank Ivanovich; he's the reason I was late."

"What do you mean?"

"Frank has been arrested. He's been in the Virginia City jail for the past twenty-four hours. His one allowed phone call came in through one of our agencies."

A.C. stared in disbelief. "What's the charge?"

"Murder."

"My God, murder? Who?"

"Someone named Orvis Mooney. But don't worry, we got Frank released, though it wasn't easy; they seem to be very serious about it. We had to get the Attorney General of Montana involved. There was no arraignment set, no hard evidence brought forward, only an unsubstantiated report of an altercation."

"I knew about that. Who reported it?"

"An anonymous tip."

A.C. shook his head. "I can't believe Frank would resort to murder." *Would he? Had he learned something?*

"Oh, I'm certain Frank didn't have anything to do with it," said Dunway.

"How can you be certain?"

"They found the body."

# The Jeweler

Following General Dunway's directions, he made his way back to Huguette's office on the second floor. He took the elevator this time.

"A.C., how did the meeting with General Dunway go? I hope it was productive."

"More than that, Huguette, it was damned fascinating. He's a force of nature. After his presentation, together with your discussion earlier this morning, I have a completely new appreciation of rocks."

Huguette laughed and ushered him into her office, every inch of which was filled with books, papers, magazines, artifacts, models, and on one high shelf, a small bust of what A.C. assumed to be James Smithson.

"I'll keep you but a minute," she said, "to say goodbye, but also to give you this." She picked up a small piece of note paper with a name and address written on it and handed it to him. "While you were with the general, I made a call to the jeweler who made Stony's ring, Nathaniel Woodmont. He's agreed to meet with you. It's a short distance away, a mile or two, near Dupont Circle. Can I get a cab for you?"

A.C. took the note and tucked it into his pocket along with the ring. "No need; I'll grab an Uber. And let me say before I go, in spite of my poor attempt at humor a moment ago, I can't tell you how much I appreciate your assistance. You've been extremely helpful. And I've had a grand time, thanks to you, and the general, of course."

"I'm so glad we could help. Especially if it in any way allows you to find out what happened to Stony, and your friend."

"You will be among the first to know, should I discover anything."

***

The trip to the jeweler's took about ten minutes, including the wait for the ride; very little traffic these days, A.C. mused on the way. He stopped outside the storefront and looked in through the front window at an empty display. The ornate gilt lettering on the front door read "Presidential Gems" and below that, in slightly smaller letters, "Nathaniel Woodmont" with a logo identifying him as a Certified Gemologist Appraiser, American Gem Society. A.C. pulled up his mask and went in. As he opened the door, a small bell rang somewhere in the shop.

Nathaniel was standing behind a counter at the rear of the small shop. He was a youngish man with dark hair, slicked back in a retro-Thirties style, nattily dressed in a white shirt, dark pin-striped suit pants with a matching vest, wearing gold wire-rimmed glasses and a small goatee. Spread out in front of him was a soft gray cloth holding several pieces of small jewelry.

"You must be Mr. LaFleur," Nathaniel said, looking up. "Oh, yes, I'm sorry." He quickly reached under the counter and brought up a mask—light gray silk, from the look of it—and slipped it on. "Such a nuisance."

A.C. walked towards the counter. "I agree. But apparently necessary. And yes, I'm A.C. LaFleur. Huguette said you'd be expecting me. I appreciate your time, and apologize for the short notice."

"When she told me what you wanted to see me about, my first inclination was to decline." His speech, soft but intense, was as neatly clipped as his hair. "Perhaps I should have."

"There's still time."

133

"I know what's going on in Montana, of course. I have friends there. It all sounds very edgy, possibly even dangerous for anyone with the bad sense to get involved."

A.C. stepped back and raised his hands. "Listen, I understand why you might be leery about seeing me. I've had an eye-opening morning myself. There's a lot more to this than I thought. But it's important, and I believe you can be of real help."

Nathaniel fastidiously wiped at the corner of one eye with the end of his little finger, sighing theatrically. "Well, it is for Huguette. And for Stony, of course." He pursed his lips. "I'm going mad with boredom during this horrid shutdown. I've been allowed to stay open, thank the gods, but business, as you can imagine, has been dreadful. So, anything remotely interesting…" He walked out from behind the counter, head cocked to one side. "You have the ring?"

A.C. took it out of the box and handed it to him.

"One moment." Nathaniel walked back behind the counter and brought out a small goosenecked LED lamp. Taking a loupe from his vest pocket, he bent down to examine the ring. He gave another sigh, subdued this time, and straightened up.

Impatient with Nathaniel's posturing, A.C., a bit abruptly, asked, "And?"

The jeweler put on what A.C. took to be a contrite look. "I'm sorry I was somewhat short with you earlier. I was hoping…well, I don't know what I was hoping. This is the ring I made for Stony last fall." He handed it back to A.C. "Poor Huguette. She was so hopeful. Well, what am I saying? Poor Stony. Huguette told me the circumstances surrounding its discovery, of course. I just didn't want to believe it. And given the additional reasons for your investigation, which she also explained, I will be glad to assist in any way I can." While A.C. stored the ring away, Nathaniel beckoned for him to come around to the other side of the counter. "Let's go to my office where we can talk."

A.C. was not surprised to see that Nathaniel's office was neatly arranged. The walls were nearly all covered with rows of small cupboards and drawers; the few open areas were taken up by shelves, each containing several small, carefully arranged jewel boxes. Obviously, everything had its place and that place was precisely the right place. A large oak desk took up the center of the office, its top completely clear. Nathaniel indicated A.C. should take a seat in one of the cushioned chairs at the outer side of the desk. A.C. sat down slowly, still apprehensive, but glad to see the change in attitude, while Nathaniel settled into the antique office chair on his side of the desk.

"Knowing what the stone was," he said, gesturing at A.C.'s coat pocket, "I never should have made that ring. Or more correctly, I shouldn't have put my mark on it. It could be traced back to me."

"Why is that a problem? What is it about it that makes it dangerous? Cursed like the Hope Diamond?"

Nathaniel smiled thinly. "I wonder." He put his hands flat on the desk. "What do you know about the stone?"

"Assume I know nothing."

"Very well. The gem is pallavine, a meteoric mineral closely related to another meteoric crystal called olivine. Several billions of years old, falling to Earth from the asteroid belt that orbits out between Mars and Jupiter. The example in Stony's ring is an extremely large and beautiful example."

"I've heard a little about these crystals, from Jamila—the friend of mine who was murdered in Moonlight."

Nathaniel gave a small gasp. "Oh, yes. I am so sorry."

"Thank you. I'll be honest—as sorry as I am about Stony, my more immediate concern is finding Jamila's killer."

"I understand."

"Please go on. Wait, one question. You said pallavine and olivine are related. Why is pallavine so much more valuable? What's the difference?"

"Just what I was getting to. Olivine—named for its olive color—is extremely abundant in the Earth's crust. It's even used industrially; but for our purposes, it is the source of the gem peridot, sometimes called chrysolite. Olivine is also not uncommonly found in meteorites. Pallavine, however—named for the German scientist who first discovered it, Peter Pallas, in Russia, in 1879—is extremely rare. Only forty-six meteorites containing pallavine have been discovered. All of those but one shattered on impact. That means any large pallavine crystals contained in those other forty-five meteorites shattered into tiny fragments. Obviously, that makes it impossible to cut and bevel anything as beautiful as the example in your pocket." He held out his hand across the desk. "The ring, please. Let me show you how beautiful it is."

While A.C. retrieved the ring, Nathaniel opened a desk drawer and brought a small lighted magnifier. Taking the ring from A.C., he held it up between them and handed the magnifier to him.

"Pallavine, while very similar to its mate olivine, has a much more subtle coloration, an olive green, but with bright yellow highlights. That is part of what gives it its unique color. More important is the fact that pallavine is doubly refractive." A.C., who had been bending over intently studying the gem, looked up briefly. "That means the light splits into separate rays as it passes through the crystal, in effect creating a doubling of the facets. The crystalline structure is also highly complex, often containing many needle-like inclusions—material trapped inside of the crystal body—which also contribute to its iridescence."

A.C. straightened up and handed the magnifier back to Nathaniel. "Extraordinary. I hadn't really appreciated the depth before, the brilliance. Truly beautiful."

"Yes; but it is its rarity that makes it so valuable. I said earlier only one large meteorite didn't disintegrate when it hit the Earth; that meteorite was found in Indonesia, near a village called Jepara. Other pieces of the same meteorite have been found, but nothing containing pallavine crystal large enough to be cut and faceted. Jepara pallavine gems are the rarest in all of human history."

"I have been told something of pallavine, but once again, I didn't realize quite how special it is." He pointed at the ring. "Is that where Stony would have gotten it? In Jepara?"

"Possible, but unlikely. The Jepara meteorite is solely owned by a small German company, and as far as I know, nothing more of any significance has ever been found there. I suppose the company could be contacted for information, but they are very close-mouthed about their dealings."

"Any ideas on who could have been a middleman?"

"There would have been no middleman. Too dangerous."

"For the middleman?"

"Yes, but also for the buyer. Something this rare, especially given the recent interest, would cause too much talk."

"Could he have found another source?"

"Again, possible, though very unlikely." He paused, reconsidering. "Although I suppose, since the likelihood of obtaining it from the Jepara meteorite is also extremely small, that may be the only reasonable assumption."

By the look on Nathaniel's face, A.C. could tell this did not sit well. "Suppose he did have some raw crystal. What would have been involved in turning a chunk of it into a gem like the one in the ring?"

"Olivine and pallavine are relatively soft minerals, on the Mohs scale, between six and seven. As a comparison, diamond is a ten, ruby and sapphire nine. So, it is easier to work with than something like diamond, but still would require some time. There are several cutters I know of in New York City who could do it." Nathaniel picked up the ring and turned it around in his hand admiringly. "Speaking of that," he said, "this ring is not unique."

"No?"

"I made a second one, at the same time, last fall, the second being slightly smaller than Stony's. Also, regrettably, with my mark." He tilted his head and raised his eyebrows. "Mr. LaFleur, do you also have the second ring?"

There was a long pause as A.C. thought back to the circumstances Doc had described regarding his first meeting with Abigail. It had been the similarity of the ring he'd found on the side of Lone Peak with Abigail's ring that had led him to conclude the bones were those of her missing brother. "Can I get back to you?" he finally equivocated.

Nathaniel appeared to quickly grasp that any knowledge of the second ring was not immediately forthcoming. "Of course."

A.C. seemed relieved to have dodged the bullet on this one. He went back to a previous thread. "Mr. Woodmont, are you worried about this because of the rarity of the stone, or because of a supposed curse?"

"Stony wouldn't tell me where he obtained the pallavine, as

we've discussed. He must have known the risks of bringing the stone to me, but we have had a close business relationship for many years. Therefore, he knew he could trust me implicitly. And the chance to work with pallavine was irresistible, regardless of the danger. As for a curse? Well, who knows?"

A.C. reached up and adjusted his mask—it had crept up under the bottom edge of his glasses. "Excuse me. Like you said, a damned nuisance. Anyway, we were talking about where Stony might have acquired the pallavine. Would it be possible to tell Jepara pallavine apart from pallavine from a different meteorite?"

Nathaniel carefully passed the ring back to A.C. "Almost certainly. Someone with the right tools and the requisite knowledge would be able to perform a comparative analysis."

"I'm glad I didn't know all this earlier," A.C. said as he took back the ring. "I've been carrying this thing around like it was just another clue."

"You're beginning to understand the issues."

"Let me run this past you. Say, Stony made a find on his own, something comparable to the Jepara rock. You're saying he wouldn't try to sell it right off, especially not using a middleman; too dangerous. And depending where he found it, there could be serious ownership disputes. So, it would have to be done very discreetly on his part, face to face with an equally discrete and extremely knowledgeable buyer. On the QT, as we used to say."

Nathaniel smiled at this. "That's right. Well, Mr. LaFleur, I believe I've told you just about everything I can about pallavine, and about the ring—well, the two rings, to be more precise. But I have a question for you."

"Go ahead."

"For my own peace of mind—besides Huguette, how many people have seen my jeweler's mark on this ring?"

"Well, the person who found it, obviously. Other than that, I can't guess."

Nathaniel looked thoughtful for a moment, then asked, "How is it that it is not being held by the authorities?"

A.C. had expected the question earlier. "No interest. As far as the Sheriff is concerned, Stony's disappearance is very simply explained: what is known out West as a backcountry misadventure. Wolf or grizzly attack, a fall, some type of accident or other mishap. It's a severe environment; there are many ways to die out there. We were advised to retain possession of the ring, unless a claim was made against it at some point."

"Well, that puts my mind at rest."

A.C. slid his chair back from the desk. "Mr. Woodmont, thank you for your time and expertise. You've been very helpful."

"I'm glad I was of service." He took a business card from a drawer and handed it to A.C. "Please contact me if you need anything else. I wish you the best of luck with your investigation."

As they approached the front door, Nathaniel stopped and turned to A.C. "Do you recall I told you I have friends in Montana?"

"Yes, you mentioned it."

"I have a recommendation for you. Do you go through Billings on your way home?"

"No, but I could probably arrange it. Why?"

"Make a stopover in Billings, and from there drive down to a small town called Red Lodge; it's about an hour's drive. Get a room at the Pollard Hotel there, it's right on Main Street. Once you're settled, have someone direct you to Bearcreek; it's a small town right outside of Red Lodge, six or seven miles. Plan to get there in the early evening, around dinner time, go to the Bear Creek Saloon and Steakhouse, on Main Street, and ask for a man by the name of Card Daniels."

"Carl Daniels?"

"No, Card, c-a-r-d."

"And why am I going there?"

"I think Card can give you some insight into what's going on out there right now. But other than that, you're in for a good time."

"How do you mean?"

"Oh, let that be a surprise."

***

As A.C. stood on the sidewalk waiting for his Uber ride, he'd all but decided to ignore Nathaniel's mysterious recommendation to visit Bearcreek and go straight home. But the longer he stood there, the more he began to feel a diversion might be just the thing to relieve some of the anxiety that had been building up ever since he'd arrived in Washington.

Montana was supposed to have been an escape from the stress of dealing with the pandemic in New York. Even in a small city like Oswego, the pressures of day-to-day living had started to wear him and Maggie down. Doc's invitation had come at the perfect time. He'd certainly not planned to jump into another extensive and probably fruitless investigation; but the circumstances demanded it. By the time the Uber car pulled up at the curb he'd changed his mind. Whatever awaited him in Bearcreek, he was ready for it.

A.C. felt quite a large twinge of guilt when he called Maggie and told her the revised plans. As a nurse, she'd been apprehensive enough about the trip to begin with; now A.C. was going to be off roaming around Montana increasing his exposure. He assured her he'd take all necessary precautions. Given the reduction in air travel, rebooking the flight had been no problem. At the same time, he arranged for a rental car in Billings, which was a bit more problematical, given the confused directives and constant alterations in interstate travel rules. In the end he'd been able to convince the agent to approve the reservation. He arranged to drop the car off in Bozeman, where Maggie would pick him up.

As the plane taxied out for takeoff, A.C. reviewed some of what he'd learned: meteorites attract as many crooks as poorly guarded banks; in the underground gem and meteorite trade, single, clandestine transactions are the norm, typically no middleman; and pallavine was a hell of a lot more exotic, and more valuable, than he'd thought.

The plane was not surprisingly first in line for takeoff. The thrust as they barreled down the runway pressed A.C. into his seat; simple physics, but somehow comforting after the whirlpool of facts, theories, and the scenarios of potential global conflict he'd just been swept up in. At least some things were constant and predictable.

Where did the ring fit into this? Why would Stony want such a thing? The simple knowledge he was wearing a crystal of such rarity and geological significance that put any diamond, ruby, or sapphire to shame? That would be hubris, vanity; from the way Huguette talked about him, that didn't fit. It was not the type of gem worn for show; Nathaniel had said as much. Or was it something more subtle: the deep appreciation for something possibly forged during the creation of the solar system, something understood for its own sake, not for display, but a way to connect to the whole of creation.

Possibly. But as romantic as Stony was, A.C. reminded himself, he was still a treasure hunter, a dealer. Had Stony found another chunk of the Jepara meteorite? Nathaniel didn't think so, but did say it was faintly possible. A.C. remembered Abigail saying Stony had been in the Sahara right before he'd come to Moonlight, and that his search there had been a bust. Was that true? Or had he found something, something he knew he could sell in Moonlight much more quickly than in Africa? Apparently, anyone worth their salt as a meteorite hunter had descended immediately on Moonlight, along with everyone else. A perfect market.

A chime sounded. "Ladies and gentlemen, the use of approved portable electronics is now permitted."

Only momentarily distracted, A.C. went back to his theorizing. There was no doubt the arm Doc had found on the ski slope was Stony's, based on what he'd just confirmed with Nathaniel. But had Doc jumped to the wrong conclusion, just as Jamila had said? A pallavine ring didn't necessarily prove Stony had been murdered, even if there were circumstantial reasons to think so.

Okay. Back to how Stony had such a ring. Assume he'd found a new source of pallavine. If it had been the Sahara, he would have had to get it out undetected, passing through various African and/or Asian and/or European countries, all with customs requirements with lesser or greater degrees of associated risk. And then he would have had to get it to the "cutters," as Nathaniel called them, in New York, then to Nathaniel to have the rings made—wait—had Nathaniel ever said precisely when he'd made the rings?

*Did I even ask him?*

"May I offer you something to drink, sir?"

A.C. jerked his head up, momentarily disoriented. "Drink?"

"Yes, sir. We have water, beer, and wine."

"Any scotch?"

"No, sir, I'm sorry; nothing else at this time."

*Oh, yeah, pandemic rules again.* "Okay, skip it, I guess."

She moved on down the aisle.

*Where was I? Last fall.* He remembered Nathaniel mentioning he'd made the ring in the fall. While Stony was on the way to Moonlight? No, Abigail said he'd gone directly to Moonlight after she'd telexed him. The ring would have to have been made *after* he'd been to Moonlight. The timeline was tight, but doable. *Note to self: check date with Nathaniel.*

Okay, making progress here. That leaves open the likelihood of Stony finding the pallavine in Moonlight, barely after arriving there. He was, according to everything he'd learned, tops in his field. Both an extraordinary geologist and treasure hunter. Indiana Jones in real life. He'd gone there looking for the usual—collectable meteorites, certainly, maybe even gold and diamonds, but that was always a longshot, at least in significant quantities. A more distant possibility was meteoric olivine; more desirable than the terrestrial version, but still not particularly valuable.

That leaves pallavine. Stony was one of the few geologists on Earth who would instantly recognize it. Could he have found a pallavine meteorite? That quickly? Fortune favors the brave—that was the common formulation, but A.C. had his own version—luck is that condition in which opportunity meets preparedness. Stony could have used that phrase as a resumé.

*The ring.* Proof of a new source of pallavine. Hidden in plain sight. Safe to carry around.

Until someone tried to take it off his finger so hard it twisted bone.

# Pig Racing

"Take I-90 west to Laurel, then get off on 212," the car rental agent explained. "Red Lodge is about forty minutes from there."

He turned down the offer of a Chevy Suburban (a hundred-and-eighty-dollar upgrade), thanked the agent and walked ten minutes to the rental car lot to get his Toyota.

The drive was as easy as the agent had said. In less than an hour he was parked on Main Street in the first open space he found, in front of the Montana Candy Emporium, which looked to be in an old movie theater—HUCKLEBERRY CARAMELS was on the marquee.

The Pollard Hotel was hard to miss, three stories high and taking up the whole corner and half the block on the other side of the street, behind him. The expanse of dark red brick, green awnings under brick arches, and a large green POLLARD sign featuring the silhouette of a moose made it even more obvious.

The lobby was paneled in dark pine and dominated by an ornate wooden staircase, furnished with dark leather-upholstered chairs, antique mission-style tables, and a saddle. After he'd registered, the desk clerk was called away momentarily. While waiting for his room key, A.C. skimmed through a historical brochure. The hotel was the first brick building in Red Lodge, built in 1893. It had hosted several famous occupants: Buffalo Bill, Calamity Jane, and a character with a most unusual name, even for

Montana's wild west: Liver Eatin' Johnson. After some thought, A.C. recalled his more well-known given name, Jeremiah.

The clerk returned with the key. "Room seventeen," she said. "You'll be sharing with one of our resident ghosts. No extra charge." The room was tastefully decorated, comfortable, and reasonably priced. He didn't notice the ghost as he unpacked his toiletries and freshened up; perhaps they didn't appear until after midnight. But, so far, so good.

The ten-minute drive to the Bear Creek Saloon and Steakhouse (located in the town of Bearcreek, all one word—he wasn't sure why they were spelled differently) wound through yellow scrub and not much else; there was an occasional ranch building or small house, a scattering of old ramshackle mine buildings. Once in Bearcreek, he drove past the saloon, which was at the far west end of town, and through Bearcreek itself, to see what else was there. As it turned out, not even as much as he'd seen on the way in. A couple of dilapidated buildings, a stand-alone post office, a tiny pink bungalow, and he was out of town. He turned around and went back, parking in the dirt lot on the side of the saloon.

Getting out of the car, he began to worry if Nathaniel had given him a bum steer; the Bear Creek Saloon looked as rundown as most of the rest of Bearcreek, what there was of it. It was a large oblong building made of rough planking, with a corrugated red tin porch roof hanging from the front wall. The front door was a dark opening at one end of the wall.

Once inside, A.C. looked around with obvious relief at the clean and bright interior; old-fashioned white walls, tin-stamped ceiling, and large wooden tables. What really caught his eye, however, was the bar, a beautiful long expanse of dark wood, with a curved section at one end, and huge polished columns setting off the large wood-framed mirrors on the back wall.

As he walked to the bar, he noticed no one was wearing a mask, so he left his in his back pocket. *Guess I shouldn't mention this to Maggie.* A tall woman with a long blond ponytail came over as he sat down.

"Hi, I'm Sil. Welcome to the Bear Creek Saloon."

"Thanks. I'm A.C."

"Glad to meet you. Did you come in over Beartooth Pass?"

"No, I came down from Billings."

"Okay. Beartooth is the other way, towards Yellowstone. Where you headed after you leave here?"

"Big Sky."

"Well, you should definitely take the Beartooth Highway. Great drive. Now, what can I get you?"

"I see a bottle of Famous Grouse back there."

She turned and reached back for it. "Neat?"

"No, if you don't mind, I'll instruct you on how to make what's called a floater."

"Sure thing, cowboy," she laughed.

"Small glass, filled with ice, and spring water to up near the rim; then float a layer of Grouse on top."

"I can handle that." She moved to the other end of the bar and filled a glass with ice.

While she was making his floater, two sloppily dressed, scruffily bearded characters sidled up next to A.C., one on each side. One of them leaned in close.

"Better watch out for that one," he said in a low voice. "Seen her lick the spit off a feller's tonsils last New Year's Eve." The second man elbowed A.C. in the ribs and laughed, as A.C. leaned forward as far as possible to distance himself from the two of them. He began to revise his opinion of the Bear Creek downwards as they walked away, laughing.

Sil brought over his floater. "A refined, sensible drink. Don't get much call for that around here."

A.C. pointed to his two new friends. "Those two over there; what's their story?"

"Don't know them. They've been here since before lunch, were drunk soon after, and have been at it steady ever since. I saw them come over here a minute ago; they give you any trouble?"

"No. I own a bar in New York, so I've seen it all before. Just surprised to see that sort of east coast rubbish out here in God's own country."

Sil laughed at that. "Let me know if they bother you." She

started to move away.

"Before you go, can you tell me where I can find Card Daniels?"

"You know Card?"

"No, I was just told he would be here and that I should look him up."

Sil pointed across the bar to an open door leading to a raised deck. "That's him over there."

A.C. leaned back to see someone sitting at a table by himself at one end of the deck. He fit right in with the general atmosphere of Bearcreek—beat up cowboy hat, worn out jeans, untucked plaid shirt, and the sorriest-looking pair of boots he'd ever seen. "Not what I expected."

"Oh, don't worry," said Sil, seeing A.C.'s apprehensive look. "I know he looks a little rough around the edges, but give him a chance."

"An acquired taste?"

"Something like that."

"Thanks." He picked up his floater and made his way out to the deck, which was crowded with people lined up against an outside railing overlooking an oval dirt track. At the center of the oval was an infield covered with river rock, surrounded by a wire fence. At one end stood a bronze statue of a pig. A roofed chain-link cage sat on the track near the statue. The outside edge of the track was bordered by colorful advertising billboards. At one end was a pen full of pigs.

"Excuse me, are you Card Daniels?"

The man looked up. His face was as brown and beaten as his boots, but his eyes were bright blue and twinkling. "Today I am."

Not quite sure how to react to that, A.C. hesitated before introducing himself. Card didn't seem to mind waiting. "My name is A.C. LaFleur," A.C. finally said. "Nathaniel Woodmont in Washington D.C. referred me to you."

"How is old Nate?"

"Fine, I guess. I don't know him well; I was there on business."

"You don't strike me as a jeweler type."

"No, I'm a detective. Retired now, but working on a murder case. I was hoping I could ask you a few questions."

"Well, now, I don't believe I've murdered anyone for quite some time now."

"No, I'm sorry. You see—"

Card let out a laugh and slapped the table. "Sit down, partner. What's that you're drinking?"

"It's called a floater; Famous Grouse floating on spring water."

"Sounds like it's worth a try." He waved Sil over. "Sil, I'll have one of this gentleman's floaters, and keep them coming."

"Only one more for me, if you please. And the tab's on me."

"That's what I like to hear!" said Card. "But you'll need to drop a C-note on top of that."

A.C. looked up at Sil with a puzzled look. "He'll explain," she said as she went back to the bar.

"Okay, what is the hundred for?"

"Why, to bet on a pig, of course!"

A.C. looked out over the railing at the dirt track, comprehension slowly dawning. "You said—bet on a pig?"

"This is a pig racing track, you know."

A.C. shook his head in wonderment. "No, I didn't know that. Nate failed to mention it." He looked over at Card, bewildered. "This is legal?"

Card laughed. "Oh, the betting part was challenged once— thanks, Sil," he said as she brought over the drinks, "so we got a law passed allowing what's called a sports betting pool. Pigs, gerbils, or hamsters only, and it has to take place outside. Sanitary reasons, I guess. And, this is the real kicker, it applies only to incorporated towns with a population of one hundred or less."

"Which qualifies Bearcreek."

"Exactamundo. We're the only pig racing town in Montana!"

"This is why I love Montana!" A.C. said, shaking his head again, this time in admiration. "So, the price of you answering my questions is a hundred dollar bet on a pig?"

"Right again. Well," Card said, waving his hand

expansively, "feel free to bet more if you like."

A.C. looked out at the track and saw a group of pigs being herded out of their holding area towards what he'd first thought was some sort of cage, but which turned out to be the starting gate. A.C. smiled over at Card. "They're lining up. Any hot tips?"

"Number six, Bacon Bits. One of my pigs."

As the six pigs in the current race were being lined up, the noise level of the crowd increased as people jostled for a place along the rail and the entrants were announced over a loudspeaker. Card pointed A.C. in the direction of the betting window. Just as he got back to the table, the familiar "call to post" bugle call sounded, and they were off.

In less than a minute, the pigs were at the finish line, to great acclaim. Bacon Bits came in last.

A.C. looked at Card. "Well, I've been to a rodeo and two state fairs, and I've never seen anything quite like that."

"Don't it just beat all?"

"But I have to say, Card," A.C. said, frowning, "I'm pretty disappointed in Bacon Bits."

"Oh, I knew she'd prob'ly lose," Card answered, smiling broadly. "She's the youngest one out there. Scared of the bigger pigs, so she always waits until they start running 'n get out of her way."

"But—"

"Anyway, the winner only gets fifty percent of the pot—the rest goes to Carbon County high school scholarships."

"Okay, fair enough." He sipped at his floater. "This means we get to talk now?"

"Sure. But the next race is about to start. Want to give it another shot? Another one of my pigs in running—Hog Handles."

"Why don't I just donate the hundred?"

"Suit yourself. But Hog Handles, I got to tell you—"

"Enough. Here's the hundred. That about wipes me out; I hadn't planned on a gambling trip when I came out here."

"I like your style, LaFleur. And I've been pondering..." He raised his drink. "I like these, what d'you call 'em, floaters. And I recognize your name, now. You were mixed up in that Pony deal a year or two back."

"That's right."

"Don't worry, I won't try to pump you about it. Or ask for any more juice. What do you want to know?"

"Before we get into that, can you satisfy my curiosity? How did you end up here, in the middle of nowhere?"

"The short version?" A.C. nodded, gratefully. "Army brat, no real home. Started out in college majoring in finance—I know, hard to picture. But drifting around the country a lot, seeing all kinds of different places, different landscapes, climates, I got interested in geology. Finance was a damned straightjacket, anyway. So, I switched to geology. Graduated and went into the treasure hunting business, in the U.S. and Canada to start with, then all over the world. How I ended up here—no, that story's way too long—anyway, now I buy and sell mineral futures; appropriate, given the history of mining in this part of the country."

Sil dropped off two more floaters. A.C. tried to correct her, but was having a hard time making himself heard above the noise of the race going on. Sil signaled they were both for Card; A.C. smiled and gave her a thumbs up. As soon as the noise died down—Hog Handles had come in second—he returned to Card's story. "When you were exploring—treasure hunting—what sort of things were you looking for? Oil, gas? That seems to be the usual course for geologists."

"Nope, never got into the fossil fuels, so-called. I was more into gemstones, at first, then took a stab at planetary geology, and started investing in asteroid mining futures. But here on the ground? Hunting for meteorites."

*Ah, this is the reason Nathaniel sent me here.* He paused, reflecting for a moment on what Caleb Dunway had told him. "That's a viable business, asteroid mining?"

"Will be, someday."

"What's legal out there, in space?"

"Everything. Until it's not. The treaty situation is a bloody mess, to say the least. Take future asteroid mining, for example. Supposed to follow the Law of the Seas—finders' keepers, just like in non-territorial waters. Well, not too hard to say outer space is non-territorial. At least for now. There's a 1967 U.N. space treaty—I love to quote the full title—'Treaty on Principles Governing the Activities of States in the Exploration and Use of Outer Space, including the Moon and Other Celestial Bodies'—but not every country signed up. Not that it means all that much. It's usually considered a sort of non-armament treaty."

"Does it apply to stuff coming down to Earth from outer space?"

Card tilted his head in thought. "It's not clear," he finally said. He looked at A.C. "If it's that Moonlight murder you're investigating, you may be facing some uncertainty when it comes to the ownership of the meteorite."

A.C. tried not to show his surprise. "You know about it."

"Word gets out, among serious meteorite hunters."

"What kind of uncertainty?"

"The old railroad laws. Clear as cow flop, or the space treaty."

"Which you're suggesting could lead—is leading to—the violence cropping up in Moonlight. Will it get as bad as Virginia City in the gold rush days?"

"Hopefully not. All these mad rushes—gold, mineral, meteorites, whatever—they play themselves out. With meteorites, once the primary body is found, interest drops off just like that, like throwing a light switch. It's basic economics. Eventually, changes in supply and demand, legal and other external forces—bad guys, for example—upset the balance."

The circus atmosphere of the races still going on below them had not distracted Card from their conversation, but had, apparently, increased his interest in floaters. He raised his glass, gazing at it in seeming contemplation, then completed his thought. "Seems Moonlight's at a pretty high pitch at the moment."

"What about Moonlight diamonds? Important?"

"Diamonds are easy: I'm short on 'em. They're important only to the extent terrestrial diamonds have become passé."

"I've heard this story before."

"Then you know it's true. COVID has only made it worse. It's only things like the billion-year-old Moonlight diamonds that are desirable. It's not going to be enough to bring back the industry, but still, that's what's driving outfits like De Beers. They know they're missing out in the traditional market and are looking for alternatives."

"How can Moonlight diamonds compete with their own Kimberly pipe diamonds?"

"One, no social or cultural baggage. Two, low exploration cost and a growing market niche." Another sip of floater took it to the bottom, requiring a wave to Sil. "You're familiar with what's going on at the Bozeman hangar?"

A.C. answered carefully, hoping to learn more than he knew. "Not intimately familiar, but yes, I know of it."

"Well said. What I know," he said, leaning over to cut through the clamor of pig racing surrounding them, "is that the Moonlight diamonds are being trafficked there, cash on the spot, then flown to New York to the famous Diamond District. Daily. Pretty cool operation, if you're into that kind of thing." He pulled the second floater over to him, stirred it with his finger, and took a sip. "Could get used to these."

"What about Moonlight gold?"

Card's usually affable smile twisted into a conspiratorial grin. "Gold. I'm long in it. In the current market I call it unaffordium and unobtainium. The virus has been as disruptive in gold as in diamonds, but with a different twist. Dealers are sold out, closed, or both. Credit Suisse, which has minted its own bars since 1856, has told clients don't even ask. London's bankers are chartering private jets or begging for space in military cargo planes to get bullion to New York. Wall Street is asking the Royal Canadian mint for help."

A.C. had heard enough to confirm what he'd already known to some extent, and decided it was time to get back to the murder. "You said earlier you'd heard about the meteorite that hit the house in Moonlight. Did you also hear the sheriff has written it off as an opportunistic break-in and an unplanned subsequent murder?"

"He's almost right. It probably was about the meteorite. Not unplanned, though. I think someone had cased the joint and got the timing wrong, thinking no one was home. I've heard the sheriff thinks whoever the killer was is long gone. I doubt it. But the meteorite, cracked open like a hard-boiled egg and nothing of real value found—well, I don't think they'll be back."

"You said you were a meteorite hunter," said A.C., deftly switching gears. "Did you know Stony MacLeod?"

"Previously, only by reputation. But I got to meet him when he stopped by here on his way to D.C. last fall; he said he was on his way to visit Nate. That was before Stony went missing, of course." Card looked long and hard at A.C. before asking, "You think he's dead, don't you?"

"Yes." The last pig race of the day had just finished, to the accompaniment of much Montana-style hooting and hollering. A.C. leaned in. "His sister Abigail is still searching for him…but…well, he's been missing for a long time. I think at this point she'll be happy just to find his remains." He considered telling Card about the arm in the snow but decided it would only confuse things. He already considered himself lucky Card hadn't pressed him on why he had been visiting Nathaniel. That could have led to the ring, and even more questions. "Did Stony say anything about what he was doing here?"

"Not much. Strong and silent, like me." They both had to laugh at this. "One thing was kinda odd," Card continued. "He wanted to talk to me about Japanese property law."

"What does that have to do with anything?"

"In Japan, maybe other places too, I don't know, if someone buys a stolen good unknowingly—unknowingly in quotes here—if after three years there has been no legal action related to the item, then the buyer is free and clear—they own it. I think Stony was thinking about peddling something to a Japanese citizen. To avoid repercussions down the line."

"How did he appear to you when he was here? Did he give you any indication he was having any trouble?"

"Nope, nothing I saw. Given what I know of him, he wouldn't let on if there was. He was a pro, knew the rules: avoid partnerships, fences, and romance." He took the last swig of the last floater. "Keep away from romance, that should have been number one."

A.C. finished his drink. "Races over?"

"Yeah, that's it for tonight. Guess I'm going to have to work with ol' Bacon Bits, get her mind right."

"Let me know when she's ready. In the meantime, thanks for the time and the information. And the entertainment. I think I got my two hundred dollars' worth." He scraped his chair back but didn't get up. "Any more wisdom to impart before I go?"

Card leaned forward in his chair and put his hands flat on the table. "Give it up. Hate to see a nice fella like you come to a bad end. Same advice I gave to the Farrells. Stay out of it, it's getting too dangerous."

"The Farrells? Paul and Paula?"

"That's them. A mutual friend sent them to me for advice, just like you. They bet a C-note apiece on Bacon Bits—twice." Card chuckled. "Paula was sure the pig would run better the second time, after a warm up race, and figured the odds would be better."

"How did it turn out?"

"Like betting on instant replay."

"What kind of advice were they after?"

"Where to sell their stuff. Told them I'm no fence, it's too dicey. What I *did* tell them is for someone in their position, as amateurs? Unload it as quickly as possible and don't worry too much about the price. I don't know, that hangar operation might be what they need, but then again…" He let the implication that Paul and Paula might be in over their heads hang in the air.

A.C. stood up just as Sil came over. "Any more floaters, guys?"

"Not for me—two's my limit. I need to get back to the hotel and get some rest if I want to get an early start in the morning." He reached for his wallet. "What's the damage?"

"On the house," she said, nodding over at Card.

"Professional courtesy," Card said, as he stood up.

"Card, I can't thank you enough. It's been a perfect afternoon."

"I'll walk you to your car."

As they came around the edge of the building into the parking lot, they saw the two barflies that had buddied up to A.C. staggering to their car, laughing hysterically, bragging to one another about all the clever things they had done that day. Card and A.C. watched as they got into the car, then got out and switched places, fumbling for the keys, which the first one had dropped on the ground, finally getting the car started. Back tires spinning in the dirt, they backed out of their parking spot in a cloud of dust and headed for the road.

Before they even got out of the parking lot, A.C. and Card were startled by the sound of a siren, very close by. A sheriff's car pulled up out of nowhere, angling in front of the car, blocking its exit. By this time, several other patrons, along with Sil, had come out to watch, cheering like a pig race was going on, as the sheriff's deputies got both drunks out of the car and bent over the hood.

Card walked with A.C. to his car, on the other side of the lot. A.C. got in, closed the door, then opened the window. Card was still standing there, and he leaned over and put his hand on the doorsill. "You know, partner, I'm afraid this might be the only justice you're going to see here in Montana. I've seen too many meteorite hunters walk free—theft, assault, even a murder. Okay, alleged murder, but everybody knew the score. Keep in mind it's a closed system, and outsiders beware."

"Sobering words." A.C. put a hand on the sill next to Card's. "One last thing."

"Sure, partner."

"Did Stony ever say anything about pallavine?"

Card leaned down closer. "Steer clear, my friend. Anyone who knows anything will tell you—it's cursed."

# PART 3: NO SYMPATHY

"Pleased to meet you, Hope you guess my name…"
— Mick Jagger, Keith Richards

# Vanishing Acts

Not far south and west of Red Lodge, the Beartooth Highway snakes its way up above Rock Creek via a series of three hairpin curves, then meanders up and down and to the east a bit before the road levels out and angles back southwest. A.C. thoroughly enjoyed the drive, mentally thanking Sil for the advice. This scenic route would only take a couple of hours longer than going back up to I-90 and then west to Bozeman. Interstates were the same everywhere, in A.C.'s opinion, and he never passed up an opportunity to strike out on the road less traveled.

Before he left the Pollard Hotel, he skimmed a brochure on the Beartooth Highway he'd found at the front desk—approximately sixty-six miles, closed due to heavy snow from early November to Memorial Day, variously called the "All-American Road," the "National Scenic Byway," the "Beartooth Scenic Byway," (this by the National Park Service), and "the most beautiful highway in the world," (source unknown). It is one of the highest elevation roads in the continental United States, which makes sense, given that the Beartooth mountain range is one of the highest overall, with twenty peaks over 12,000 feet. What really caught A.C.'s attention was the mention that, geologically, the Beartooth range contains some of the oldest and rarest minerals on Earth, over three billion years old. Maybe not quite as old as the Moonlight meteorite, but respectable.

What he hadn't realized was that the torturous hair-pinned section of roadway he'd just driven was not Beartooth Pass. He finally hit the actual pass not far past the Beartooth Basin Summer (!) Ski Area. After navigating four more one-eighty degree turns, he spotted the Beartooth Pass Vista Point sign just in time to pull off onto the short dirt access road.

He was glad to get to the viewpoint, which opened out onto a postcard-worthy view of more forested areas. He was initially surprised at how desolate the landscape he'd been driving through had been—not a tree or shrub in sight for miles, just barren hills with a scattering of various-sized boulders and an occasional jumbled outcropping of larger sharp-edged rocks. Then he remembered he was well above timberline. *Sil didn't warn me I'd need oxygen, for crying out loud.*

Ominously tall marker poles—at least fifteen feet, he estimated—bordered the outer edge of the road. He was used to heavy snow—lake-effect snows along the shores of Lake Ontario are legendary—but still. Large patches of snow filled sheltered nooks and gullies like miniature glaciers.

He shivered a bit as he stood next to the car taking in the view but didn't feel like digging into the trunk for his jacket. *Cold up here, even in June.* He looked back behind him, noting the contrast between the lush forests he saw in the distance—the environment he'd become accustomed to in Moonlight—and the isolation of the landscape surrounding him. He gained a new awareness of the harshness of Montana, the unforgiveness of winter, the fragility of life at the extremes. *No one could last out here all winter, no matter what kind of survival skills they might have. Not even Stony.*

As he got back into the car, he had a sudden thought. The skeletal remains Doc had found still had not been officially identified, but the evidence of the ring (withheld from the authorities) made that unnecessary. Based on what he'd learned from Nathaniel Woodmont, Stony must have found the primary segment of the pallavine meteorite before winter set in—the ring practically proved that. Even given what little he knew about Stony, he thought he knew him well enough to understand his mindset. To someone like Stony, every situation of apparent disadvantage has within it an inherent advantage. The trick is in knowing how to use it.

With the onset of an early, harsh winter, Stony had been confident his find was safe for the foreseeable future. Subzero temperatures, an average snowfall of over four hundred inches, blistering winds—no one would be looking for anything in Moonlight until the next spring. In the meantime, the ring was the perfect sales sample, easy to carry, easy to hide when necessary.

With a grim smile, A.C. came to a new realization. Stony had never intended to overwinter in Moonlight, or even in Montana.

*But if that's true, why was he scattered all over the side of Lone Peak?*

***

The Beartooth Highway led him to Cooke City, where he stopped at the Bearclaw Bakery for a take-out pastry and a cup of coffee. A couple of blocks down the street, he went past the Cooke City Montana Museum, but as he'd arranged to meet Maggie at the Bozeman airport, where he'd drop off his rental car, he reluctantly took a pass.

Maggie was waiting in the parking lot across from the rental car drop-off area. He tossed his travel bag into the back seat and climbed into the passenger seat. "Hi, honey," he said as he buckled his seat belt. "What's new?"

She leaned over with a quick welcome-home kiss. "Stay masked up the whole time?"

"Sure. But back to what's new; how is Doc?"

"Right after you left, he started sliding downhill. I was afraid he was going to slump back into his depression. Fortunately, I got a call from a couple of his friends at the golf club, Nick Berasi and Greg Wagner, asking how he was doing, and was there anything they could do? I said he could probably use some sort of pick-me-up, if they had something in mind. They ended up taking him out to lunch with the new Moonlight golf course designer."

"Oh, who's that?"

"David McLay Kidd."

"I thought he was the head of Lone Mountain Land Company."

"No, that's *Matt* Kidd."

"This isn't going to be easy to keep track of, two Kidds."

"Well, just remember that David *McLay* Kidd, the golf designer, is from Scotland. His company is DMK. He's very famous; he even designed a course at St. Andrews. Everyone in Moonlight is very excited to have him here."

"So, did Doc enjoy himself at lunch? Did he get out of his slump, as you called it?"

"Yes, he came back from the club much improved, very chatty. I think this new golf course is just what he needs to get his mind off things, meteorite hunting, Jamila, all of it. He can't stop talking about it."

"That's good to hear." A.C. shifted in his seat. "Glad it's not far to Moonlight; I've been sitting in a car all day. So, what else is going on?"

"Abigail disappeared."

"Abigail! What the hell?"

"Yeah. She just vanished, for two days, no texts or calls."

"Was she lost out in the woods? She could end up like Stony."

"Well, at this point no one knows where she was. Just as I was leaving to come down to pick you up, I got a text from Frank. Apparently, she contacted him and said she's back in Moonlight, or at least on her way back."

"So, a bit of excitement while I was gone."

"Oh, there's more. The Farrells seem to have gone missing as well. No one's heard anything from them for several days."

"That doesn't sound too serious. They're certainly not obliged to keep everyone up to date on their actions."

"But up there, A.C., people tend to let everyone know what they're doing. It's a very close-knit community. If the Farrells left without telling anyone, feelings would be hurt."

"Well, I wouldn't worry. There will be a good explanation, I'm sure. They seem very level-headed. Nothing to worry about."

"If you say so." Maggie gave him a sidelong look; his reassurances had not sounded all that convincing. "I still haven't told you the worst of it."

A.C. twisted in his seat again, this time more out of concern than discomfort.

"How bad is it?"

"Frank's involved." Before A.C. could say anything, she went on. "First, just like Abigail, a few days later Frank went missing. He was gone for a day and a night, no texts or calls, and then he suddenly reappears at the doorstep. We had no idea what had happened to him. Abigail said he'd gone out that morning as usual but hadn't said anything about going anywhere. We were all very worried maybe he'd fallen in the woods somewhere, or done something rash…" She trailed off.

"Is this when the other shoe drops?"

She nodded. "Size thirteen."

"Go on."

"There's been another murder in Moonlight."

***

"Mooney," said A.C., brightly "And Frank spent the night in the Virginia City jail for it."

Maggie gasped, veering slightly off the side of the road before recovering. She glared at A.C. "How did you know that! Oh, sometimes, A.C., I could just—!"

He suppressed a chuckle—it *had* been a dirty trick. "I'm sorry," he said. "I didn't hear about it until right after Frank was released."

"You could have called!"

"I guess I thought you already knew, or I would have mentioned it when I called."

Maggie was not mollified. "That reminds me--you didn't call at all, other than to tell me to pick you up two days late."

"I know, and I apologize," A.C. said, this time sounding quite sincere. "No excuses. I just got so wrapped up in this thing…"

161

They drove on in silence for some time, on the long, boring stretch south of Four Corners, before Maggie trusted herself to speak again. "I suppose you know all about it then? The murder?"

"Actually, no," A.C. answered. "I haven't even talked to Frank. The information came secondhand, through his military connection in D.C."

"Shall I tell you about it?"

"Please."

"He was found dead on Moonlight property, out where the new golf course will be going in." She paused, a quizzical look on her face. "What was Mooney doing there, anyway? I thought the interest was focused on Lone Lake!"

"Good question," replied A.C. "I need to talk to Frank, get a better idea of what's going on. Who found Mooney, by the way?"

"An associate of David Kidd's, doing some preliminary scouting. The poor guy was really shaken up at first, but I had a chance to talk to him and he seemed to be doing okay. He even half-joked about it—he said the job was already hard enough, trying to design a course with ski trails crossing the fairways, allowing for home sites, and oh yes, it has to be just as beautiful as the Reserve at Moonlight, but more playable. And provide a way to handle the additional effluent waste water. Then on top of all that, stumbling onto a dead body." She laughed rather glumly. "Funny if not so horrible. Anyway, he went home to Oregon for a few days to take a break. Maybe things will have calmed down by the time he gets back."

"That's my fear—not only is the madness not slowing down, it seems to be accelerating." He settled back into his seat and took a deep breath. "We're all going to have to start being more careful."

"Oh, A.C., you really think it's going to get worse?"

"If history is any guide."

"Well, everyone will be at dinner tonight. You can get the details of the murder and Frank's part in it, firsthand. And you can fill us all in on what you've learned."

"Do you think Doc's ready to get involved?"

"Ready or not, it's something he needs to do."

# Golf is Not for Everyone

The conversation on the deck during cocktail hour, through a sort of unconscious mutual agreement, had been light—A.C. related his experience at the pig races; Maggie discussed plans to go down to Ennis soon on a shopping excursion; Doc was keenly, if quietly enthused at the possibility of a DKM-designed course in Moonlight; Abigail nattered as usual. Only Frank, going heavy on the reverse floaters, remained quiet.

The casual mood carried on into dinner, although a bit more subdued. As Maggie cleared the dishes after everyone had finished, Frank pushed back his chair and looked slowly around the table.

"You all know I didn't do it."

"No one here thinks you did, Frank," said A.C. "As I understand it, there are certain circumstances that rule you out."

Frank raised his eyebrows. "Such as?"

"Tell you later." He turned to Abigail. "By the way, Abigail, wel—"

"I didn't kill him either," Abigail blurted out.

A.C. blinked in surprise, as the others turned their heads towards her as well. "Well, no, of course…but anyway, welcome back." He took a sip of wine. "Where were you? You had people here pretty worried for a couple of days, from what I understand."

"Oh, well. Okay. Yes, that was thoughtless of me. I should have…anyway, I went back to D.C."

"Sort of sudden, wasn't it?" Frank asked abruptly.

"I know, I know," said Abigail, and then went on, pleadingly, "but you don't know how hard it's been, these last weeks, searching for Stony with so little chance of finding him." She straightened in her chair. "But I still haven't given up, not completely. I want to keep looking. I can't believe he's dead, but at the same time I know I might never see him again...does that make sense?"

Maggie had come back to the table by then. "Of course, dear. We all know how close you two were. It's understandable that you would be struggling with everything that's happened."

"Thank you, Maggie," Abigail said. "That's exactly it, I've been struggling. Trying hard to stay positive. That's why I went back to D.C.; I needed to do something to try to get past this, something practical and pragmatic, even if difficult."

"Which was?" prompted A.C., after nothing more seemed to be forthcoming.

"This is very hard to talk about," Abigail began.

"It's okay, Abigail," said Maggie. "We're here to help."

With a slight shake of her head, Abigail finally said, "I cancelled the lease on his apartment. And that meant I had to go there and clear it out." After a pause, she continued. "There was almost nothing there. I knew he didn't like to tie himself down with a lot of stuff—he was away so much of the time—but I hadn't expected it to be so...austere. I've never mentioned this, but I've made certain inquiries with the sheriff's department here. They suggested I try to find something that might have traces of Stony's...DNA..."

"Why is that, Abigail?" asked Fuentes. A.C. looked over sharply, surprised by Doc's sudden interest.

"They said they have some..." she faltered. "They wanted something to try to match to some unidentified remains found earlier this year. But there was nothing, not a hairbrush, not even a dirty coffee cup."

"Did they say what they have?" Fuentes asked.

"No." She suddenly sounded defeated, resigned to never knowing what had happened to her brother.

"You said you were going to keep looking," said A.C. "How much longer?"

"Oh, I don't know. There are some areas in Moonlight I still haven't covered."

Frank leaned forward. "As far as I know, Abigail, there's only one area of Moonlight you haven't searched. There's been quite a bit of activity up there recently." He glanced away, then back to Abigail. "It's where Mooney was found with a bullet in his head."

Abigail looked around in alarm. "Activity! What kind of activity?"

"Surveying," Fuentes said. "That's where the new golf course is being laid out."

Abigail seemed to not understand this at first. "Golf?"

"That's what I was talking about earlier, out on the deck," he said, enthusiasm creeping back into his voice. "They've been out there getting a firsthand look at the topography, trying to get a feel for how things will translate from an initial topo map layout to the detailed computer-aided design. At that point, they'll lay out everything from tee boxes to fairways to bunkers, cart paths, greens—even the clubhouse and parking lot."

"They've already started construction?" Abigail asked.

"Oh no, too soon for that," he replied. "Probably just looking at where to put a road into the site. The building season will close down before they're ready, but then it's full bore in the spring."

"These maps," she asked, "how detailed are they? Do they show, oh, big rocks, areas of fallen timber, things like that?"

"Sure" Fuentes said, now completely absorbed in the topic. "The amount of detail is amazing. But the real work will come later, using computer-aided design tools."

"Wow," said Abigail. The others sat by, wondering where this would lead. "Fascinating. Who has these maps? Or is there something online?"

"Well, Greg—Greg Wagner—is the one who is doing most of the initial work. Before the designers really get into it, he's responsible for giving them the basic data they'll use. He's got the maps in his briefcase—never lets them out of his sight—and is in constant communication with the design firm."

Abigail looked around her distractedly. "Really! Oh, I don't understand what anyone sees in golf. It's so stupid." She stood up. "Maggie, thank you for a wonderful dinner, but I have an early morning." She turned and walked away, then stopped on her way to the foyer and looked back over her shoulder. "See you tomorrow, Frank?"

***

Once Abigail was gone, they moved into the living room, A.C. and Maggie on one couch, with Frank and Fuentes each in his own chair. Spanish Peaks gleamed almost iridescently in the early evening light, reminding A.C. of the glitter of Doc's Rock, sitting forlorn and battered on the now rarely visited patio. The others sat quietly as well, gazing out the window.

Frank broke the reverie. "So, what happened at the Smithsonian, A.C.?"

A.C. glanced over at Fuentes. "Are you ready for this, Doc?" he asked. "Don't want to push you."

"Don't worry, A.C.," he replied. "As I'm sure Maggie would agree, in her role as nurse and psychological advisor, we can consider it therapy."

Maggie smiled at this. "Doc, you don't know how glad I am to hear that. I agree; engagement could be exactly what you need right now."

Fuentes nodded his assent. "Go on, A.C., fill us in."

"Okay. Frank, thanks for breaking the ice, just now and in D.C.; the arrangements you made were perfect. Huguette Martine, the docent at the Smithsonian, gave me a personal tour of the gem gallery, as well as relating the history of the institution. General Dunway explained the geopolitical aspects of everything surrounding meteorites, and beyond. I had no idea there was so much interest in extraterrestrial mining, with the same sort of thing going on here, with all this meteorite hunting. Then there was the jeweler in D.C., Nathaniel—extremely helpful—and on the way back—sorry, Maggie—I made a side trip to Bearcreek to meet with an expert, with the improbable name of 'Card,' on all things

166

mineralogical, including meteorites. Oh, and before I even left for D.C., I spent valuable time with some local experts: a fellow named Al in Alder Gulch who mines garnets, and a sweet gal in Bozeman named Bingo who taught me about Yogo sapphires."

"You really *did* stay busy," said Maggie, with the first real hint of forgiveness she'd shown since he'd returned. "Sounds like it was a fruitful trip."

'It really opened my eyes to a few things. The big picture boils down to this: people get crazy when lured by the prospect of vast riches just lying around to be picked up, or even if a considerable mining effort is required." He looked at Frank with a grim smile on his face. "Even murderous."

"Couldn't have happened to a nicer guy," panned Frank.

Maggie gave them both a reproving look. "This sounds very serious, A.C.; is it really that bad?" As she said this, she happened to look over at Fuentes, who had lowered his head and was studiously staring at his shoes. "Oh, Doc. Of course, it's that bad."

He looked up. "It's okay, Maggie. I understand exactly what A.C. is getting at."

Clearing his throat unnecessarily to signal a shift in the conversation back to generalities, A.C. continued. "Like the gold fever in Virginia City back during the Civil War. Murders, vigilantes, hangings." But then he unavoidably brought them right back to the current situation. "And I think Moonlight is teetering on the brink."

A.C. proceeded to relate some of what he'd learned from General Dunway concerning the intense competition between various global players regarding gems, rare earth elements, novel mineralogical compounds, and various meteoric elements, including pallavine.

Frank interrupted. "What is pallavine? I've never heard of it."

"It's an extremely rare meteoric crystal. It's related to a more common mineral called olivine, or peridot. It's a beautiful light green color."

Frank sat back in his chair. "Whoa. We've been finding tiny green crystal shards in our concentrates. I've just been throwing them away. Is it valuable?"

"It's one of the rarest gems on earth, or even in the universe; and so, yes, large crystals are extremely valuable."

Frank sat back, looking a bit stunned. "Wow."

"Wow, indeed," said A.C.

"Now I'm getting scared," said Maggie. "I've heard some jewels are cursed."

A.C. unconsciously patted the jacket pocket still containing Stony's pallavine ring. "I don't know about that. Cursed or not, they can be dangerous to hold."

Sensing he'd taken things about as far as he could for the time being, he concluded with what turned out to be a combination of warnings. "Some of the parties involved in the search for these compounds—gems, elements, whatever—are extremely ruthless, and also well-financed, often with dark money, either privately or through shadow government agencies." He lowered his voice. "As for justice for Jamila? My new friend in Bearcreek cautioned there is no likelihood of that, and by going forward with this we only bring danger to ourselves."

# Number One Suspect

Dawn shrouded the peaks across the valley with a fine mist, vaguely pink against the dark forest below, the sky and clouds above shading upwards from a bright orange band along the ridge to mauve to a dusty blue.

A.C. was up before the rest of the house. He sat quietly on the couch and gazed out at the morning as it slowly took shape, sipping strong coffee and reflecting on the previous night's conversation. The threat they all faced might seem to be like smoldering embers, but he knew from experience what might appear to be cold and dead can flare up dangerously at any moment. He'd somewhat reluctantly taken on the task of fire warden. The thought of what might lie ahead had awakened him early and sent him to the living room, staring out the window looking for…well, if not answers, then at least direction.

He started involuntarily at the sound of his phone ringing. It was sitting on a side table, where he'd left it the previous night. *Never get used to this perpetual connectivity.* He struggled a bit getting up off the couch, like the old man he knew he was but didn't like to admit, even to himself. By the time he got to it, the phone had stopped ringing. He didn't recognize the number; as he held the phone, the message alert sounded. He dialed voicemail. "Hello, A.C., sorry to bother you. It's Huguette from the Smithsonian. Please call me."

Appreciating the short, to-the-point message, he called her back immediately.

"Hello? It's A.C. LaFleur. I just missed your call."

"Hello, A.C. Thanks for calling back. I'm sorry to disturb you at this hour, I know it's early there."

"I was up." He paused. "Not that it's a problem, but how did you know how to contact me? I'm very parsimonious with my number."

"General Dunway didn't think you would mind."

"No, of course not! I apologize for not leaving my number with you when we met. Rude of me."

"Not at all." There was a long pause, and as A.C. ran through a hastily composed list of possible reasons she would be calling, he had a sudden and unwelcome sense of dread. The intuition proved correct, as he heard Huguette say, "Nathaniel Woodmont has been killed."

By the lack of an immediate response, Huguette felt perhaps she'd not presented this news in the best possible way. But then again, what would have been any better?

A.C. quickly processed the information, falling back on skills he'd practiced for over forty years as a detective on the force. "How?"

"He was found in his shop, strangled."

"When?"

"The day you were there."

A.C. looked down at the floor in dismay. "My God. We joked together about a curse, but this…"

Huguette waited a moment, then prompted. "A.C.? There's something else, something you may not have realized yet."

"Yes?"

"Don't be surprised if you are contacted by the authorities. You were the last one to see him alive."

# It's Everywhere

A.C. steadied his slightly shaking hand—*nothing to worry about, he told himself*—and carefully poured another cup of coffee. He glanced up at a sound from the driveway. Carrying his coffee, he opened the front door to find Geno just about to ring the bell.

"Geno. Good morning," A.C. said, walking out to the front porch.

"Good morning, A.C. Sorry to look in on you so early."

"No problem." A.C. glanced over his shoulder back into the house, lifting his coffee cup in invitation. "Coffee?"

"Thanks, but no, no time."

"What's going on?"

"I'm trying to locate several people. Have you heard anything from the Farrells?"

"No. Maggie mentioned they seem to have left without telling anyone. I told her she shouldn't worry."

"Well, I have a bad feeling."

"Because?"

Geno looked around, as if trying to decide how much he could say. Then he turned back to A.C. "What do you know about the airport hangar up at Bozeman? I'd be surprised if you haven't heard anything, frankly."

"The subject has come up. What exactly do you think I might or might not know?"

"It blew up last night. Not just blew up," he amended, "*really* blew up. Jet fuel feeding it, hot as hell, fire trucks couldn't get near it. Melted the corrugated steel roof. It's still burning in spots."

After a moment's reflection, A.C. asked, "And your take on this is…?"

"Not good. It's a large private hangar, identity of lease holders currently unknown. Three jets, in and out at various times. At least one of the jets was making regular flights to New York City."

"Tell me something I don't know."

"These flights are transporting jewels—Moonlight jewels—to buyers back in New York."

"I said, something I don't know."

Geno looked offended. "How much *do* you know?"

"Never mind. Not enough, obviously. Please go on."

"Okay. Some Moonlight families—as well as LMLC executives—asked me to bring a packet of jewels to the hangar and then accompany them to New York. Hand them over at the other end. I was told to go to jet number such and such—"

A.C. interrupted. "You really did this?"

Geno glanced down, as if bit ashamed. "Once."

"Were you expected to bring back cash?"

'No, nothing like that."

"Then what? You had another bad feeling?"

"More than that."

A.C. waited patiently for Geno to explain. After a long uncomfortable silence, he continued.

"Armed guards at both ends. And on the jet."

A.C. tried to process what Geno had been telling him, but he felt he lacked sufficient data. He thought back to how the conversation had started. "How do the Farrells figure into this?"

Geno seemed relieved to get back to uncompromising ground. "They may have been there." Then he shifted back and forth on his feet. A.C. had never seen him so agitated. "I think they were there," he said, at first unwillingly, then more confidently. "I'm pretty sure they were there. In the fire."

"But you have no proof of that."

"No; they're just starting to sift through the debris now, as things start to cool off. It's just a feeling, I guess, but given what they've been involved in…" He shrugged, as if to say, *where else could they be?*

"Geno, have you considered having a partner with you at all times?"

"No, not really. Why?"

"Things have changed here. It's not the Moonlight you know and love. But maybe you aren't quite ready to believe it."

Geno nodded. "It has changed."

"And it's becoming more dangerous." A.C. spread his arms out, encompassing all of Moonlight in a simple gesture. "What are you seeing out there? Day to day?"

"I see what you're getting at," said Geno. "There is a growing interest—or should I say, an 'exploding' interest—in the green crystal."

"Pallavine."

"Is that it?" asked Geno. "Pallavine? No one seems to know much about it, but there sure is a lot of interest. After the big storm last week, it seems to be showing up everywhere. A lot of water came down off Lone Peak, like a giant sluice. The Kramers found some on the South Road. The Levine kids even found some at Ulery's Lake, on the beach."

"That's what's driving the madness. It's making my job harder than ever. I'm wrestling with two main obstacles to my investigation, and if I can't overcome them, I'm afraid I'll never catch up with Jamila's killers."

"What's holding you back?"

"Okay, one; let's say this was a Federal investigation, DOJ, whatever. Plenty of resources to throw at it, like FBI, forensics, surveillance. It's very common for the Feds to have an informant working for them, willingly or not. And there are plenty of ways to get people to cooperate: immunity, RICO, IRS. I don't have those kinds of resources to fall back on."

"And two?"

"The local authorities have decided—practically predetermined—this was a simple burglary gone bad. So again, I have no support, no backup, not even any interest."

"So, what do you do now?"

A.C. sighed. "Old school detective work. I have to grind through what little I know about the crime, go back to my interviews, over and over, until I find the mistake."

"Mistake?"

"It's a cliché, but there's no such thing as a perfect crime. Well, it's a cliché because it's true. Every criminal makes at least one mistake, and now it's my job to find it. That's my one chance of solving this thing." He raised his hand, signaling there was something else he wanted to ask Geno. "Earlier you said 'several people.' Who else is missing?"

"One of our employees didn't show up for work this morning. It's too early to go into panic mode, but I have another one of those bad feelings; something isn't right."

"Well, it's probably nothing."

"I hope so. Anyway, gotta go." He turned away, then looked back. "Let me know if you hear from the Farrells?"

"Of course."

"And good luck with those obstacles."

"Thanks. And you think about getting a partner."

# Ain't Superstitious

A.C. watched as Geno drove out, then went back into the house wondering what the third thing would turn out to be this morning, humming the old Howlin' Wolf tune to himself: *Ain't superstitious, black cat just cross' my trail.*

When he got back into the house, he saw that Fuentes was out on the deck.

"Morning, Doc," he said, holding the door open. "Up with the sun, huh? I'm getting another cup of coffee; need a refill?"

"Sure, thanks." Fuentes held out his cup. A minute later, A.C. came back out with the coffees and sat down across from him. "Here you go."

Fuentes nodded his thanks. "A.C., can I ask you something?"

"Sure."

"Where are you with Jamila's murder?"

*Number three.* "It's complicated," A.C. answered guardedly.

"I thought you hated that phrase."

"I do, but it's the only thing I can give you at this point."

"Still, you must be making some progress."

A.C. studied the rim of his coffee cup. "I may be closing in on something."

"Is there something I can do to help?"

"Absolutely, if you're up to answering some questions."

"I really need to help, so ask away."

A.C. took a sip of coffee, organizing his queries. "First question: Jamila's computer, who could it talk to?"

"That's an interesting way to ask that question. It was disconnected from the cloud. Everything was going to a local disk array, so no outside communications."

"If not to the cloud, could it talk to something locally, within the house?"

"Only to me, to my computer. She had given me some programs I could run remotely to kick off a processing job. I think she was also manually storing results there, as a backup. Oh, an automated system would notify me if something failed, or send me a batch of results after they'd finished. Again, as a backup. She didn't want to lose anything, but also wanted to stay off the grid."

"Okay, next: she was mapping the location of the main strike, right?"

"Yes."

"Have you examined any of her data since…well, have you looked at anything recently?"

"No. I've been trying to not even think about it."

"I understand. But it would be very helpful if you could look at it for me."

"I don't know how that could help, but if it's important, I'll do it today. Anything else?"

"One other thing. There is another thread I'm following. Something that's been rattling around in my head ever since my meeting with Huguette." He blinked, reminded of something else that had happened in D.C. He started to tell Fuentes about the jeweler, then decided against it; no need to muddy the waters. "I'd like you to track down a name for me."

"Sure. Who?"

"See what you can find on anyone named MacLeod, residing in Washington, D.C."

Fuentes furrowed his eyebrows. "MacLeod? As in Stony? What are you looking for?"

"Oh, you know, the usual: family history, background, contact information, anything you can get." Sensing another question, he raised his hand. "Probably nothing; just a loose end."

Fuentes nodded vigorously. "I'm on it. I'll get back to you shortly with whatever I find. Even *stat*." He smiled, something none of them had seen for a while, and went back into the house.

A.C. remained there for a minute, gazing over at the couch where he'd seen Jamila so often, sitting there working on her laptop. He stood up and involuntarily looked down at the patio where Doc's Rock sat, now covered with a small blue tarp.

*Black cat just cross' my trail.*

# Lowest Common Denominator

After Fuentes left, A.C. soon found himself up out of his chair, pacing back and forth across the deck. Pacing was not his favorite pastime. Not only was it boring, it seldom did anything to improve either his disposition or his thought processes. He much preferred to sit quietly, in a darkened room, arranging his thoughts systematically. This morning that had not been possible.

*At least I've got Spanish Peaks in view at each end of the circuit.*

Finally tiring of what was threatening to become a marathon-length pace, he went back into the house. Maggie had come down and was sitting at the kitchen bar.

"Good morning, Maggie," he said, trying to put a cheerful note into his voice, if for no other reason than to shake off his gathering gloom. As he did so, he sensed the opposite of cheer radiating from Maggie's downturned face. "Hey," he said, "what's wrong? You look so sad."

She looked up with lowered eyes. "You're right. I'm in a proper funk, trying to figure out what to do with Jamila's things. Or whether I should do anything, or not. I'd like to help Doc deal with it, but I don't think he's ready, and I don't feel like I can just go in there and do it for him. Clothes, hats, scarves, personal stuff in the bathroom he hasn't touched yet—I snuck in there the other day to look—jewelry. All that. It's all so personal. I would feel like I'm intruding, but at the same time…" She trailed off, then went on dispiritedly. "And everything in her office. I guess he'll have to deal with that on his own. I don't know enough about computers; I'd probably make it worse."

She put her head in her hands. Without looking up, she asked in a soft voice, treading lightly: "How close are you?"

A.C. walked over and put his hands on her shoulders. A light squeeze told her all she needed to know.

***

Frank brought in lunch a little after one. Cold cuts—roast beef, sliced turkey breast, pastrami, four different kinds of cheese—real cheese, none of that imitation crap foisted off by grocery store delis—lettuce, fresh sliced Roma tomato, pickles, condiments, and homemade potato rolls.

"Bit of a challenge, baking up here," he'd said as he came in, sounding like an apology, but the rolls were perfect.

It was a quiet lunch, everyone contemplating the current situation in their own terms.

Frank had filled them in earlier on his arrest, but there were a lot of unanswered questions. What had Mooney been up to at the site of the new golf course? Who had reported the altercation between him and Mooney, leading the sheriff to arrest him? He knew only that there had been an anonymous call put in the night before Mooney was found. He also found out Mooney's camp was close by and had been ransacked. That led Fuentes to speculate it could have been the two seedy-looking characters they'd seen with Mooney at the Wilson the night they met Abigail. Frank agreed, and almost suggested they could have been the ones who killed Jamila, but he'd stopped himself in time, changing the subject to the latest products from his sluices.

Maggie was still struggling with how best to help Doc without pushing him back into seclusion. He'd been making remarkable progress, but remained understandably fragile. The improvement in his mood had been especially evident today, as he expressed his enthusiasm about helping A.C. with some research.

179

She saw the prospect of his being of real value to A.C. sparkling in his eyes like afternoon light on Ulery's Lake. At the same time, she was also worried over A.C.'s state of mind—she thought he was close to floundering, afraid of any misstep, which had put him uncharacteristically on edge. Everyone could feel it. And just how careful had he been on his jaunt around the country? Should she make him get tested?

A.C. had retreated to the basement in search of solitude. Fuentes had made good on his promise to get back to him *stat* with the information he'd asked for, and A.C. had been wrestling with the implications the rest of the morning. He had to make it fit within what he considered strict boundary conditions: Moonlight, meteorites, and murder. His method was simple, and one he'd relied on for years: the best solution is that which depends on the smallest number of assumptions. It was an analytical technique called Occam's Razor; the simplest explanation is usually the right one. He was finally ready to lay out his conclusions.

***

Maggie broke the silence. "A.C., you were out on the deck this morning pacing like a tiger in an old-time circus cage, battering yourself against the bars. Frank—well, I never know exactly what you're up to, but that shifty look you've had lately tells me you're on to something, or think you'll soon be on to something, if only you could tell us. And Doc—and I'm very glad to see this—even you have become preoccupied with something, at A.C.'s instigation, I know, but whatever it is, I'm all for it because it seems to have pulled you out of the depression I was afraid you were starting to enjoy."

Maggie put her hands on her hips, which was not exactly the dramatic pose she was going for, since her hands remained below table level, and in a calm but demanding voice, addressed A.C. in particular: "Now, do you have a better idea than the sheriff—who's only interested in putting this whole thing behind him, apparently—do you know what really happened?"

"The sheriff—Doc's Rock—the whole thing, it's all my fault," said Fuentes, but perhaps with less conviction than previously.

"That's bullshit, and you know it, Doc," said A.C., leaning forward in agitation. "Sorry for being so blunt, but I think we all know the so-called 'grab and go' theory is nothing more than a lame attempt at CYA brought about by a less than optimum investigative environment. This COVID scare has thrown everyone into a bunker mentality, as far as reasonable decisions go, and rather than doing their job, they are content with hiding behind the shield of supposed unacceptable risk to avoid taking any responsibility."

"Tell us how you really feel, A.C.," said Frank.

"You of all people should know exactly what I mean," A.C. exploded. "I mean, Christ on a bike, Frank, they arrested you for killing Mooney! How stupid was that?"

Frank flinched, abashed for possibly the first time in his life. "Sorry. Didn't mean to make light."

A.C. took a deep breath, settled his shoulders, and sat back in his chair. "Okay, now that the air has been cleared, I'll address Maggie's concerns. Here's a summary of what I learned on my cross-country tour. Al at the Garnet Gallery—echoing the general feeling in the community—is convinced the sheriff is right, it was nothing more than a crime of opportunity, motivated by the celebrity of the hunk of rock sitting down there embedded in the patio, which is, aside from the diamonds and as a collector's item, worthless. Card Daniels, of pig racing fame, also believes in grab and go, but with the proviso that the perpetrators are professionals and still in the area. Both the sheriff's department and Card believe the murder will remain unsolved. Then there's Orvis Mooney, another pea under the damned mattress, one that is still keeping me awake at night."

Frank half-stood out of his chair in an obvious burst of uncontrolled excitement. "I've solved it!"

"What?" said A.C., still a bit annoyed with Frank. "So, you've solved Mooney's murder, is that it?"

"No, no, of course not," said Frank in exasperation. "Not Mooney! Who cares about Mooney? I'm talking about Jamila!"

"Frank, slow down," cautioned A.C. "We're willing to hear what you have to say, but you're going to have to lay it out for us. Calmly."

"Okay, this is how I see it." He pointed behind him, towards the road above the house. "There's a house up on that hill with a view down to where we're sitting right now; no obstructions, trees cleared to create line-of-sight, a perfect vantage point. They were watching the house, waiting for the right opportunity. They saw Doc leaving the house with someone—a female—in the car with him. This is the day Doc and Maggie went to Ennis shopping. But they thought it was Jamila in the car with Doc—at the time, they didn't know you and Maggie were visiting, A.C. So, they thought the house was empty. Unfortunately," he said as he glanced over at Fuentes, who was sitting quietly, head down, "that wasn't the case."

"You haven't said who it was, yet, Frank," said Doc, without raising his head.

"The Farrells! They must have thought we were getting too close, and they went to ground. Vamoosed. On the run. All we have to do is track them down."

A.C. stood up and started pacing again, stopped himself and sat back down, his face screwed up as if in pain. Frank looked over at him intently, trying to decode the look. He'd known A.C. a long time, known him well, he thought, but this anguish was something new.

"That's an interesting theory, Frank," A.C. finally said, evidently with some effort. *Has Frank gone off the rails?* He reached up and took off his heavy, black-framed glasses and rubbed his eyes. "A theory I have to admit I had not considered. But then, I have information regarding the Farrells that you do not, Frank."

"And what would that be?" Frank asked, careful to keep his voice neutral.

"Geno told me this morning, before the rest of you were up and about, the Farrells probably died in a Bozeman airport hangar explosion last night."

This produced the surprised reaction A.C. had expected, and he held up his hands to quell the barrage of questions. "I hadn't heard about the explosion, either," he said, "and Geno didn't give me any details. News reports are focused on the sensational as opposed to the useful, as usual. But it doesn't surprise me, given the level of insanity that seems to have descended on this area." He paused, and the pained look in A.C.'s face Frank had seen moments before began to show itself again.

"When the fireball exploded over Moonlight last summer," A.C. began, "it set off a series of events none of us here could have ever imagined, or contemplated. Multiple murders, one personal and tragic." He paused, then went on, his voice rising. "Ever since that night, there's been nothing but rampant idiocy; from you, Frank, with your toy sluices, to the moronic Moonlight land company actions, all the deluded treasure hunters, both legitimate, like poor Stony, and Mooney-style vultures, the scavenging global interests, mega-corporate wheelers and dealers, covert and not-so-covert foreign government interests, shadow money and midnight jet couriers, even local security involved in the madness…"

He stood up abruptly and left the room, leaving everyone sitting at the table in stunned silence.

***

It was almost two hours before he came back to the dining room, led up the stairs by the hand by Maggie. The others had remained at the table for a time, speaking in low tones, then scattered throughout the house. Maggie rounded them up, and when they had settled, she and A.C. took their places at the table.

"I won't apologize for what I said a bit ago," A.C. said, "only for the way I said it."

Profuse denials of any offense taken continued for some time, until A.C. held up a hand. "I appreciate your indulgence. But now let's get back to our discussion.

"To start with: assuming the Farrells were victims of the explosion leaves open the possibility Mooney was behind Jamila's murder. Now that he's dead, proving that would be next to impossible. If, however, as Frank opined, the Farrells did not die in the fire and are the perpetrators, their trail is getting colder by the minute. Of course, the official position, as much as I distrust it, is still a possibility; there are enough crazies around here to make anything possible. It could have been a random, unplanned attack, in which case we have nothing to go on. Or it could have been professionals, in which case we are still behind the eight ball."

Maggie drew back in distress. "Oh, no, A.C.! This is never going to be solved!"

"I didn't say that. Early this morning, I asked Doc to do some research for me, in two different areas. One, I asked him to examine Jamila's data. No one had looked at her latest results, not since that day. And two, I asked him to do a biographical search on someone living in Washington, D.C." He saw the confusion on both Frank's and Maggie's faces deepen. "But before I get into that, we need to go back a bit." He pointed in Frank's direction. "It's something Frank and I discussed early on. By the way, Frank, sorry if I disparaged your prospecting earlier, but I need you back, and focused."

Frank bent his head in acquiescence. "You can count on me, A.C."

"I never had any real doubt." He went on, his manner becoming more deliberate as he spoke. "Something at the murder scene has bothered me from the very beginning. As they were moving the body—I am so sorry about this, Doc."

Fuentes could not hide his stricken look. He lowered his head and gestured to A.C. to continue.

"As they moved the body, I noticed a small area of *livor mortis*—a bluish splotch of discoloration—on two areas: one on her torso, and one, darker blue, on her lower back."

Maggie looked at A.C. quizzically. "But that means—" She halted in midsentence, familiar with the physiological process, but not quite able to work out what he was getting at.

"It has to do with the way blood pools in various parts of the body, as it cools." A.C. looked over at Fuentes, who was still sitting head down, but was hearing his explanation calmly.

"It means," A.C. finished, "the body was moved after death."

***

Frank was the first to speak up. "I recall the conversation, A.C.," he said, "but at the time you were convinced it pointed to Mooney."

"Not convinced," A.C. qualified, "only that he was our prime suspect. But there was more to that conversation, Frank. One of her shoes had fallen off." He saw Frank nodding in agreement. "Between her office, or maybe the deck, and the front door, while she was being dragged there. And Doc's Rock was smashed for the same reason the body was moved."

"I'm still not following you, A.C.," said Maggie.

"Okay. Remember the scene that day? The first to arrive was a young, inexperienced deputy. His initial report to the sheriff is what quickly established the official version of events. Too busy, too distracted by COVID, or whatever, the department's response was determined by a rookie cop jumping to unwarranted conclusions.

"Now, look at the scene from the viewpoint of the killer. We know the body was moved, most likely moved from the deck, where Jamila typically sat with her laptop, running her data processing programs. The meteorite in the patio—given the connotations, I am beginning to tire of calling it Doc's Rock, by the way; I think we need a new name—in any case, it's downstairs on the patio, two flights of stairs and a room away, hammered and cracked, but for no apparent gain. The attack on the meteorite was simple misdirection. An attempt to divert attention from the real focus of the attack."

Doc looked up. "Jamila's computer."

"Right."

"That's why you asked me to look at it today. Because you suspected there might be something there."

"Right again." He held out his hands, inviting him to continue. "Are you up to it, Doc? Want to explain what you discovered?"

"Just the day before, Jamila had set up..." he started to explain, then stopped abruptly.

"Are you sure you want to do this now, Doc?" asked A.C.

Fuentes took a deep breath. "I'm okay. He continued, though a little shakily. "She had created some automated notifications, alerts that came to my computer, so I could keep up with the progress of the image processing, and even help her out. I hadn't even looked at my computer until this morning, when A.C. asked me to look at her data. There was a message on my system—it had come in that morning—saying that the latest data run had aborted for some reason. That's what she was working on that morning, finding the error so she could restart the program. But she never got the chance." He looked over at Frank. "Could you make me a floater, Frank? A real one, not one of yours."

Frank smiled broadly. "Coming right up. Anyone else?" A.C. raised his hand for a floater, and Maggie asked for a glass of wine. Frank got up to get the drinks.

"Thanks," said Fuentes. "Anyway, there was also a message from Jamila about what she'd been able to determine at that point; this was right before the program crashed. She'd found the location of a main strike, in the area of the new golf course. Her coordinates describe an area with a radius of slightly less than a mile, so very precise."

Frank brought over the drinks. "Don't keep us in suspense," he said, setting one down for both Fuentes and A.C. "Where is it?"

"Right in the middle of the site of the new golf course." Fuentes took a sip of his drink, laughing softly. "She said in her message now we'll have more to look for than my lost golf balls."

Frank had in the meantime gone back over to the kitchen bar to retrieve his own drink. "She could really pinpoint it that well?" he asked.

"I was surprised myself, even as familiar as I was with what she'd been doing," said Fuentes. "I shouldn't have been. She was brilliant." He suddenly paled and looked around at the group. "I'm sorry. There's a lot more, but—" He got up and walked hurriedly into the back bedroom, leaving his floater behind.

Maggie began to stand up to follow, but A.C. waved her back into her chair. "Leave him for now." She sat back down, staring at the empty chair where he'd been sitting. "He's been doing so well," she said. "I hope this doesn't set him back."

"He'll rally," said A.C.

"How likely is that someone could find the meteorite without Jamila's data, A.C.?" asked Maggie.

"I'd say very slim," he answered. "Since no one's found it by now, it must be in pretty rough territory. LMLC has started roughing in an access road in the area, but that's about it. We also need to keep in mind that with winter approaching, the window is rapidly closing on both the meteorite hunting season, and my investigation."

"You were told by the general you met with in Washington," Maggie continued, "it could be extremely valuable. Is that because of the rare earth elements you talked about, or maybe those exotic compounds? You said he was quite emphatic about its possible value on the international market, if it contained those things. Is that what the murderer was looking for?"

"If that were the case," A.C. answered carefully, "the meteorite in the patio would have been removed more completely, possibly to be taken off for detailed analysis. Since it was left behind only slightly damaged, that tells me whoever it was already knew it is not particularly valuable, again confirming the damage was meant as misdirection.

"Maggie, you've brought us to a crucial point: what was the murderer after?" He paused for several moments, seemingly unaware of the drama he was creating as he rehearsed his next remarks. "We now know, thanks to Doc's efforts this morning, Jamila's computer contains the data pointing to the location of the main strike, somewhere on the site of the new golf course. Mooney was killed near there. We also know something much more valuable than diamonds or gold is suspected to be a component of that meteorite, something infinitely rare and beautiful, namely, pallavine. The gem in Stony's ring is pallavine; it's the ring that caused his finger to be brutally fractured, the ring which, cursed or not, undoubtedly led to his death.

"Pallavine is the common denominator. The jeweler who made Stony's ring, Nathaniel Woodmont, was found murdered in his shop, apparently only hours after I left him. In fact, I'm a suspect." He did not pause at the surprised exclamations prompted by this news. "That brings me back to the ring Doc saw on Abigail's finger the night he met her at the Wilson, a ring I have never seen her wear since, despite her telling Doc how dear it was to her; a ring set with a stone cut from a crystal of pallavine."

In the silence that followed, A.C. continued his explanation. "Before Doc left the table, he was about to tell you about the other critically important item he uncovered for me. Something Huguette Martine said during my visit to the Smithsonian has been nagging at me ever since my visit with her. So along with asking Doc to check Jamila's data, I tasked him with tracking down a name in Washington, D.C., the name MacLeod. There weren't as many as I expected, just a handful, most of no particular interest. He located multiple records for Stony—Daniel—MacLeod, who is as well-known as Abigail claims. Colorado School of Mines, articles in the Smithsonian Magazine, membership in the International Meteorite Collectors Association and something called The Meteoritical Society, and so on. But what Doc found out about Stony's sister was the key. Abrielle MacLeod—"

Maggie couldn't contain herself. "Abrielle? Who is Abrielle? What are you talking about?"

"Abrielle MacLeod," A.C. went on steadily, ignoring the interruption, "is twenty-six years old, unmarried, a rising star at a prestigious law firm in Washington, D.C., the adopted sister of Stony MacLeod, also adopted. As children they frequently visited the Smithsonian together. Her nickname, given to her as a child, and known to everyone acquainted with her, is Abber."

Maggie stared at him, bewildered, unable to frame a coherent question.

Frank, by training and experience well accustomed to unexpected shifts in the level and quality of field intelligence, did not immediately accept the new information at face value, and also knew the right question to ask. "How was this confirmed?"

"I called her up and talked to her."

At this, both Frank and Maggie sat back in their chairs, stunned, and almost in unison cried out, "Then who the hell is Abigail?"

A.C. sighed heavily.

"I have no idea."

# It's Four PM – Do You Know Where Your Golf Pro Is?

Before A.C. could explain further, the house phone rang. Maggie answered, then handed the phone to A.C. "It's Geno. He says it's urgent."

After listening a moment, he told Geno to hold on. "Has anyone seen Greg Wagner lately?" he asked the group. Negatives all around. "No, Geno, no one has heard from him, why?" After a short pause, he turned to them again. "Greg has been missing for over thirty-six hours. Geno has been down in Ennis, checking with Greg's dad; he's on his way back to Moonlight now. The rest of the team is spread out all over the area, searching."

A.C. went back to his conversation with Geno. "Yes, of course, we'll let you know if we hear anything. Do you need any help?" A pause. "Okay, Geno, will do." He broke the connection. "He'll call if they find anything. Said there's nothing we can do for now." He handed the phone back to Maggie. "This is ominous."

"What are you thinking, A.C.?" asked Fuentes.

"About something Abigail said the last time we saw her. 'Golf is stupid,' or something like that."

"What does that have to do with anything?" asked Maggie.

"For someone who thinks golf is stupid, she seemed awfully interested in the maps Greg has been creating. And she abruptly switched the focus of her search from Lone Lake to the site of the new golf course. Doc, the imaging data on Jamila's computer—how was the location of the strike specified?"

"Just latitude and longitude, within a small radius, like I said."

A.C. looked around the table with a sudden and obvious dread clouding his face. "Has anyone seen Abigail lately?"

No one had seen her for two days.

A.C. pushed his chair back with a jerk, bumping the edge of the table, sloshing floaters and wine in all directions. "Maggie, where's the phone?"

"Right here, A.C. What on earth is the matter?" She handed him the phone, then returned to mopping up her wine with a napkin.

A.C. began poking at the phone ineffectually. "Doc, how do you do redial on this thing?" he asked Fuentes, holding it out and shaking it impatiently.

"Give it to me," said Fuentes. "Who do you want to call?"

"Geno! Redial Geno!"

Fuentes handed the phone back to A.C. as soon as Geno's phone began ringing. "Geno!" A.C. practically shouted into the phone. "How close to Moonlight are you?" He began pacing around the room. "What? Just getting to Jack Creek? Not good. Geno, get back here as fast as you can. Greg is very likely at the site of the new golf course. No, the proposed course, the new one! Geno, we have to get out there—Greg might already be dead." By this time, Fuentes and Frank were also up out of their chairs, listening and watching as A.C. continued giving Geno instructions. "Call the sheriff. We'll try to call you back with more exact coordinates in a few minutes, as soon as we're on our way." He hung up.

"A.C., what the hell!" yelled Frank. "What's going on?"

"It was Abigail. She killed Jamila. And now she's got Greg."

The stunned silence lasted only a few seconds; then they all broke loose at once, loudly proclaiming disbelief, shock, and concern in equal measure.

A.C. held up his hands, waiting for the storm to pass. Once they had quieted down somewhat, he explained. "Abigail got the coordinates of the main strike from Jamila's computer, but she didn't know how to go about using them until she heard about the detailed maps Greg was creating for the golf course designers. She needed Greg's maps to find the meteorite. I'm betting she's kidnapped Greg, forced him to lead her out there. Hopefully he's unharmed, but if he resisted, she could do something rash. I think she's becoming desperate; all these weeks without finding anything, knowing that every day she stays here makes it a little bit harder to keep up her charade. I don't know; maybe she sensed I was getting suspicious, getting close to tripping her up. I might have pushed her into this."

"I still don't understand—" began Maggie, only to be cut off by A.C.

"No time." He pointed at Fuentes. "Doc, get those coordinates." He turned to Frank. "How are you set, Frank? Are we ready for trouble?"

"Everything we need is in the truck, locked and loaded."

"Good. Because I remember someone telling her to keep a round chambered in that old handgun of hers."

"Well, how was I—"

"No blame, Frank! Just a reminder we have to be ready for anything." He wheeled around to where Maggie was sitting. "Maggie, you stay here in case—"

"Not on your life, A.C. I'm going."

"Okay, okay." He looked around. "All right, we need to move fast. Let's go!"

As the door closed behind them and they walked quickly across the driveway, they heard Frank muttering. "Who are you, Abigail?" he asked himself. "Who are you to come into our lives like this, like a destroying angel, like a medieval curse?" As he opened the door of the pickup truck, he gritted his teeth. "No matter," he growled. "Whoever the hell you are, you're mine now."

# Put `er into Low Gear, Frank

Once they were on their way, Maggie repeated her question. "How did you know, A.C.?"

"Occam's Razor," he said. "It started to come together after my visit to D.C.," he began, "with a chance remark made by Huguette, as I said. We'd finished our tour of the museum, and I'd just shown her Stony's ring. This naturally led to a discussion of her relationship with Stony. When I mentioned that 'Abber' was here in Montana with us, she was surprised, but recognized the nickname right away. But when I used the name 'Abigail,' she seemed confused for a moment, then brushed it off as failing memory. We even joked about it. I didn't think anything of it at the time, but I kept going back to it—what had caused that momentary confusion? Doc made the crucial discovery this morning, when he located the real Abber, Abrielle MacLeod. Along with everything else, that left only one reasonable conclusion, the one that fits all the facts without making any unnecessary assumptions.

"The name was really Abigail's only mistake," he went on, "though an easy one to make—she'd probably seldom heard Stony call his sister anything but Abber, and simply misremembered her real name when it came to putting together the fake identity. Who she really was, and what her connection was to Stony, I don't know. It's obvious she created the alias to get access to Moonlight without arousing suspicion. She certainly made it convincing. We were all taken in by her."

"Stony didn't just go missing, then," said Maggie. "She murdered him, too."

"And Mooney," A.C. said.

The truck rocked violently from side to side as Frank turned onto the newly bulldozed access road leading to the proposed site of the new course.

No one voiced the thought they all shared. *Please. Not one more.*

***

The big pickup rumbled to a stop.

"That's Greg's truck!" exclaimed Fuentes. It was tilted at a sharp angle off to one side of the primitive road, the right front wheel buried in a deep ditch.

"I'll take a look," said A.C., climbing out of the rear door. A minute later he came back. "Nothing," he said, leaning into the cab. "Just an empty briefcase lying on the floor. They must have gone on from here on foot. Let's go!"

"No, get in, A.C.! I can get around it."

A.C. jumped in and closed the door as Frank twisted the steering wheel hard to the left. "Hang on, everybody!" A second later, the left front side of the truck bounced high into the air. "Big log over here," said Frank, as the rear end bounced just as hard as he cleared the log. "Road looks better ahead."

"Thank goodness!" Maggie's first four-wheeling adventure had her clutching the hand-holds tightly.

"Doc, did you get through to Geno? Is he far behind us?" A.C. asked.

"No answer. He must be in a dead zone," Fuentes replied. "It could be an hour or more before he gets up here."

"And the sheriff?"

"They're on their way, but I'm not sure how far they can get up this road."

The truck suddenly stopped again.

193

"Now what?" said Maggie, peering over the front seat. "Oh."

A large outcropping of smooth stones blocked their way forward. Heavy trees lined both sides of the road. "How close are we, Doc?" Frank asked.

The navigation system had been put into GPS coordinate mode. Fuentes leaned over to take a closer look. "At least another quarter of a mile, maybe more, depending on where they are within the likely radius."

Frank looked down at the drive controls on the steering wheel. "Time to see if what they advertise about this thing is real," he said. "I'm going into 'rock mode.'" He toggled the control, then edged the truck forward slowly. The big turbo diesel engine throbbed as the front wheels inched up the front of the huge boulders. The back tires spun madly in loose soil for a second before getting a grip on the harder rock underneath. Maggie was white-knuckled, holding her breath.

The truck bounced sharply as one front wheel dropped into a crevasse on the top of the outcropping. The back tires screeched, propelling the truck forward with a jolt.

"Everyone okay so far?" Frank asked. Affirmative replies from all encouraged him to keep going. "Down the other side!"

Getting down the back side of the obstacle was even trickier than the way up, but Frank knew what he was doing. "Don't worry, Maggie, we're not going to tip over!" he called out at one point. Finally, they were back on somewhat level ground, in a small meadow.

"Which way, Doc?" asked Frank.

"Well, straight ahead. But it doesn't look like we can go too much farther," he said, pointing ahead of them. A rugged ridge of rock, much higher and longer than the boulder field they'd just navigated, stretched across their path a couple of hundred yards ahead, and the meadow they were in tapered off into deep woods to the left.

"Alright. I'll drive us up to the edge of the meadow, then I guess we're on foot after all. Damn."

After Frank had driven them as far as he could, he stopped and they all clambered out of the tall truck. At any other time, they would have enjoyed the beautiful scene: afternoon sun glowing in the meadow, dark shadows trailing away from the bordering trees, Lone Peak gleaming high above them.

"This way," said Fuentes, referring to his handheld GPS and pointing to the right. "Over that ridge is our best bet." He stood by anxiously while Frank pulled some gear out of the rear cabin.

"Catch, Maggie," he said, tossing a small backpack her way. "First aid." She nodded her acknowledgement. "I hope we don't need it," she said.

"A.C., here's something for you. Beretta, nine-millimeter, locked and loaded, as promised." A.C. took the pistol, which was in a shoulder holster, and carefully slipped it into place, giving it a pat of familiarity. Frank then put another small pack over one shoulder, and on the other slung a small Weatherby hunting rifle. "Ok, Doc we're ready to go."

***

Alternately overheated and chilled, they struggled their way across the first ridge, then another smaller outcropping, before moving into the shade of Fan Mountain. As the late afternoon dragged on into early evening, A.C.'s hopes began to sag, along with his stamina. He and Maggie were both falling behind at times, but were determined to continue the search.

They turned north, traversed a shallow ravine, then angled back towards Lone Mountain. The ground was more level now and they made good time.

"What is the GPS telling you, Doc?" A.C. asked as they stopped for a quick rest.

"We're there, damn it!" Fuentes in exasperation. "We're at practically the exact coordinates Jamila laid out."

A.C. took off his glasses and rubbed his eyes with the back of his hand with apparent fatigue, but a gesture Maggie recognized as one of defeat. "Guess I've led you out here for nothing," he said dejectedly. "Not to mention failing Greg. Wherever he is."

"A.C.," Maggie said gently, "we're not done yet. We've covered only…what, Doc, maybe a third of the possible area?"

"At least half, no, a bit more," said Fuentes. "But you're right, Maggie, it's much too soon to give up. I'm sure Jamila's coordinates are damned accurate, but it's not like she had a crystal ball or something. There's a margin of error, and we're well within that margin. We just need to keep going."

"Geno and his guys, and the sheriff's department, they must be out here somewhere by now," said Frank. "If we don't find them, they will."

Fuentes rechecked the GPS coordinates. They had circled back to nearly where they had started.

***

They spread out a bit in order to cover more ground, keeping about fifty feet between them. When Fuentes heard Maggie scream, he tripped over a root, scraped his wrist on a jagged rock, and got a mouthful of moss when he hit the ground. Dragging himself to his knees, he called out, "Maggie! Are you alright?"

"Over here!"

Fuentes scrambled to his feet and ran to where Maggie was waving her arms. When he got there, it took a moment for him to comprehend what he was seeing.

Greg was slumped against a tree, his head hanging down, unmoving. A thick chain wrapped around his waist held him semi-upright. His hands were tightly tied in front of him with yellow nylon rope.

He was unconscious, but alive. His face, swollen and blotchy with bug bites, showed signs of being beaten. Dried blood caked an eyelid and one cheek.

Maggie had quickly regained her composure and was rifling through the first aid kit while Fuentes cut the rope binding Greg's hands. She pulled out a roll of gauze, tore open a small packet of Betadine antiseptic, and gently wiped clean a ragged wound on Greg's forehead. He stirred spasmodically as she worked but remained unresponsive.

A.C. and Frank arrived moments later. Frank stretched out his arms, motioning downwards with his hands, cautioning silence.

"She's got to be close by." He whispered. "And she's obviously heard us by now."

A.C. pulled the Beretta out of his holster and looked around. "Frank, what do you—"

Frank cut him off. "There's something out there," he said urgently, pointing off into the trees. "Stay here and take care of these two." He pulled the rifle off his shoulder. "This is mine, A.C." He ran off soundlessly into the forest.

As Maggie continued to minister to Greg, he slowly regained consciousness. With what appeared to be an immense effort, he spoke, his words slurred and indistinct. "No, don't…no…I don't know, I…please, no…" He closed his eyes for a moment, then looked up at her. "Who…where…"

"It's alright, Greg, you're safe. She's gone. We'll get you out of here."

"But what…"

"It's okay. Just relax."

He took a deep breath and his eyes seemed to clear. "Maggie?"

"Yes, it's Maggie. Doc is here, too."

Greg looked up, slowly coming around. He suddenly craned his neck frantically, trying to look over his shoulder, first in one direction, then the other, wincing as the chain cut into his waist. "Ahhh, jeez that hurts."

"Don't worry, Greg, she's not here."

"Doc!" Greg brightened at the sound of Fuentes's voice.

Fuentes bent down and put his hand on Greg's shoulder. "We're here. We'll get you out of this."

They could see relief flood Greg's face as the realization he had been found hit him. "Oh, my God, Doc. How did you find me? What happened? Is she—?"

The sharp crack of a rifle shot made them all jump. The following echo rolled through the forest eerily, slowly fading until the only sound was their rapid breathing and the soft breeze rustling the tops of the surrounding firs.

Moments later, Frank walked out of the woods, the rifle pointing down at his side.

"Is he okay?" he asked, kneeling beside Greg.

"I'm fine, Frank," Greg answered weakly. There was a long silence. Then he looked up and asked, "What was that shot?"

"Later, Greg," said A.C., looking at Frank, signaling the same question with his eyes. "Let's get you out of here first." He reached back behind Greg and rattled the chain. "Looks like you're locked in here, partner."

"Ah. Where's my truck? It should be close by. There's a key in the toolbox." He laughed. "She used my own damn lock and chain; can you believe it?"

Fuentes quickly located Greg's truck. They had missed finding him immediately only by about fifty yards. After unchaining Greg, he and Maggie helped him to the road, explaining their vehicle was not far from there, just past the end of the road. As they helped him up into the cab of his pickup, they heard a siren wail off in the distance.

"I ran into this ditch intentionally," Greg told them, "trying to slam her into the dash." He winced at the effort, bruised where he'd struggled against the chain and the rope binding his wrists. "Bad idea. Didn't work, obviously. I think it just made her mad, and it shook me up, too. Made it even easier for her to drag me out into the woods and chain me up." He settled into the seat of the pickup with relief. "Of course, she had a gun pointed at me the whole time." He coughed weakly. "Why in hell did she do this to me? I gave her the maps."

"How long have you been out here?" asked Fuentes.

"Since yesterday. Just about froze to death last night. She chained me to the tree and left me here. Never came back. I sat here all day, wondering what it would be like to starve to death." He flinched as Maggie continued to treat the wound on his forehead. "I think she's crazy. I knew she'd come back any minute and..." His voice broke as he tried to go on.

Maggie consoled him as best she could, shivering at the thought of finding him dead. "You're safe now."

Greg slumped in the seat, his head falling back as he sighed deeply. "Son of a bitch," he croaked. "What a day."

***

Frank reappeared soon after Fuentes and Maggie had taken Greg away; A.C. was standing there waiting for him.

"Well?" A.C. asked.

"She found it, all right," Frank said. "Jamila's coordinates were spot on. It's sitting in a small crater. A lot bigger than Doc's, and even in the shadows you can tell it's full of diamonds. The whole thing sparkles." He pointed back the way he'd come. "It's just off in the woods there."

A.C. peered intently in that direction. "What about Abigail?"

Frank held up a clenched fist. Reaching out to A.C., he slowly opened his hand. Lying on his palm was Abigail's ring.

A.C. picked it up gingerly, as if it might burn his fingers. "You killed her?"

"Nope."

"But we heard the shot!"

"That was to drive off the pack of wolves. Six or eight of them."

"Wolves!" A.C. shuddered with a sudden premonition. He was almost afraid to ask again: "Abigail?"

"She was lying next to the meteorite with a gun in her hand." He stopped and took a deep breath. What he'd seen had obviously shaken him. He pointed the barrel of his rifle at the base of the tree next to them, where the chain that had bound Greg was still lying in a soft bed of pine needles.

A.C. immediately got the implication. "Greg somehow lived through one night," he said solemnly, "but he never would have made it two."

Frank nodded once, slowly. "And it wouldn't have been much longer before Abigail was—"

"Scattered," A.C. said quietly. "Like Stony."

199

# Failure to Fire

The morning chill on the deck was being countered with hot coffee with Bailey's, liberally supplemented by glazed doughnuts.

"A toast," said A.C., "to Greg!" They raised their coffee cups.

Greg had called earlier. He'd just been released from Big Sky Medical Center with instructions to take it very slowly for the next few days, drink plenty of warm fluids, and most emphatically, do not go in to work. He'd been extremely close to hypothermia, but fortunately had no other injuries beyond some serious bruises and bug bites. Of course, he'd called from the golf club.

They all looked around at the sound of "Sorry!" as Frank came out onto the deck. "Over slept."

"Coffee in the kitchen, Bailey's on the bar," said Maggie.

"Fantastic. Be right back."

"What was Frank carrying?" asked Fuentes.

"Looked like something the cat dragged in, whatever it was," said Maggie.

Frank came back out on the deck carrying a large clear-glass tumbler.

"That looks like more Bailey's than coffee," said Maggie.

"Do I detect a note of disapproval in your voice?" Frank countered.

"It's the nurse in me; I can't help it."

"I had a hard day yesterday!"

"Didn't we all," said A.C.

"Frank, what the hell *is* that?" asked Fuentes, pointing to the tattered, gray bundle Frank had dangling from his free hand.

Maggie leaned forward with a start of recognition. "Is that Stony's backpack!?" A.C. had told her Huguette's story of Stony as a young boy, and how he never went anywhere without his pack.

"Sure is." He held it out. "I found it in Abigail's room. And regardless of what Sheriff Moreland thinks, I was never in there before, okay?"

That brought the laugh they all needed.

"How do you know it's really his?" asked Maggie.

"For one thing, look at it. It's in tatters. It's was lying out there all winter. For another, I found his passport in a closed zipper pocket."

"Anything else?" asked A.C., the first to realize the implications.

"Maps. Well, pieces of maps. Mostly illegible. But one that might be—might be," he stressed, "the area up around Lone Lake."

Fuentes jerked back in his chair. "Lone Lake?"

"Yeah, isn't that where Abigail had been searching? Before she stole Jamila's data?"

"Yes, that's right," said Fuentes.

"That's not all," said Frank. He reached into his pocket and pulled out a big wad of bills. "Several thousand dollars, stashed under her bed. She must have been selling diamonds through that operation in Bozeman. My diamonds!" he added in a pique. "Hey. Do you think she's the one who blew up the hangar?"

"Not likely," said A.C. "She wouldn't shut down her own pipeline."

"She was running it?" exclaimed Fuentes.

"No proof, yet," was all A.C. would say.

In the pause following that maddeningly enigmatic statement, Maggie raised a question that had been on all their minds. "Are we ever going to know what happened to Stony? Or is this yet another case of justice denied?"

"At the risk of repeating myself—" replied A.C.

"When has that ever stopped you?" Frank couldn't resist interrupting.

"—justice is where you find it. Seriously, though, I've been giving it a lot of thought. This is the best I can come up with." A.C. took a long drink from his cup, the dregs, as it turned out. "Is there more coffee?"

"Hold on," said Maggie, "I'll go get it."

They waited impatiently as Maggie refilled his coffee cup and he poured in a generous dram of Bailey's. "Okay," he said, settling back in his chair, "this is how I see it. Stony, as well-traveled as he was, may not have had the best instincts when it came to women. And we all know how beautiful and beguiling Abigail was. Based on what little she told us that was remotely close to the truth, I think they probably met in Chad. A romantic relationship followed. Then she telexed him about the strike in Moonlight, and he was here by himself a few days later. A combination of innate genius and pure luck led him almost immediately to the pallavine meteorite. He scrambled to have the two rings made, traveling back and forth to New York City and D.C. over the space of a few days. Then he had Abigail join him here in Moonlight, and gave her the ring. That was his undoing.

"It was something Card Daniels said that triggered the realization, like in the old film, she'd done him wrong. Card said there are three things to avoid in the meteorite hunting game: partnerships, fences, and romance. Stony violated two out of three. After wooing her with a pallavine ring, the romance must have soured. He refused to share the location of the second meteorite strike. At some point—this is conjecture, since we can't know for certain, but I'd argue more like an educated guess—something happened up by Lone Lake. Was it simple misadventure, like Stony falling off a cliff, which she quickly took advantage of? Or more calculated?"

"I know what I'd vote for," said Frank.

"However it happened," continued A.C., "that's when she tried, unsuccessfully, to wrench the ring from his finger, creating the spiral fracture Doc always knew was suspicious. Then, either in shock due to the accident, or panic at her first murder—if it *was* her first—or maybe it's getting dark and wolves are howling and she doesn't want to get lost in the woods at night…? In any case, she must have left him there, only to realize later he'd been carrying the map to the meteorite. She went back, but it was too late. The wolves had finished the job on Stony."

"And the backpack was nowhere to be found," said Frank.

"Right. So, over the winter, she cooked up her 'Abigail' scheme. Poor Abber, bereft and alone, searching relentlessly for her missing brother. Doc conveniently provides a pass into Moonlight. Frank even more conveniently gives her a place to live."

"She knew the backpack was somewhere close to Lone Lake," said Fuentes, "that's why she kept searching there. And somehow, she found it."

"Yes," said A.C., "but Stony's maps, what was left of them, were useless, as Frank just showed us. Even without knowing about the pack, though, we know as soon as she found out Jamila had located the main strike, she figured Jamila's data was all she needed to find the main body. Which she did; it just turned out to be the wrong meteorite."

"It all fits, A.C.," said Fuentes. "We'll never know the details, but it's a very plausible story."

"What about Mooney?" asked Maggie. "Where does he fit in? Just another gold fever victim?"

"Oh, he was exactly as Abigail described, a murderous claim jumper. And based on what I heard from General Dunway, and what little Frank has been able to learn, it's clear it was Abigail who reported the fight between Frank and Mooney. We know it wasn't any of us."

"Why would she have reported it?" asked Maggie.

"To divert suspicion away from the real killer," replied A.C.

"Which was Abigail," said Frank.

"That's right, Frank, with a weapon that was not recovered. But we'll come to that in a minute. Abigail killed Mooney—a single shot to the head—then called in to report Frank's little altercation from the day before. We've already seen how willing the sheriff is, in the present circumstances, to take the easy way out. Okay, I admit they're in a difficult situation, but Abigail sure knew how to take advantage of it. She couldn't risk having the sheriff come in and seal off the area as a crime scene, not before she found the meteorite.

"With Frank in jail, and not expecting him to be released so soon, she thought she had time to finish things off. First, and this was a panic move on her part, she flew to D.C. and killed Nathaniel Woodmont, thinking he could connect her with Stony. When she got back here and found out Frank had already been released, she started worrying about getting into the golf course site again, especially after hearing Doc talk about the accelerating development plans. She realized she could use Jamila's data along with Greg's detailed maps and overhead drone photos to find the meteorite. Most of the rest, you know."

"What do you mean, 'most' of the rest?" asked Fuentes.

"One reason we know Abigail killed Mooney is what Frank found when we rescued Greg. Remember the rifle shot?"

"You said that was to scare off a pack of wolves, right, Frank?" Maggie asked.

"That's right," Frank replied. "But what we didn't understand right away is why Abigail hadn't used her gun to try to drive them off before they attacked her. When I found her, she was lying on the ground half-devoured with the gun still in her hand."

"How does that relate to Mooney?" asked Fuentes.

"To begin with," explained Frank, "Abigail told me she had a gun, and I offered to look at it for her, to make sure it was clean and in good condition, and so on, but she never brought the subject up again and I forgot about it. Until I saw it lying next to her, and examined it."

"Being very careful not to leave any fingerprints or disturb the scene in any way," added A.C.

"Right. It was a Colt pistol, model M1911, to be exact, also known as the Colt Government. Single-action, magazine-fed, chambered for a .45 caliber cartridge. It was standard issue for the U.S. Armed Forces until 1985. Heavy and hard to handle, especially for someone her size, and out of date. Who knows where she got it? Anyway, as soon as I looked at it, I knew right away what had happened. Failure to fire."

"Which means?" asked Maggie.

"There was a round in the chamber, but it failed to go off. There was a mark on the primer—the end of the bullet—where the hammer struck. Old gun, old ammo—she pulled the trigger but nothing happened. The primer was bad."

"Okay," said Fuentes, "that explains how the wolves got to her, but what about Mooney?"

"I also checked the magazine. There was one round missing."

"And undoubtedly," said A.C., "ballistics testing will show it was the bullet that killed Mooney."

This was a lot to take in all at once.

Fuentes was the first to say something, "What a fool I've been. I didn't suspect a thing, not until I looked up the name MacLeod in Washington D.C."

"It wasn't just you, Doc. She took us all in."

"So, it's finally over."

"Not quite. I have to make one more trip to D.C."

"A.C., what on earth for?" asked Maggie plaintively.

"There are a couple of Stony's things I need to deliver to Abrielle."

Maggie nodded. "I'll go with you this time," she said, "if only to make sure you wear a mask!"

# Superfecta

Before leaving for Washington, A.C. went back to the Garnet Gallery in Alder.

"A.C., that you?" Al hobbled across the dirt parking lot of the Garnet Gallery towards A.C.'s car, a sack of gravel under each arm. "Hang on, let me get rid of these." He carried the bags over to the shed and flopped them down, clapped his hands free of dust, and came back over to the car. A.C. had gotten out and was standing there, waiting.

"Al, why are you still breaking your back hauling that stuff around?" he asked. "I thought you'd sold out a year's worth of harvest."

"Hell, they came back and bought up three years. I'm just finishing off some good-looking stuff I had lying around. Then I'm out of here for a while." He clapped A.C. on the shoulder. "Say, there's a good poker game going every Saturday night, up in Pony. See you out there?"

"Sounds tempting, but I'm heading back to New York soon."

"Well, that's a damned shame. We could use more like you around here. We heard all about the Moonlight murders, your part in all that. Got what she deserved, if you ask me."

"I had help," he said, shifting uncomfortably from one foot to another, "and justice is where you find it, sometimes. Anyway,

Al," he went on, "I came out to ask you about the garnet deal you made; now you tell me it's even bigger. What's going on?"

"I'd say it has a lot to do with the lady folk up on that mountain of yours."

"You mean Moonlight?"

"Right. They're not satisfied anymore with ball caps and golf shirts with fancy logos; they want jewelry." He held up a hand to deflect the question he'd anticipated. "Not just any jewelry. Custom-made, designer stuff. Made with Montana gold and gemstones. They want the Trifecta."

"You've got me there, Al."

"Yogo sapphires, Ruby Gulch garnets, and Moonlight diamonds. And it's not just rings and such, oh no. There's a new market for all kinds of gewgaws: copper napkin rings, gneiss paperweights, who knows what, all encrusted with the Montana trifecta. Not just locals, either; governors, senators, millionaires, billionaires, billionaire's wives—they all want in on it. But the key to this is the Moonlight meteoric diamonds. That means dealing with the diamond merchant's wife."

"Diamond merchant! In Moonlight?"

"Just like in New York City, but with a big difference; no discount. Oh, yeah, she's a mover and a shaker, and is pulling all the strings. She and her husband got in on it early, and now it looks like they've cornered the market."

A.C. gave him a quizzical look. "A husband-and-wife team, you said?"

"That's right. Farley? Farrand? Something like that."

"Farrell?"

"That's it."

"Gosh, Al," said A.C., "I'm sorry to say they may have been killed."

"No!"

"You heard about the explosion at the airport? They were apparently caught in it."

"I'm sorry to hear that." After a moment's reflection, he added, "It's going to change things."

"Yeah, well…"

"Anyway, somebody else will pick it up." He paused. "There's something else."

"What's that?"

"They're finding some sort of green crystal up in Moonlight. Rumors are it's even more valuable than diamonds."

"Is that so?" A.C. said, his voice neutral.

"Say, that makes it more like a superfecta, right?"

"Sorry?"

"Well, a trifecta, that's picking the top three finishers. A superfecta, that's even harder. You have to get all four." He looked up. "That could be bad," he said thoughtfully. "I have the feeling you're in for more Virginia City trouble up there."

"What do you mean, Al?"

"Murders."

"Oh, Al. I hope to hell not. I can't take any more."

***

Early the next morning, A.C. and Maggie left for Washington, D.C. A.C. was glad to have her along; he thought it would make the difficult visit to Abrielle a little easier.

It had been a more grueling trip than his previous visit, complicated by airline schedule changes, scrambled hotel arrangements, and a lost rental car reservation. After a fruitless argument at the rental car counter ("You know how to *take* the reservation, you just don't know how to *keep* the reservation..."), he bagged the rental car and called Uber. When they finally got to the JW Marriot it was well past midnight, and they both fell into bed without even completely undressing.

Abrielle MacLeod lived in Georgetown, which was close by to both the hotel and the Smithsonian. A.C. wasn't sure why he had even tried to rent a car, other than old habits die hard; all their business could be easily accomplished using Uber and Lyft.

They started out early the next morning. A.C. resisted the impulse to ask the driver to take them past Presidential Gems on their way to Abrielle's; there was nothing to learn, and it would just depress him. He was sure Maggie wouldn't be interested either.

As the car made its way slowly down 33rd Street NW, A.C. recognized her townhome from the online street view he'd looked at previously. "Here it is," he said, "on the left."

"Oh, yeah," the driver replied. "Uh, no place to park. Okay if I just stop here?"

"This is great, thanks." Maggie took care of final payment while A.C. lugged himself out of the back seat of the small car.

As they walked to the front door, A.C. unconsciously patted the inside pocket of his sport coat, making sure the rings were there. Maggie carried the pack.

"Beautiful neighborhood," said Maggie.

"She must be doing alright for herself," he replied, in an admiring, not an envious, way.

Abrielle opened the door. She was tall, looked nothing like Stony (of course, he reminded himself), dressed just as he'd imagined a top-flight Washington lawyer on her day off would be— stylishly, professionally, and comfortably.

A.C. was taken by an attack of speechlessness. He thought he'd been prepared for this. Maggie quickly took over.

"Ms. MacLeod? A.C. and Maggie LaFleur."

"Yes, of course," Abrielle said warmly as she opened the door. "Please come in." They were spared any awkwardness by her forthright manner. "I'm so glad to meet you both. How was your trip here?"

"Oh, it was fine," said Maggie.

"We're just glad to be here at all," said A.C., earning him a warning glance.

"Well, I can't tell you how much I appreciate it. Please come in to the living room." Abrielle led them into a smartly decorated room just off the foyer. While they seated themselves, she said, "As I told you when we spoke several days ago, Mr. LaFleur, I had given up hope of ever hearing anything. The Montana sheriff's department, while very apologetic, gave me really nothing to go on. I understand they are working under severe constraints, but I had frankly expected more."

"I understand completely," said A.C. "As an ex-detective, I can only tell you that given the circumstances, they were doing their absolute best." A white lie never hurt in cases like this.

Maggie had seen Abrielle eyeing the pack she was holding on her lap. "I expect you recognize this?" she said, rising slightly and holding it out towards Abrielle.

Abrielle stood and walked over to take the pack. She bit her lip. "Not much left of it, is there?"

"Unfortunately, no," said A.C. "It spent the winter out in the wilderness."

"As did Stony, I understand." She quickly raised her hands. "Oh, please, don't misunderstand me. After hearing nothing from him for so long, and unable to get any definitive information, I never really expected to hear from him again. Or learn anything about what happened to him. I'm glad I finally have an answer. And some little part of him."

A.C. decided this was as good a time as ever; he hadn't expected to have a good opening. "I have something else that belonged to him," he said, reaching into his coat pocket.

"Yes, I know," Abrielle said, unable to disguise the sadness in her voice. "The ring you told me about."

A.C. held out a small cloth jewelry bag. "I have it here," he said, "along with its mate. He had two rings made, one for him, and one for…"

"You don't need to explain, Mr. LaFleur; I've already decided what should be done with it. With both of them. I don't even want to see them, honestly."

A.C. waited for her to elaborate, slowly placing the rings back into his pocket.

"They should go to Huguette," Abrielle said. "Or more properly, to the Smithsonian."

A.C. was again speechless.

Maggie came through for him. "That's perfect, Abrielle."

***

The last stop was the Smithsonian, now with a purpose beyond a friendly visit. Huguette met them on the steps, at the same spot as before.

"It's good to see you again, A.C," she said. "Though I have to say I'm a bit surprised to see you back so soon." She turned to Maggie as A.C. introduced her.

"My wife, Maggie." They exchanged socially acceptable waves in lieu of a handshake.

"So glad to meet you!" Huguette said, then turned towards the entrance and invited them to follow her into the building.

Once in her office, A.C. got down to business. Their return flight left in just three hours, and he didn't want to miss it, not after their recent experience. "I won't keep you long," he said as he sat down. "I have something for you." He pulled the small package from his inside coat pocket and pushed it across the desk.

After Huguette opened it, her reaction was what he had expected. "Oh, my." She sat for a long moment, speechless. She reached out and pulled the gift closer. Hesitantly, she picked up one of the rings. "This was Stony's." A.C. nodded. Huguette placed it carefully back onto the wrapping paper and picked up the other ring, identical but slightly smaller. "And this?"

"That ring was given by Stony to the woman we knew as 'Abber,' or more correctly, Abigail. False Abrielle."

"Oh, my." Huguette had obviously run out of words. She turned the second ring over and over in her hands. "It's just as beautiful as the first," she said.

"Nathaniel made them both."

She placed the ring back on the table with the other, gently. "I'm sorry Nathaniel is no longer with us; I'm sure he would have liked to have seen them again. But then again, given the tragedy surrounding these two gemstones, maybe not." She frowned. "But I don't quite understand. Shouldn't these go to Abrielle?"

"We've just come from Ms. MacLeod's," A.C. explained. "We had a personal item of Stony's to give her. I also offered her the rings, but for understandable reasons, she turned down the offer. She suggested the museum would be a more appropriate place for them."

Huguette was still trying to understand the import. "How generous." She picked up the other ring and admired it, turning it over in her hand. "Yes," she said, now definitely more animated, "first, of course, they'll go to the lab for detailed analysis and documentation. Then, I think, a private showing to a select group of benefactors. Once on permanent display—" She stopped in midsentence. "May I make a suggestion? To be approved by Abrielle MacLeod, of course."

"Of course."

"I'd like the donor plaques to read Daniel 'Stony' MacLeod and Dr. Jamila Sayvetz. Would that be acceptable to you?"

"Very appropriate. I'm sure Ms. MacLeod will agree. And Dr. Fuentes will also be pleased, I'm sure."

"Thank you."

A.C. rose from his chair. "We'd best be going; I have a quick meeting scheduled with General Dunway before we head back."

"Of course, don't let me keep you."

As they reached the door, he turned back to her. "What about the curse? Will you feel safe with the rings here? If the Hope Diamond is cursed, surely those two rings must be."

"Oh, definitely. But I look at it this way—as national museum specimens, they'll belong to everyone. It's only those who take sole possession who are in danger."

"That sounds right."

Huguette stood up behind her desk. "Thank you, A.C. Please come back and visit these two little jewels from space soon. You're always welcome. And I'm very glad to have met you, Maggie."

A.C. tipped his head, Maggie gave another little wave, and they closed the door behind them.

***

Once out in the hallway, they took the elevator down to the first floor. A.C. turned back and forth a couple of times before getting his bearings. *Okay. Dunway's office is that way.*

Maggie held back as A.C. started down the hallway. "I'll wait here," she said.

212

"You sure? It will only take a few minutes. He won't mind."

"No, you go ahead. I'll stay here and browse the exhibits."

"Okay, be right back." He headed off down the hall.

The general's greeting was embarrassingly effusive. "A.C., you old war horse! Come in, come in. You've been damned busy!"

"And still standing, barely," A.C. answered, as the general gripped his hand in greeting. The general motioned for him to sit down across from him.

"Nonsense!" Dunway said. "Always knew you were the man for the job. Which brings me directly to the reason I wanted to see you. I believe we can help each other."

"Whatever I can do," A.C. said, "within reason, of course."

Dunway smiled. "Oh, don't worry, nothing extreme. To start with, on my side, you've been completely cleared of any involvement in Woodmont's murder."

"That's a relief, thank you."

"Consider it professional courtesy. More than one department was involved—three-letter agencies, I think you call them? The evidence from Woodmont's security cameras, both infrared and visual, show you alone with him, and leaving him very much alive." He pushed a photo across the desk to A.C. "What I want from you is an identification. Do you know who this is?"

A.C. picked up the photo, studied it for a second or two, then laid it back down on the table. "That's a hard question to answer."

"How so? Do you recognize her or not?"

"Of course. That's Abigail MacLeod."

"The difficulty being…?"

"Just who the hell was she, really? It would be nice to know, even if just as a matter of formality. The forensic lab in Billings has the body—what's left of it—and DNA analysis confirmed what we already knew—she was definitely not related to Stony."

The general pulled the photo back across his desk and slipped it into a folder. "All we know is that she killed Woodmont. Facial recognition is very good these days, but so far we've turned up nothing. Is there anything about her from the time she spent in Moonlight you think would help us trace her identity?"

A.C. shook his head slowly. "Nope. She had us all fooled, right up until the end. I only figured it out based on a comment by Huguette concerning Stony's sister's real name. Until then we took what she told us at face value." He blinked slowly. "She was very convincing."

"No doubt. No idea of her motive for killing Woodmont? He seems to be only tangentially connected to all this."

A.C. reflected for a moment, then replied, "I suppose she just wanted to keep any information concerning Moonlight pallavine from getting out. We still don't know exactly where Stony found it."

"Did she know you visited Woodmont?"

"I don't know how, but yes, she must have known."

"Well, we've started tracking down all of Stony's known associates, along with a raft of other meteorite hunters and, well, geological adventurers, I'd guess you'd call them. We're obviously interested anyone who worked with her in the past, and not just for identification purposes; they could be just as dangerous. Knowing who she was will give us an advantage when—not if—something like this happens again. I have no doubt we'll find out who she was before long."

"Let me know if there's anything I can do."

"Of course." He pushed his chair back and stood up, an obvious indication the meeting was over. A.C. stood and moved to the door.

"Thanks for coming by, A.C.," Dunway said. "Oh, by the way, there's someone in Montana who has some good news—well, never mind, you'll find out when you get back there. Travel safe."

# Aiming Stone

The airport was quiet, as was usual these days, and Fuentes was waiting for them outside.

As soon as they got into the car, A.C. in front, Maggie in back—her choice—Fuentes started grilling A.C. "How did it go? Everything okay with Abrielle?"

"Yes, Doc, she's taken it all very well. We left the pack with her." He paused. "She didn't want the rings." At the inquiring look from Fuentes, he just said, "I'll tell you about it later. But I had excellent news from General Dunway—I've been cleared of all suspicion in Nathaniel Woodmont's murder."

"Was there ever any doubt?"

"In certain quarters, yes. But the general was able to squelch it before it went anywhere." He settled back into his seat.

Fuentes looked over at him with a sly look on his face. "You can't guess who dropped by this morning."

"I never guess."

"Well, if you *did*, in this case you'd be wrong."

"Tell me!"

"Paula Farrell!" He loved it when he could really and truly surprise him—it happened so seldom.

A.C. was definitely surprised. "But I thought…"

Maggie leaned forward over the front seat. "The Farrells?"

"I don't believe it," A.C. said.

"You said yourself no evidence had been found placing them at the hangar site that night."

"It was hopeful thinking. I was sure they'd bought it."

"Nope, they're back in Moonlight," Fuentes assured him.

"I'll be a son of a bitch."

"Yes, you are, sometimes," said Maggie from the back seat.

"Enough of that," A.C. said, smiling back at her. "Paul and Paula. They're okay? Where in hell have they been?"

"We'll have to wait until tonight to find out. She was in a hurry; her phone was ringing the whole ten minutes she was there, and then she rushed off to work. They're coming over for cocktails tonight. I also asked Geno. Now just relax and enjoy the trip home."

A.C. leaned back to look at Maggie. "It does feel like home, doesn't it?"

"It can be, if you like," she replied. Since converting the 1850 House from a full-time restaurant to a limited special events venue, they'd often talked about selling and getting out of Oswego. They couldn't think of a better place to go than Moonlight. With the proceeds from the sale of the restaurant combined with their savings, they'd be able to manage it.

He reached back behind the seat for her hand. "Let's do it."

***

Cocktails on the deck—more or less socially distanced—started at five.

Geno was the first to spot the Farrells as they walked in. "Oh, my God! Paul! Paula! I thought you were…"

"Dead?" asked Paul. "Yeah, we heard we were supposed to have been blown to kingdom come in the hangar explosion." He glanced over a Paula. "There are some who would not be sorry."

Before Geno had a chance to interrogate them further, A.C. came out onto the deck.

"I can't say I'm not damned glad to see you," he said to them, "But bloody hell! What have you been up to? It can't be good."

"Nice to see you, too, A.C.," said Paula, laughing. "Paul, do you think we can tell them what we've been doing?"

"Is it illegal?" asked A.C. "You know I don't cotton to illegal; it's part of the job description."

Above the general laughter, Paula said, "We've been in Lake Huron."

Frank, who'd just brought out the first tray of hors d'oeuvres, overheard this and broke in. "You mean *at* Lake Huron."

"No!" Paul insisted, "*in*. We've been prospecting for puddingstone."

"Okay, Paul," said A.C. "Now you're starting to annoy me. Puddingstone? What the hell is that?"

"It's a conglomerate, also called plum-pudding stone. Very common in Michigan, the Great Lakes, all around there. Anyway, we'd heard reports of puddingstones veined with gold lying in the shallow water around Lake Huron. Of course, we had to investigate."

"Of course." A.C. was barely restraining his impulse to reach out and throttle them both for making him believe they were dead.

Paul went on, oblivious to his near second death. "Can't give you an exact location, but we've been out there searching, knee-deep in water for hours on end."

Paula spread out her arms dramatically. "This could be as big as Moonlight diamonds!" she exclaimed.

Fortunately, given A.C.'s increasing exasperation, the doorbell rang, and he took the opportunity to break away to answer the door.

"Bingo!" said A.C., rushing over to her. He forcibly resisted the desire to grab her in a bear hug, reluctantly settling for the socially acceptable fist-bump. "It's good to see you! Everyone, this is Bingo Brennaman. Bingo, what are you doing here? I thought you'd busy lining up a graduate program somewhere."

"That's on hold. I've accepted an offer from General Dunway as a government field agent here in Montana. My first assignment is the meteorite out on the new golf course site."

"So, this is the good news he mentioned!" She smiled in agreement.

Paul stepped forward. "Bingo, is it?" She nodded. "This meteorite, could it be, uh, that is, is there any indication that it's, uh, pallavine?"

Bingo shook her head. "Nope, nothing like that. I've already done some preliminary thin-core samples. It's nickel-iron. Oh, with a lot of microdiamonds. But nothing real exotic."

"No rare earth elements?" asked A.C., dreading an affirmative response.

"No, nothing unusual. But still beautiful. Those cores, when the sun hits them, it's just fantastic, the way they flash and sparkle. Like nothing on earth." She smiled. "Literally."

Fuentes had been sitting back, listening intently to the back and forth. "Bingo, what happens with it now, the big meteorite?"

"Lone Mountain Land Company owns it, of course," she said.

"For now, at least," remarked Fuentes. He was thinking back on all the conversations related to the ambiguity of mineral rights and railroad ownership issues.

"Sure," agreed Bingo, "but assuming the legal issues get resolved, Nick—the golf pro at Moonlight Reserve—said it will stay right where it is. The course designer, David Kidd, wants to use it as an aiming stone."

Fuentes's eyes brightened at this. "Because Nicklaus has aiming stones at the Reserve, on two and twelve."

"Right! On the new course it's going to be the aiming meteorite!"

# Brown Kiwi

"Once more to Ulery's Lake, A.C., before you and Maggie head back east?" Fuentes asked. "We'll have it all to ourselves this time of year."

There had been frost on the grass that morning, with early snows predicted for the whole of the next week. Winter was moving in early just as it had the year before, driving the treasure hunters to warmer climates—there was news of a large strike in South Sudan. Had Stony still been alive, it's where he would have gone next, A.C. thought, since by now his business in Moonlight would have been completed. Or perhaps not, given that he'd presumably already found the ultimate treasure. Maybe he would have decided to retire the Indy persona and move on to a more sedate existence—assistant curator of the gem and mineral division at the Smithsonian, perhaps, or on retainer to General Dunway as the resident expert on all things meteoric. But those chances, along with everything else, had been denied him.

"Good idea, Doc," replied A.C. after a moment's thought. "Maggie is busy packing, and I know better than to kibbitz; she has very definite ideas about how things go into a suitcase. Me, I just pick it up and put it in. Let's go."

They passed one other hiker on the trail down, but once there, Fuentes was proven right; it was deserted. Tiny ripples scuttered across the surface of the lake, giving the mountains reflected there an effervescent aspect. They settled into two of the large Adirondack-style chairs on the small platform which jutted out towards the lake, glad they'd brought along an extra layer.

"There are a couple of things I've been wanting to talk to you about, Doc," said A.C. "And I hope they won't bring back unpleasant memories."

"You know you can talk to me about anything, A.C."

"I appreciate that. First, though, I want to tell you how glad we all are to see you beginning to enjoy life again. And that you've finally accepted the fact it wasn't Doc's Rock that brought on Jamila's murder."

"Thanks. I know that now, though it hasn't been easy. But a large part of my recovery is due entirely to your efforts. And very elegant efforts they were." A.C. smiled at the reference to their departed friend's philosophy of life, what the Professor had called "the elegance of effort." He had instilled in them a profound appreciation for the value of not simply making an effort, but making that effort count for something larger and more lasting than the immediate result.

"I'm grateful I could make a difference. It doesn't always work out that way." After a minute, he continued. "Doc, that day I asked you to check out Jamila's computer, you said there had been some messages from her, notifications from her programs that came to you after she was killed."

"That's right. She'd set it up so I could help out with the analysis."

"And you were able to get the results of the AI image processing that had been running on her computer. That's how we found the meteorite on the site of the new golf course, when Abigail kidnapped Greg."

"Right again."

"But you left something out."

"Yes," he admitted. "The final processing run had crashed, as I told you. What I didn't tell you is that I was able to successfully rerun it that morning."

A.C. looked over at him intently. "Jamila had been talking about having difficulty making sense of what she was seeing," he said, "and that there appeared to be two distinct paths. Two fireballs, coming in over Moonlight simultaneously, but in different planes."

"Sounds like you've anticipated what I'm about to say."

"I have. And the inescapable conclusion I've come to is that there was a second meteorite." A.C. stood up and walked to the edge of the deck, looking out over the lake. "Where we found Greg, and what remained of Abigail—that meteorite is of common nickel-iron composition. Oh, a lot of microdiamonds, but other than the size of the meteorite itself, nothing out of the ordinary. That's why they're willing to leave it in place as an aiming stone." He turned back to Fuentes. "It's not what I expected to find there."

"No?"

"No. What I expected to find was the meteorite that provided the pallavine Stony used to make the rings. But you already knew we wouldn't find it there, didn't you?" He gave Fuentes another searching look. "It's out there somewhere, though, isn't it?" he asked, pointing towards Lone Peak.

Fuentes stood up and walked over next to A.C. "I've known for a while now. Jamila's coordinates were extremely good, but it's a big area. That's what I've been doing on my long hikes these past couple of weeks, looking for it." He stretched out his arms. "It's this big. And it's full of pallavine. Big crystals sticking out all over, like little translucent green windows."

"It really is in Moonlight, then. Aren't you afraid someone is going to find it?"

"It's in very rough terrain. It's like Howard said in *The Treasure of the Sierra Madre*: 'We gotta go where there's no trails at all - where you can be positive that no surveyor or anybody who knows anything about prospectin' has ever been there before.' I've fixed it so no one is going to find it. Not right away."

"How can you be so sure?"

"Kiwi."

This produced a blank stare. "What?"

"Shoe polish. Brown and black shoe polish. I've matched the color of the meteorite exactly, covered up the crystals. It looks like a plain old rock now. I also piled up brush and dead timber to cover the scar it made in the forest floor when it hit. It will stay hidden long enough for the snows to move in this winter and bury it completely. Oh, I know I can't keep it hidden forever. There's a lot of data out there—satellite imagery, meteorological data—someone will eventually track it down. There are also the flakes of green crystal being washed down the slope, an obvious clue to its location. The treasure hunters will be back. That's why it's important I stake my claim first. With Jamila's data to back me up, I believe I can make a good legal case for possession."

"Then what? Have you thought about what owning that thing could bring about? Even without anyone knowing it was there, it's left a trail of misery." There was a short silence as A.C. shifted his shoulders uncomfortably. "Then there's the curse," he finished lamely. He'd run out of reasonable objections.

"I've been thinking about it a lot, A.C. And I don't believe in a curse any more than you do."

"But what would you do with it?"

"Well, my first impulse, when I finally found it, was to have Frank get me enough C4 to blow it back into space where it came from."

"Understandable," said A.C., then qualified that by asking, "but you wouldn't really do that, would you?"

Fuentes laughed. "Just a quick fantasy. The thought of it made me feel better for a few minutes, but no, I wouldn't do that." He paused. "The other day I heard Maggie hinting she might like some of this new Montana jewelry that's getting so popular."

A.C. turned to him, wide-eyed. "Holy cats, Doc! You wouldn't make another ring!"

Fuentes laughed even harder. "Don't worry. A bad joke."

A.C. walked away from him, then turned back. "Listen, Doc, seriously now, what are you going to do?"

Fuentes sat back down in his chair. A.C. followed a few seconds later and sat down next to him, still a little ruffled. "Seriously, now," he repeated.

"The one thing I want more than anything," Fuentes said, soberly, "the reason I'm so intent on claiming it, is to protect it. I don't want to see it go to someone like Abigail. And I don't want it commercialized. Maybe it should go to the Smithsonian, with

Stony's rings. Or maybe cut it up into a few smaller pieces that would not individually be so valuable, and distribute them to various museums—the Colorado School of Mines, maybe, and other natural history museums."

"I have to say I'm relieved—that sounds more like you. But what if you don't end up with it after all, what then?"

"There always C4."

"Frank will never let you blow it up."

"Probably not."

"You don't want to sell it, but you have to keep it away from the pirates. Tough nut to crack."

"Tell you what, A.C. Let's get you and Maggie moved out here before the snow gets too deep. Then we'll have all winter to figure something out together." He stood up, stretching. "Ready to head back?"

"Sure." A.C. pushed himself up out of the low chair with a groan. "I wouldn't call these the most comfortable chairs on the planet."

"They're built for style, not comfort."

"One of the many small things wrong with this world."

Fuentes clapped him on the shoulder. "Let's go home."

"I'm with you, Doc."

"As always, A.C. As always.

# Acknowledgements

We had many collaborators in writing this book. Invaluable editing services were provided by a large number of dedicated and thorough copyreaders, proofreaders, and content reviewers, from all over the world. Others very graciously allowed us to use them as inspiration for various characters appearing in the book (of course, strict resemblance to actual persons is neither intended or implied). In all cases we are greatly indebted to everyone who contributed their time and effort.

*U.S. editors*: Sandy Fountain, Melissa Levine, Bernie and Jody Dan, Dave and Fern Servais, Abigail Kull (Moonlight Basin, MT); Otis and Joy Kramer (Brawley, CA); Ed and Robin Orazem (Wellesley, MA); Ellen Doyle (Grosse Pointe Farms, MI); Arthur Handley (Saranac Lake, NY); Tod Kull (Davenport, IA); Adrienne Abbott, Geoff Chase, Sarah Massey-Warren, Greg Kok (Boulder, CO); Deb Abbott (Cripple Creek, CO); Randy and Melanie Palmer (Mesquite, NV); Kenneth Nagel (Grand Rapids, MI).

*Overseas editors*: Jeanette Noble and Graham Young (Monifeith, Scotland); John and Kim Ramsay (Loch Tummel, Scotland); Keith McCloskey (Dublin, Ireland); John and Chris Middleton (Huddersfield, England); Scott Lewis and Marilou Roth (Toronto, Canada); Gerard and Kerry McMahon (Apollo Bay, Australia); Jonathan and Margaret Doyle (Canberra, Australia).

*Appearing in the book*: Paul and Paula Farrell; Greg Wagner; Nick Berasi; Geno Lantagne; Emily Melton; Mandy Hotovy; Ashley Quande; Bridget French; Matt Kidd; Kevin Germain; David McLay Kidd (DMK Golf Design, Inc); Jorge Morales; Ryan O'Connor; Rich Jorgenson; Monte Johnsen; Chris Morris; Austin LeFave; Huguette Courcelles Bradley; Madison Brenner; Della and Joah Levine; Ethan and Carter MacFadden; Lola and Peyton Morris; Ella and Jack Smith; Caeden O'Connor.

Cover design by Steve Abbott. Photo credits: Moonlight Basin (entrance gate) and iStock (meteor and gem).

www.ingramcontent.com/pod-product-compliance
Lightning Source LLC
Chambersburg PA
CBHW061512120726
48001CB00004B/1300